Northern Vet

GENEVIÈVE MONTCOMBROUX

Whippoorwill Solitude Publishing

ISBN 978-1-987946-31-4

Cover: mmontcombroux

Published by Solitude Publishing

solitudepublishing@gmail.com

To all the dogs that so enriched my life

Contents

CHAPTER ONE

Author's Note: Indigenous people, particularly those in remote settlements, when speaking English rarely use contractions. They say, "I cannot" rather than "I can't." This is reflected in the novel. Also, the citizens of Canada's Yukon Territory refer to the region as "Yukon." Outsiders tend to call it "The Yukon." This, too, is reflected in the novel.

The red pickup swung into the yard and came to a halt in a spray of snow. Brooke killed the engine and jumped out, shock written on her face.

"My dogs? Where are my dogs?" Her words reverberated in the frigid air.

Harnesses in his hands, her husband Seth turned to face her. "Come and admire my new team."

The breath was sucked out of Brooke's lungs. A wave of anger roiled up. Near exploding, she stammered, "Where are my dogs?" She pointed to the empty pens beside the cabin. For emphasis, she slammed shut the truck door.

"I had a buyer. Sold them."

"You did what?" Rage constricted her throat.

Seth continued harnessing the eager huskies. "Just what I said. Sold 'em. We can't keep mutts that can't race. Not like my new Iditarod team. These beauties are finally gonna land me in the winner's circle."

Brooke stepped onto the covered porch. "You piece of crap! You had no right to sell my dogs. Mine, you hear? Not yours! I want them back. Where did they go?"

The dogs that were already harnessed grew impatient. They barked and jumped in the air, raring to go. The snow anchors barely held.

Ian Campbell and Vince Bergen, their neighbors from two miles away, who had come to see Seth's new team, rushed to restrain the sled before the team took off on its own.

Seth hitched the team leader. "Don't fret. They were just a bunch of old rescues that couldn't race if they tried."

Trying for calm, but with an icy tone, Brooke dropped her travel bag on the porch. "Where are they? I want them back." Her anger mounted another notch. "You, lowlife! You took advantage of my being away at my father's funeral to do your dirty deed. You're beyond despicable."

Seth made a mock gesture of despair for the benefit of the males present. "Women! They know nothing about business."

Ian let go of the sled now that Seth was standing on the runners. "You sure did good getting these guys from Dan up at Big River. He wouldn't sell to me."

"He only sells to the right people. You're too fat."

Ian's features twisted into an annoyed grimace.

Brooke's fury surged again. "You, jerk! One last time, where are my dogs?"

"In good hands. I've had enough of doing no better than the twentieth place. And renting a team isn't going to help me win the Iditarod."

The powerful huskies, feeling the looseness of the restraints, barked at the top of their lungs and stretched the gangline to breaking point.

"Tell me where my dogs are or I'll shoot you." She grabbed the rifle from the peg by the cabin door, where it hung when they were outside. Their protection in summer against a visiting grizzly or in winter, if an ornery moose thought of attacking a dog team.

Seth laughed. "You'd better shoot the two old dogs that are left. Nobody wanted to buy them." He let slip the brake and his team bounded forward in a blur of motion.

Brooke brought the Marlin to her shoulder. Before she could take a bead on her husband, the firearm was pulled from her grasp. Man and dogs disappeared down the snow-packed trail. She whirled round. Dexter Weiman stood beside her, holding the rifle out of her reach. His dark eyes locked on her gray ones.

"Dexter, what are you doing here?"

A disarming smile floated on his lips. "I was coming to borrow a neighborly cup of sugar." He kicked the snow off his boots.

"I'm not in the mood for jokes, cheechako."

He lifted one shoulder in a lopsided shrug. "Yep, that's me, the tenderfoot. At least until the end of winter when I become a bona fide sourdough. Is that how it works?"

"If you last that long."

Jimmy Redhead took a couple of steps toward her. "I think I can find out where your dogs went."

A tear rolled down her cheek on hearing the gentle voice of the Tlingit First Nation. Dexter put his arm around her shoulder. At the end of summer, he'd moved into the cabin next door, if two hundred yards away could be considered next door. He said he wanted to learn all about sled dogs and races.

Vince headed to his truck. "Okay, folks, I'm off. Thanks a million, Jimmy, for taking care of my lead dog."

"Me too. I'd better get going." Ian's eyes lingered on the six one-year-old husky pups poking their noses through the fence. He was about to say something, but clamped his jaw shut and hauled himself into his truck.

With a sigh, Brooke turned to Jimmy. "Thanks for acting as a vet today. What was wrong with Vince's dog?"

"A torn dewclaw. I removed it. I've fed the pups."

As if they understood his words, the youngsters let out excited howls.

His arm still around her shoulders, Dexter returned the rifle to its peg on the wall. "I figured I'd save you from going to prison."

She sighed. "I was fully prepared to shoot him."

"I figured you were. That's why I intervened."

His gentle tone and sincere compassion defused the last of Brooke's anger.

A wail came from deep in her chest. "No, no..."

Julot and Nana, the veteran dogs, answered with a long sad howl. She cried on Dexter's shoulder. Several racking sobs later, she lifted her head. "Sorry, your coat's all wet now."

"It'll dry."

"Let's go in. I'll make coffee."

The kettle was simmering on the stove. Automatically, she spooned ground coffee into the top of a French coffee pot and filled it to let the boiling water filter through.

"This old French *cafetière* is my prize possession, after my dogs. It makes the best coffee ever."

Dexter added a log to the stove and Jimmy slipped into the cabin. Although it was already three months since her father died when his boat capsized during a freak storm off the coast of the Bahamas, it had taken all that time to negotiate the return of his body and get it back home. Her husband's treason tore anew at her heart, already torn by her father's unexpected death.

Brooke placed three cups on the table while Jimmy took sugar from the shelf. He cut slices off the sourdough loaf he had baked that morning and brought them with a dish of butter to the table. Jimmy had come to her cabin every day to look after the dogs while she was away.

"Thanks. Now, I've got to find my dogs. I must phone my lawyer to get a divorce."

A smile etched Jimmy's rugged face. "We can find the musher who bought your dogs. He had personalized license plates, which read *Dream On*."

Brooke's eyes widened. "That sounds vaguely familiar." Galvanized, she rushed to her computer. "*Dream On* kennels. I should find it." Luckily, the internet connection came to life. Moments later, she leaned back on the chair, deflated. "Not a thing. It's not a working kennel, obviously."

"I still think we can find him," Jimmy said.

Brooke gave a discouraged shake of the head. "How? Yukon Territory is not exactly small. We can't go to every community and ask if anyone has seen a truck with *Dream On* plates transporting a bunch of dogs."

The Tlingit drew himself to his feet. "I have friends. I'll get the word out."

"*Gunalshéeh*," Brooke said.

With a trace of a smile on his lips, Jimmy said goodbye. Shortly afterwards, Brooke heard the yips of his dogs and watched through the window as his team vanished beyond the trees.

"What does that word you said mean?"

Brooke smiled. "It means you're kind and generous. There isn't really a word for thank you in Tlingit, but *gunalshéeh* is an accepted translation."

"You speak the language?"

"Just a few words I picked up from Jimmy. It helps me get along with our aboriginal friends. Now, when did my jerk of a husband sell my dogs?"

"Yesterday."

"I must check how much money I have to buy my dogs back."

Dexter frowned. "We must find them first."

"Did you see the truck, too?"

He lifted his hands in defeat. "I saw a dark green dog truck go up the road, but didn't think too much of it. Trucks coming to your home clinic are nothing unusual. When I heard the ruckus the dogs made, I thought maybe a grizzly had intruded."

"Didn't they tell you grizzlies hibernate until March?"

He shrugged and gave a sheepish grin. "Anyway, I saw the same truck going back. Dark green. But I was too far away to see the plates. I swear Jimmy has a pair of laser eyes in the back of his head."

"And today you came to my rescue. I've got to thank you."

"This morning Jimmy said he ought to tell me about the sale and did. Right away, I knew there might be trouble. So I cut across the back way on snowshoes."

"Silent and efficient." The remnant of a sob shook her chest. "What would a man want with a mismatched bunch of old huskies, including the four young Canadian Inuit dogs I rescued? Those are guaranteed to give anyone trouble. They may even have found a way to escape by now."

Dexter buttered another slice of bread and sprinkled it with sugar. He pushed it toward Brooke. "You've had a shock, but you must keep up your strength. What do you mean, they could have escaped?"

"Julot and Nana, out there in the pen, are their parents, so part of their pack. Those dogs will do anything to stay together. Their pack mentality is super strong."

He whistled. "And they'll find their way home even though they traveled in a transporter?"

"You've seen the air holes in the dog boxes. The dogs smell the landscape."

Eyes wide in admiration, Dexter clicked his fingers. "They escape and smell their way back."

"Exactly. Those dogs can detect an *aglu* one mile away. That's how keen their sense of smell is."

"What's an *aglu*?" Dexter wasn't embarrassed at showing his ignorance.

"A seal breathing hole in the Arctic sea ice. Inuit hunters rely on their dogs to find seals."

Like a student who suddenly understood, he nodded. "And the others? How many?"

"Four Alaskan huskies that were injured, and three that didn't work out. The racers were only too glad to leave them for me to re-home."

"But sled dogs are not pets."

She swallowed the last mouthful of sugary bread and butter. "No, they are certainly not pets. They are athletes. I rehabilitate those who can no longer race, train them to be good canine citizens and find someone or a family who likes hiking and skiing. The huskies are working dogs. Like all athletes, they need plenty of exercise. After a while, they adapt. They become loyal companions."

"But not the Inuit dogs?"

"No way of turning them into pets. Inuit dogs are a primitive breed and are best left that way. Those animals came from Outside. They didn't adapt to the southern climes, or rather the owner didn't adapt to them."

"Excuse-me. *Outside*?"

For the first time since her return, Brooke laughed. "Outside is anything beyond Yukon's borders."

"One more thing to remember before I can graduate to sourdough status."

She smiled. This tall man with muscles bulging under his sweater was endearing. Although she didn't have any expectations, she checked her cell phone. "Since there is no cell coverage here, I've got to go to Donek to phone the bank in Whitehorse."

"I'm heading that way. Can I give you a ride? We can make it before the bank in Whitehorse closes."

She let out a breath. "Thanks, that would help a lot."

The big jeep didn't take long to get to town through the shortcut over the frozen creek. Dexter parked outside the veterinary clinic. "I'll meet you here when you're finished. I'm going to the post office."

Her assistant greeted her with a smile soon extinguished. "Is something upsetting you?"

"Not half, Erin! My worthless husband sold my dogs."

"No!"

"I must phone the bank to get a loan to buy them back when we find who bought them, then my lawyer. I'm getting a divorce."

"It's about time, too."

To her relief, the bank was still open in Whitehorse. Not long after, Brooke stormed across the waiting room floor. She shook her fist. Mrs. Marsh and her placid Labrador looked up in surprise. "That jerk emptied our account. They can't give me a loan. I have no security. Why on earth did I agree to a joint account? There's next to nothing left in my personal savings account."

His business over, Dexter had come in and chatted with Mrs. Marsh. He turned to Brooke. "Maybe you don't charge the mushers who come for veterinary care half enough money."

With an apology to Mrs. Marsh and her Lab, he placed a comforting arm around Brooke's shoulders and forcibly walked her outside. Still holding her, he guided her across the street to the hotel restaurant. She crumpled onto a chair and held her head in her hands. A deep sob shook her. She brushed her hair back and took a deep breath.

"Some of the racers can't afford full vet fees. I'm more concerned about the dogs' welfare. Small matters can turn to big matters in the middle of a race with poor outcomes for the dog, and the musher, really."

"You're too generous and I can't change that, but I can help."

The waiter approached their table. Dexter smiled. "Moose steak with steamed vegetables for both of us."

Brooke raised her eyebrows, but remained silent until the waiter moved away. "I can't accept your help. How would I repay you?"

His smile revealed his perfect white teeth. "We could establish a veterinary scale of payments. Nobody needs to get a free ride. Look at it this way. If a musher can afford to run races, he has to be able to afford the care of his dogs."

"Some of them sacrifice everything just to enter the races, hoping to win enough to get a sponsor."

"Nah, it's not quite like that. This is the twenty-first century. Anyone wanting to race knows exactly down to the last dollar what it costs to run a kennel and feed dogs. They know how much money they need for race fees and veterinary expenses. If they can't lay their hands on that kind of money, they should not be racing. You have been giving in to their sob stories and letting them off lightly. In short, many of them exploit your obvious love of animals to nickel and dime you."

Brooke gave him a sober look. "You don't believe in anyone having a dream, do you?"

"But I do, only not at our expense, so we have to reorganize the clinic."

"Our? We?"

He threw her a warm smile. "That is, if you accept my help."

Head tilted, she examined him as if she was meeting him for the first time.

His smile was teasing. "Like what you see?"

The twinkle in his dark eyes drew a smile from her lips. "Where did you live before you abandoned everything to come to this backwoods place? And why come here?"

"Where did I live? In the heart of Vancouver, British Columbia. Agate Creek is a nice community, a bit off the beaten track, but close enough to Donek, which has all the amenities a guy like me would need. When I viewed the cabin in Agate Creek, I was hooked."

"Excuse my nosiness, but do you have something to hide?"

His laughter drew an inquisitive look from Brooke. A lock of dark hair fell over his forehead.

Just then, the waiter brought the food, along with a basket of fresh-baked bread. He poured water in their glasses.

She didn't start eating, but looked expectantly at her neighbor.

"Okay, confession time. I was your typical corporate executive. Tie, dark gray suit and all that. After some time, I came to the realization that I wasn't cut out for that lifestyle. For example, I would have liked to keep a dog. I had one when I was growing up. Nope. Nothing like that was possible. I reached the point where I had to quit or lose my sanity."

A quick glance at his trim body, large shoulders and capable hands made her think he spent more time at the gym than at the office.

Dexter followed her eyes. "Do I pass muster?"

She laughed. "I was wondering if you spend much time at the gym."

"Gym, yes, and skiing, bicycling. Swimming too. The city is great for that kind of thing, but I felt caged in."

A forkful later, Brooke nodded. "I think I can understand. When I was a student in Saskatoon, which has the best veterinary school in the country, by the way, I couldn't wait to get back here. But for you, why Yukon? It's a long way from anywhere."

He shrugged. "The little cabin I found was ideal. The local council was happy to get rid of it, for the unpaid taxes."

"Little cabin? It's the biggest log structure for a hundred miles around. Dare I ask how you earn a living?"

His carefree laugh resonated in the room. The few fellow diners shot curious glances in their direction.

Dexter lowered his voice a notch. "I'm okay for the time being. Right away, I spotted the potential. A roomy cabin, nestled in an unspoiled valley. Great views of the northern lights.

"Potential for what?"

"For a hotel, lodge, resort, whatever you want to call it. Tourists would flock here for the beauty, the nature, the peace and quiet."

A frown furrowed her brow. She narrowed her eyes. "Have you considered that we locals don't really want a busy resort on our doorstep?"

"Why not? Tourists bring a lot of cash. Something, I gather, mushers around here are rather short of."

"We've got our pride. We're a tight-knit dog-sledding community."

"Let's not talk any more about it, shall we? It's only an idea."

Her phone rang. Dexter was relieved. He was glad that she, and most likely the rest of the community, wouldn't want a resort. He had no intention of building one. That wasn't why he was in Agate Rock.

"That was my lawyer returning my call. I have an appointment for tomorrow afternoon, then I'll talk to the bank. I wonder if she can vouch for me to get a loan, considering what my soon-ex-to-be did."

"I have some business in Whitehorse tomorrow. How about I give you a ride?"

"Mr. Weiman, you were on your way to Donek and gave me a ride, and tomorrow you happen to have business in Whitehorse, where I have to be. Is all this a coincidence?"

Dexter replied in a deadpan voice. "Broke my sunglasses and have to get a new pair. I'll show you the bits if you don't believe me."

"Okay, I accept. I'll get Alex to come and feed the dogs and keep the stove going."

Dexter helped her with her parka. "I get the impression that young fella would rather spend his time with the dogs than attend school."

"Contrary to what it looks, he's a serious student who has ambitions to be a veterinarian. Yes, he finds school boring because he finishes his assignments in half the time. He much prefers a biology textbook to a comic book."

"That's refreshing to hear from a teenager."

***

Long before daylight returned to the territory, Brooke was up caring for her two old dogs. They were still howling over the loss of their pack. "I know, babies. I could howl too, but I'm doing something about it. I'll get them all back. Be good, now." Once more, she turned toward the east and blew the recall signal on her silent whistle. An empty gesture, but one that expressed her hope. She then fed the six pups, who were too young to have gone on Seth's training trip. "Poor puppies, it's not your fault that my husband is such an idiot. You're real beauties. You'll make someone a good racing team. That's if I can manage to find you a good home before he returns in three days' time." She lifted a gloved finger. "Actually, I think I know someone." The boisterous pups jumped up and sat expecting a treat. With a laugh, she handed them a piece of dried meat each.

Minutes later, Dexter's truck pulled into the yard. Brooke was expecting him, but not what he was driving.

"My, a nice rig! A big truck and a dog transporter. And you don't even have any dogs."

"It was an opportunity too good to miss. Business decisions should be made fast. Dogs need to be chosen slowly and carefully."

"Amen. You're a man after my own heart." She blushed and climbed into the passenger seat.

He welcomed her with a big smile. He reached into the CD compartment. "Bruce Springsteen okay?"

Grateful for the change of topic, she nodded her agreement. *And if you don't want people to take notice of you around here, just drive a truck with a dog transporter. No need for dogs.*

Chapter Two

T he bank business was concluded quickly. It didn't take them long to say no. The visit to the law office boosted Brooke's self-confidence. The capable woman lawyer put immediate measures in place to prevent her husband from attempting more damage, such as mortgaging the clinic, even though the business was in her name only. The lack of such measures had enabled him to mortgage the cabin, even though that too was solely in her name.

On the lawyer's advice, Brooke blocked her credit card and, despite the bank manager's misgivings about its legality, also blocked her husband's access to their joint account. With depressing thoughts running wild, she walked the short distance to Antoinette's, where Dexter was to meet her. The restaurant was her favorite on her infrequent visits to the capital. On this occasion, she hoped, in fact, was quite sure, that Dexter would pay for the meal. He had suggested Antoinette when she had proposed a cheaper eatery.

The subdued lighting and dark red decor soothed her tormented soul. While she waited for him, she pondered over the reasons why she had married Seth in her last year of vet school. Now she could see clearly how he had bamboozled her. The handsome young musher, unable due to lack of funds to move to Alaska, was happy to move north to Yukon with her. His irresistible smile, his devoted attention, his declarations of love, all that was part of his malevolent agenda. He must have assumed that veterinarians made big money. As a bonus, she would look after his dogs for free. She was taking over Dave Roberts' practice. Everything was set up.

How blind she had been, how naïve! She should have known not to trust a man so intent on her projects and career. A man who shared her ideals, ideals he had never expressed until she did. He coincidentally had possessed those self same ideals. What was the old saying about love being blind? She was the poster child for it.

The waitress smiled. "Would you care for a drink and a starter while you wait?"

Brooke realized how thirsty she was. "I'd like a lime juice, please. I'll wait to order."

While she waited, she pulled out her phone. "Hi, Stephanie!"

"Goodness me, Brooke! Are you in town?"

"At Antoinette's. Do you have anything for me?"

There was a laugh from her friend. "You bet! Four bags of stuff. Can I bring them to you?"

"Please do. I'm waiting for a friend."

"If it's a man, maybe I shouldn't."

"I'll tell you about it when you're here."

In no time, Stephanie bounded into the restaurant. The two friends hugged.

Stephanie ordered a mango drink. "And don't leave without the bags this time."

They laughed over a past incident. Stephanie's happy mood evaporated as Brooke told her of the disaster that had befallen her.

"I know you told me before that Seth was a slimy character. I'm sorry I didn't listen to you."

"Let's not dwell on the past. What are you going to do now?"

A sigh later, Brooke shook her head. "I'll continue with my practice. My lawyer made sure that worthless husband of mine can't cause any more damage. It'll take time, but I'll repay the debts. My lawyer said we can sue so he'll end up paying the debts, though there's no guarantee of that. Anyhow, it'll all take an awful long time."

"These things usually do." Stephanie put her hand on Brooke's. "If the bank won't lend you money, how are you going to buy supplies for the clinic?"

A silence followed, while Brooke leaned on her elbows. "I'll use more of the traditional medicine Jimmy is teaching me... I'll borrow from friends for essential stuff..." The last sentence stuck in her throat.

"Wait." Stephanie reached for her phone. "Tanya, can you pack a carton with antibiotics, disinfectant, vaccines, a box of needles, a box of gloves, and a few other items like that?" She smiled. "Good, we're at Antoinette's."

Brooke took her head in her hands. "You can't do all that. I can't pay you."

"Who mentioned money? I'm the president of the Helping Paws Club. We fundraise, we rescue, we foster, we re-home, offer vet care in remote communities and do a million other things. It includes vets helping other vets. So there it is."

Her throat too tight to speak, Brooke squeezed her friend's hand. Shortly afterwards, Tanya entered and surveyed the dining room. She came across to Brooke and Stephanie's table. "I have the supplies in my car."

Stephanie helped Tanya bring two cartons of vet supplies so they wouldn't freeze.

At that moment, Dexter arrived. After he'd been brought into the picture, he went out to open his truck. They stored the supplies and the bags of donated dog blankets and toys, except the veterinary supplies. The friends parted with the promise of a longer visit next time.

The desserts were so appetizing, Brooke, encouraged by Dexter, couldn't resist the lime ice cream parfait. Replete, she excused herself and went to the restroom. When she returned to the table, she noticed a change. Dexter was sitting bolt upright in his chair, his phone in his hand, a distant expression on his face.

He relaxed when she resumed her seat. "I just got a call from a business partner which throws a monkey wrench in the works. I have to set off for, er... Edmonton tonight. I'm happy I was able to have dinner with you. Would you mind having to take the bus back to Donek tomorrow? I've made a reservation for you at the Sternwheeler Hotel here in town. The shuttle will take you to the bus depot in the morning."

"No problem. Let me send a message to Savanah to come and house-sit for me. Savanah is Jimmy's wife."

"I've met her. A lovely woman."

As usual, there was no phone connection. She had to call Doug, the auxiliary constable in Donek, to ask him to relay a message via ham radio. When Stephanie had visited Agate shortly after Brooke's return to the community with her brand new veterinary license, her friend couldn't believe that communicating by ham radio was still necessary in the twenty-first century. Her ten-year-old, on the other hand, thought it was the most marvelous thing he'd ever seen in his whole life. Afterward, he had pestered his parents for him to join the amateur radio club. By now, not only had he learned how to operate a radio but also how to build his own set.

Dexter unloaded her supplies from his truck and carried them into her suite. The hug he gave her before leaving warmed her heart.

Alone in the quiet of her hotel room, Brooke mulled over the last two days. The question that kept churning in her mind was simple. How was she going to cope with the mountain of debt and not enough cash flow to repay the bank? They made absolutely no consideration for the fact that, as a vet, she earned an income, small she admitted to herself, but all she needed was a schedule of payments. They were not impressed by her rather modest income. Her plan as of now was to spend more time at the Donek clinic where pet owners paid the going rate, at least the majority did. How could she charge ninety-year-old Mr. Adams, when he shared the little food he had with his beloved cat because he couldn't buy cat food after paying the heating bills? When he had come to surrender his companion, she had understood his immense loneliness. She'd improvised a loyalty coupon for vet care to preserve his dignity. His cat on human food was healthier than most cats in the district. Then she had asked keen fisherman Mr. Swindley whether he had any extra fish. His enthusiastic response was heartwarming, not only the cat but Mr. Adams had plenty of fish to eat. Mrs. Swindley now happily accepted his frequent fishing expeditions. Everybody won.

Of course, her lawyer planned to arrange that she would only be responsible for half the debt, but that still represented a tidy sum, and it probably wouldn't work out. That was without taking into consideration other creditors. She remembered the pile of bills that she had put on Seth's desk, some of them marked *overdue* in red. The clinic wasn't mortgaged, but the scum had mortgaged *Doghaven*, her cherished log cabin.

CHAPTER THREE

The last light of the day was disappearing fast when the repurposed school bus pulled into Agate Creek and came to a halt in front of the café that doubled as a bus depot. Brooke jumped off and retrieved the packages the driver was extracting from the cargo space at the back of the vehicle. Conservation officer Conrad Windett came out of the café to meet her. A smile broke on her lips, then died. He had a grim look on his face. Her heart began to pound. Something had happened. She knew for certain. The privately owned bus departed, leaving a cloud of diesel fumes in its wake.

Conrad bent down. "I'll take the bags."

"What's up? I can read your face." She picked up the carton of vet supplies and started walking beside him to her cabin.

"Let's get you settled first."

"Uh... oh... that bad? But after my dogs were taken away and my bank account emptied by that worthless husband of mine, I can handle anything."

Savanah was waiting on the porch. She helped with the baggage.

"*Gunalshéeh* for staying over and keeping the place from freezing up," Brooke said.

Conrad looked her in the eyes. "It's about your husband, Seth."

"Did he cross the border and get lost in Alaska?" Her flippant tone didn't draw the smile she expected.

"Seth had an accident."

Brooke brushed back her hair. "The dogs? What about the dogs? Are they okay?"

"The dogs are fine."

She breathed a sigh of relief. "Good. So what happened?"

Conrad steadied himself with a deep breath. "Byron and I were out on a snowmobile patrol when we came across a driverless team. It was careening out of control toward us. We managed to stop the dogs."

In silence, Savanah put a bowl of soup and a mug of coffee in front of Brooke.

Conrad resumed. "We knew it was Seth's sled. It bore your clinic sponsorship logo. The sled had blood on the handlebar and on the sled bag. It had some minor damage to the side. Byron brought the team back here while I went in search of Seth. I found him farther back on the trail. He appears to have collided with a tree on a tight bend. I'm afraid the trauma was very violent." He paused looking at her stoic expression. "He was no longer breathing."

The news hit Brooke as though someone had punched her in the ribs. Eyes wide open, she stared at Conrad. Adrenaline surged in her body, numbing the effect of the news. "He must have underestimated the power of those new dogs. What now?"

"The Royal Canadian Mounted Police are investigating. They determined that he broke his neck against the tree." Conrad paused to let Brooke assimilate the information. "At first glance, it looked like a straightforward sledding accident. It wouldn't be the first time a musher slammed into a tree. Only, this time it wasn't a pure accident."

Brooke stared at him. "What are you trying to tell me?"

"Seth was murdered."

"He was what?" The air left her chest. She could hardly breathe.

"In addition to the collision, he had a bullet wound to the chest. That's where most of the blood came from."

She gasped. "Someone shot him!"

"I'm afraid so, with a high-powered rifle."

"A poacher?"

"Could be. That's why we're working with the RCMP. The autopsy will tell us more. The body was taken to Whitehorse once the nurse practitioner confirmed the broken neck, the bullet hole and the lack of life."

Brooke sighed. Reality was slowly sinking in. "She can't sign a death certificate." Conrad's words danced frenetically in her head. It wasn't possible. Yes, in the heat of the moment, she had wished him dead and even had tried to shoot him. And now he was. So tight were her hands, the soup bowl was in danger of breaking. A hand took it from her.

"Are the dogs in a pen?"

Jimmy had entered without a sound. He sat on the other side of the table. "They are all here. I checked them over. Not a scratch on them."

"Thank you."

"My wife will stay tonight. I am taking the kids home now."

Two little heads poked around the door of the bedroom. The boys tiptoed out behind their father.

With a fatalistic gesture of the hands, Brooke straightened. "Alright. What do I do now?"

"A Mountie will come tomorrow to take a deposition. You can plan the funeral, but it has to wait until the autopsy is completed."

"Of course."

Still in a daze, Brooke put the pharmacy supplies that needed to be kept cool in her small fridge until she could transfer them to the clinic, then stacked the blankets and toys in the corner of the living room she used when people brought an animal in for treatment. She'd take them over to the clinic in Donek later.

Conrad gave her a hug. "Dexter gone away?"

"Some unexpected business down south. Did Savanah tell you I was coming back on the bus?"

"She did. I'll leave now."

"Of course, you have to get back to Fletcher Creek." Her head was spinning, and she was babbling.

"Rest, now. We're all here to help."

She watched him fire up his snowmobile and leave. Back in the cabin, she let herself fall onto the sofa. "Well, this changes everything."

Savanah put a steaming dish on the table. "Eat, Early Sun. You have to keep your up strength. You will need it."

Brooke smiled at the use of the name her Tlingit friends had given her, and which made her proud. "Only if you eat with me."

"You do not think I cook all that just for you?"

Amid laughter, thought a little strained, they sat at the table. While she ate, Brooke's thoughts swirled around her head. She had just laughed despite learning her husband was dead. Somehow, she wasn't devastated. She ought to be, but only a vague sadness colored her emotions. On reflection, she had long lost the excitement that had presided over the whirlwind courtship and hasty wedding so soon after personal tragedy had left her vulnerable. She was now a widow and she shouldn't be laughing. But she could shed no tears for a husband who had used her, deceived her, and cheated her. The loss of human life, even one she labeled worthless, was a tragedy, not something she felt indifferent to. Yet, she was lacking the emotions she'd experience if a stranger was killed in a road accident.

Savanah sent her to bed and lay on the sofa to keep watch over her.

***

Her chores finished, Brooke put water to boil to make a tisane. Her coffee can was empty, and she wasn't going to buy any as part of her new austerity plan. She had plenty of herbs to make all the tisane she wanted. A knock on the door jolted her from her task.

"Come in."

Corporal Ron Larsen stepped into the living room. He removed his uniform fur cap and dropped his parka on an armchair.

"Take a seat, Ron. I've just made wild mint and raspberry tea. Would you care for a cup?"

"Thanks. It smells good."

Brooke and the police officer sat on opposite sides of the table.

"This is formal RCMP procedure. I have to ask you a bunch of what may seem like obvious questions."

"I know."

Ron carefully recorded her answers. He stopped writing when Jimmy entered and went to the clinic's fridge and left silently.

"Redhead is still your assistant?"

"My indispensable right-hand man. Someone must have come for deworming medication."

"How do you know?"

"I saw what he took."

"You've got sharp eyes to have identified what it was."

A haunted look passed over her eyes. "A necessary skill."

Ron raised an eyebrow, but went on with his questioning. "Is it correct you threatened to kill Seth Lammers after you learned he had sold your dogs? Just reply yes or no."

"Yes. Everybody must have already told you that."

"I know, but I have to put it in writing."

"Is this the moment when I ask for a lawyer?"

He smiled. "You're only a witness at this time."

"I like the distinction."

"But don't tell me you aimed the rifle at your husband."

Eyebrows raised and mouth open, she stared at the Mountie for a second. "Alright, I won't."

He smiled. He had known her since he'd been posted to Fletcher Creek two decades earlier and she was but a girl, always top of the first aid classes he taught every year. He had loved the small communities he served and had decided not to leave, passing deliberately on promotions and other assignments. "Now, I need to see and take the rifle. A Marlin 30.30, right?"

Her head swiveled to the gun cabinet. "Oh... I must have forgotten to return it to the cabinet." She looked puzzled. "It must be still..." She stood up and went to the door.

Ron followed her onto the porch.

"Dexter Weiman took it out of my hands. I don't know what he did with it. We hang it from this peg when working outside to keep it handy, just in case."

"Where is Weiman now?"

"We went to Whitehorse the day before yesterday, no, the day before that. He had business Outside. I don't know when he'll be back."

"Then that's all for today. I have to tell you not to leave town."

Brooke laughed somewhat hysterically. "Right! I wasn't even here, but I'm a suspect."

"No, not a suspect, and I'm obliged to add, at the moment."

"I have to run the clinic in Donek too, and if necessary, I go to a musher's place to vaccinate the dogs or respond to an emergency somewhere."

"I know. That's all part of *town*. Town is an urban concept. It hardly applies to our situation. I also have to question the other people who were present on that day."

Ron shrugged into his parka. About to leave, he turned toward her. "Did Seth have any enemies?"

She pursed her lips. "About a dozen or more. My late husband had a unique talent for putting people down and ticking people off."

"Totally off the record. Why did you marry him?"

She laughed bitterly. "I didn't know snakes shed their skin."

Ron squeezed her shoulder and let himself out.

Snakes. Useful animals that shed their skin, which decompose and enrich the soil. She would have her late husband cremated and would spread his ashes over the land to become fertilizer to enrich the soil. That would be the one useful thing he would have done with his life. She couldn't recall whether he had any relatives. This was a subject he had always brushed off. In the beginning, being in love was sufficient. There would be time for family later. The hurried wedding had been attended by her father and a few friends from veterinary school. Her father and Stephanie showed their disapproval, but she took no notice. She shook herself. She had work to do.

Chapter Four

In the next few days, Brooke didn't have a moment to herself, traveling to the clinic in Donek, which had become unexpectedly busier. The home clinic saw an increase number of people, most only offering support. Of course, Seth's mysterious death had made first page news in the *Gazette*, the local weekly newspaper. The rumors he had ruined her were doing the rounds of the gossip circuit. She had just returned home when Vince Bergen came to buy the six one-year-old pups.

"I'm so relieved they haven't been sold. It took me all this time to raise the money."

Brooke chuckled. "Let me guess. The bank didn't want to give you a loan to buy a bunch of dogs."

"Right! They said if I wanted to buy a snowmobile, they'd lend me the funds right away."

"That's because a snowmobile is a tangible asset that they could seize if you defaulted on the payments, but dogs? Imagine six enthusiastic sled dogs in the bank lobby."

They burst out laughing. She put the money away.

"I'll be back tomorrow, I have to finished securing the new pen for them."

"Don't worry, they are safe."

Vince had hardly gone when a violent knock on the door resonated through the cabin. Before Brooke could say a word, Ian Campbell swung the door open and yelled. "You had no right to sell Seth's team to Jerome Renard!"

With measured movements, Brooke stood up. "How dare you burst into my house! Leave immediately."

"Those dogs are mine to have." He tossed an envelope onto the table and strode out.

Panic rose in Brooke's chest. She took a deep breath, picked up the envelope as if it was contaminated. Her other hand clutched the keys to the pen padlocks in her pocket, all the while wishing that somebody would come. Was it instinct or prescience that had her lock all the pens? At the pen gate, Campbell was shaking the chain link, vociferating at the top of his lungs. The dogs unaccustomed to the threatening ruckus hid behind their dog houses.

Brooke dropped the envelope on the hood of Ian's truck. "You are trespassing and are breaking down private property. You are endangering my animals. Now leave." Her controlled voice had no effect on the enraged man who was now kicking at the gate.

He rounded on her, shouting, "Give me the key!" and lunged for her. Brooke had anticipated his move and jumped beside his truck, planning to get inside and lock the doors. At that moment, she wished she had the missing rifle in her hands. The wish evaporated when her eye caught the figure moving behind the furious man. Her whole being tensed up, but remained impassive. Faster than she could think, Jimmy Redhead pounced on Ian Campbell and sent him sprawling flat on his face in the snow.

Brook already had her phone in her hand, praying that today there would be some reception. There wasn't. Relief came when two trucks pulled into the yard.

"Need a hand, Jimmy?"

"Hmm… Could you help me get Campbell back on his feet? He slipped on the ice."

After an exchange of knowing looks, Ian was brought upright. Without looking at anybody, he grabbed his envelope and jumped into his truck and roared away.

"What's got into him?" Bill asked.

Brooke sighed. "He wants Seth's team, but Jerome bought it." Actually, he was trying to raise enough money for it, although Brooke had told him she'd rather let him have the team for free than have Campbell own it. It was no secret that Brooke's late husband had ruined her financially. Mushers who generally disliked Seth Lammers were doing their best to buy the dogs at a fair price. They respected her and many in the past had benefited from a free consultation.

"We were in my dog yard when we saw his truck. I guess we were just curious," Ed said.

Brooke smiled. They all knew that curiosity had nothing to do with their coming over. From his vantage view on top of the hill, Jimmy had sounded the alert. Charlie's ham radio was working just fine. It didn't need the internet or cell coverage. "Thanks, guys! Why don't you come in for some coffee? Oops! I ran out, but I have freshly baked scones and I can make a herbal tea."

They were all smiles. "How could a guy resist?"

In the pen, Jimmy had finished calming the dogs with his usual magic. He joined the others at the table.

***

In the early hours of the morning, a couple of days later, Brooke was awakened by an unusual noise from the dog pens.

"Not again!" In seconds, she was pulling on her quilted pants, thrusting her feet her into her boots and pushing her arms through her coat sleeves. She took a second to pick up a scalpel from the instruments drawer and put it in her pocket. If Ian Campbell was back, she wasn't going to be defenseless in front of him again. The powerful beam of her headlamp switched on, she stepped outside.

To her relief, there was no vehicle in her yard or nearby. Her light swept through the enclosures. The sixteen dogs of the contentious team pulled on their tethers and yipped, noses pointed toward the old dogs' pen where Julot and Nana were making throat sounds. Brooke pivoted. There, a black dog scratched at the fence.

"Mattoo!"

At her name, the young female ran to Brooke who crouched to hug her.

"You escaped! Where are your brothers? Where are Ooglala, Monthor and Spitzweg?"

At the familiar names, Mattoo gave a howl, immediately picked up by her parents. In seconds, the Alaskan huskies were howling too.

"Come in. I have something for you."

The dog ran to the cabin and sat on the porch while Brooke pulled a meaty treat from a box. She put a bowl of water and a small amount of food on the floor. When the dog finished wolfing it down, she bent to clip a short leash to her collar, only to discover it was missing. "Smart Mattoo, you were picketed and lunged until you were free."

Brooke reached for another collar. Since her Inuit dogs were loose in a big pen, she used breakaway collars. Those collars had a release that worked open under a sudden and strong wrenching move. She had seen too many fatal collar injuries, when a dog went on the wrong side of a tree or got his chain tied in knots, to use anything else. With the dogs settled again, Brooke dressed for the day. There was no point trying to get back to sleep. Besides, she hoped that the three males were close behind their sister.

Silent whistle in hand, she went outside again and whistled the recall signal, which carried over two miles. All the dogs took up howling again. Seth had mocked her when she had started training all the dogs with the silent whistle until the day one of his dogs had chewed through its line at night in the middle of a race and run off. Mortified, and furious because of the time he was going to waste looking for his dog, he'd plucked the whistle from his pocket and sent the recall signal. The dog came back shortly afterwards. Although Seth told her about the incident, he never thanked her for training his dogs in this way.

Brooke paced back and forth in the yard. The dogs settled down. After ten minutes, she whistled again, and the dogs howled. All of a sudden, the howling became frenetic.

"Monthor, Spitzweg, Ooglala! Come here!"

In a short time, three large bundles of fur jumped at her. Knocked off her feet, Brooke laughed and cried, hugging them. After they got treats and food, she led them back to the pen. They submitted to Julot, the boss dog, but he didn't correct them, as if he was relieved his pack was back. She marveled at the scene of the dogs' endless licking of muzzles. The boss dog was very prompt to correct the youngsters when they stepped out of line. Did he understand they had been taken away forcibly and had done their best to come back? She'd never get the answer to that question, but she liked to think so.

Back in the house, she wondered about the other dogs. What if the older Alaskan huskies had also escaped? She doubted they would have the same homing instinct as the Inuit dogs. With a sigh, she picked up a book but found she couldn't concentrate. Unable to remain idle, she went to the kitchen and began baking old-fashioned biscuits. Baking biscuits and scones didn't require much else besides flour, salt and the sourdough she kept going. Cheap and nutritious.

As she took the first tray out of the oven, howls erupted outside. By the way they howled, almost in a disinterested manner, meant that whoever was coming was still someway on the road. All the same, she opened the door in case the huskies had also escaped and come back. It wasn't them. It was a man in civilian clothes that did nothing to disguise the Mountie he obviously was. He had left his car on the road and trudged up the long driveway before mounting the porch steps.

"Ms. Porter? I'm Inspector John Whitford, Royal Canadian Mounted Police. May I have a word with you?"

"Of course, come in. It's freezing out there."

Unfazed by the visit, Brooke offered him a chair, poured boiling water into the tisane teapot and placed the plate of biscuits on the table while she continued with her baking. She answered his questions without hesitation, the way she had answered Ron Larsen's questions, though she refrained from telling him that the same questions and answers were already on file.

"You had a rifle in your hands when you threatened your husband. Is the correct?"

Brooke remembered Ron's advice. "I instinctively grabbed the rifle, but it was immediately taken away by Dexter Weiman, a neighbor."

"Where is Mr. Weiman now?"

"I don't know. He had to attend to business somewhere."

"Very convenient, isn't it?"

She tested a tray of biscuits. "Convenient for whom?"

His eyebrows rose a fraction. "For you. No rifle. No proof."

Brooke had not been born a Yukoner to tolerate the insinuations of this city dweller, even if he was an inspector. She made an about-turn. "Did you take the trouble to look at the map? My husband was killed on the way to Tootook Lake, which is more than one hundred miles north of here, while I was in Whitehorse two hundred and seventy-eight miles to the south. There's no road to Tootook lake."

The inspector appeared taken aback by her vehement response. "You can prove your trip?"

"Of course I can. I went to the bank, where I discovered my bastard husband had emptied the account and maxed out the credit line. Then I went to my lawyer to file for divorce and learned my life insurance had been cashed in. Mr. Weiman had to attend to his affairs, so I stayed at a hotel and met with a veterinarian friend. Then I took our local bus back home only to learn of... Why am I telling you all this? Corporal Larsen has already asked the questions and recorded the answers in writing. Are you not sharing files? You have no cause to arrest me if that's what you came for."

"That is not how the law works."

"Good, because——"

The arrival of a truck in the yard cut off Brooke's next words. She stood and went onto the porch. A distraught young girl jumped from the passenger side.

"My name's Vicky. Me and my parents have just moved to Donek two days ago from Montreal. We live on the Point."

Brooke led the teenager inside. "Welcome to the neighborhood."

"My mom drove me here because my dogs are not eating. They don't want to move from their houses. Can you come and save them, please?"

"Tell me about your trip." Brooke took the girl's arm, sat her at the kitchen table under the stupefied eyes of the inspector. "How long were you on the road?"

"Sixteen days because we stopped a lot."

"Did you give water to the dogs?"

"At first they drank and ate, but then they didn't eat."

"After your arrival, did they start drinking?"

The inspector tapped the table to draw the girl's attention. "If you don't mind waiting, we're busy talking here."

Startled, Vicky twisted her hands. As frosty as the air outside, Brooke turned to the inspector. "This is a veterinary emergency. You can leave now. We're done." She took Vicky's hand. "Tell me."

"They're not drinking the water, just licking the snow. I know that's not enough."

"I guess your dogs are dehydrated. I'll give you some electrolyte tablets. How many dogs?"

"Twelve."

"Boil a piece of liver, not too much, just enough to flavor the water, and put a little of that water in their bowls. Crush in one of the tablets in each bowl. Stir it well. I'll come to give them a health check right away. I've finished with this gentleman."

The girl's eyes rounded as she looked at Inspector Whitford standing by his chair, an irritated expression on his face. Vicky pocketed the tablets and ran outside to her mother.

"You'll excuse me, inspector, I have to see about the dogs."

He sighed. "I guess we're done, anyway. Your alibi has been verified."

"Thanks for telling me. Better late than never, isn't how it goes?"

He huffed. "We need the rifle as evidence. When is Mr. Weiman coming back?"

She shrugged. "I don't know. He's only a neighbor who gave me a ride. I know nothing about his life."

He handed her a business card. "When he does, if we haven't met him before, can you let him know we wish to talk to him?"

"Very well."

Unexpectedly, he smiled. "Your biscuits are delicious."

"Thanks." With a puzzled look, she watched him walk back to his vehicle on the road. *City guy! They don't park in people's driveways. Well, walk and slip on the ice.* But he didn't.

She zipped up her parka and picked up her vet's bag.

***

Brooke moved from dog to dog, examining each one carefully, all the while followed by an anxious Vicky. Brooke straightened and gave the girl a reassuring smile. "They have lost some weight but not excessively as far as I can tell without a scale. That's not surprising after a long road trip when they were confined to their boxes."

"We stopped every four hours to let them out and drink."

"Which is very good, but a ten- or fifteen-minute break to stretch their legs isn't quite the same as going for a good run. More importantly, they've come from a different climate and now have to adapt to frigid Yukon."

"That's why we traveled in winter. They like the cold better than the heat, but I understand they have to adapt."

They went over the dogs' diet and a happier Vicky led Brooke into the house to meet her parents.

The mother, Donna, a buxom woman, rushed to set cups on the table. "You'll have time for coffee?"

"That'd be welcome, thank you."

Brooke wasn't about to refuse free coffee. She sat at the kitchen table, next to Vicky who was entering the vet's visit in a log book.

"Garth! Did you find the wallet?" Donna asked.

"Here..." He stopped in his tracks. "Brooke?"

She lifted her head. "That's me." Recognition lit her features. "Welcome back to Yukon, Garth. I almost didn't recognize you."

"It's been a long time. So you did become a doctor."

Although she'd sensed a slight hesitation in Garth, Brooke smiled. "Veterinarian. What brings you back to our lost paradise?"

He relaxed and smiled. "My daughter's passion for sled dogs and racing. My mother's begging. We came into a little money and decided on the move. I have been offered the post of manager of the hotel."

"Congratulations! Your parents must be overjoyed. Now they can spoil their granddaughter."

Donna laughed. "It's all working out very well. Did you know each other before?"

That was so obvious. The thought that the woman was insecure crossed Brooke's mind. "High school in Donek. I was finishing when Garth started high school." And she was not going to tell his wife about Garth's numerous girlfriends, nor about the rumor he got one of them pregnant.

"Brooke was a science wiz and too busy with books to pay attention to guys."

Brooke nodded. So he did need to reassure his wife. "That was my well-deserved reputation. I preferred skiing forty miles than being a cheerleader. Nice to reconnect, and meet you, Donna and your delightful daughter, but you'll have to excuse me. I have patients at the clinic."

The goodbyes were brief. Brooke thanked Garth for the fee as he saw her to her truck.

"If you don't mind, I'd like to ask a question. Did Mélanie ever come back?"

"Not that I know. I didn't know many of the younger girls. After graduation most of them went south. You know that almost nobody comes back."

"If it wasn't for my parents and their insistence because of my father's health, I wouldn't have either."

She climbed into the cab. "Make the best of it."

"Ciao!"

True, I hadn't known many of the girls, but I'd been fully appraised of the gossip thanks to my mother, bless her soul. Garth is courageous coming back here after the scandal. People don't forget and don't pardon easily. He did look a bit worried, though. What about his father's health? It must be serious to bring his son back home. And accepting to manage the hotel where everybody goes at one time or another. Secrets don't exist in a small place like Donek.

Chapter Five

The maroon dog transporter that pulled into the yard was familiar. Brooke smiled. "Hi, Jerome."

He jumped from the cab. "I have about half the money to put down as a deposit."

"Fine, you can give me the rest when you win the Iditarod. I'll help load the dogs."

He scratched his head. "But I can't take them until I finish paying for them."

"Of course you can. You need to train them. I can't do that."

His worried look disappeared. "You sure? I've got everything ready in my dog yard."

She shook her head. "Don't be an idiot. Take the dogs and win. They are all micro-chipped, vaccinated and in perfect health. I'll be glad when they are at your place."

"Yeah, I heard about Campbell."

They had no difficulty loading the excited dogs, for whom climbing in a transporter meant a good run at the other end.

Brooke and Jerome fist-bumped and she went back to her dismal accounting. She didn't have time to despair as a snowmobile pulled into the yard. Conrad took off his helmet.

"What is it this time, good news or bad news?"

"I'm not sure. Larsen asked me to drop by since I was coming into the area. The autopsy unfortunately couldn't confirm what appeared obvious to us, that Seth was killed by the broken neck when the sled careened into the tree, and almost at the same time he was shot and thrown off the sled though seemed to have hung on for a few feet. There're drag marks. The coroner won't take our word for it. He has sent samples to the lab in Ottawa to see if more advanced techniques can be more precise."

"It doesn't tell where or who the shooter was, though."

"No. How long do you think somebody would be able to hang onto a moving sled in the second or two before the body is... I'm not asking this properly."

"You mean before the nervous reflexes let go? Like the headless chicken?"

"Pretty macabre, but yes."

"Death is when the brain shuts off. Then there is an electrochemical reaction of the nerves which, depending on the cause of death, could be a jerking of a limb or crispation of the fingers. So, yes, the body could have hung onto the handlebar for a couple of seconds or maybe three, especially if the body was slumped over the handlebar. It would slide off fairly slowly if the sled was steady."

"With the dogs running at twenty miles per hour, he could have traveled as much as half a mile in one minute. Am I correct?"

She frowned. "More like three hundred and fifty yards in a minute."

He rubbed his neck. "So it could be some ten yards before the body lets go."

Brooke noticed how the conservation officer was carefully avoiding naming her late husband. "Usually, a broken neck causes instantaneous death and you can have the nervous reflexes. When the brain doesn't shut off immediately, the subject will tighten its grip on whatever he is holding. Hitting a tree at speed doesn't automatically break the neck."

"And here is the sticking point. The coroner cannot establish the time of death to the minute or whether the broken neck came first or whether it was the bullet. Right now, everything is pending."

"In effect, he could have broken his neck, hung onto the sled for a couple of seconds before being shot and the body falling on the trail. Does that scenario work?"

Brooke couldn't believe she was discussing all this in such detached manner.

"It does. That's Byron's opinion."

"Since the gunshot wound bled, the bullet had to have struck within a second or two of the broken neck."

"True, dead bodies don't bleed."

She snorted. It was all too gruesome. "How does it help to know that the sled may have traveled ten feet or ten yards or thereabouts?"

"The police have asked us to help find the casing. So it gives us an idea where to begin."

"In all that snow? It'll have sunk to the ground."

"It being hot, it would have melted a hole in the snow. Being conservation officers, we have more experience of the bush. That's why they asked us. They have the crime scene secured, but need a little extra help. It will be a big step forward if we can locate the bullet casing. We once nailed a poacher by his fingerprints on a brass casing."

"But any print will burn off in the firing... no, not all. Salt residues from the skin do not burn. I guess DNA science is advanced enough to identify those minute particles."

"That's what they said. We have to work on snowshoes to avoid disturbing the scene more than necessary. I think we have a strong chance of finding the spent casing from the fatal shot."

"What if the shooter wasn't on the trail but in the bush?"

"We have a good idea of the orientation of the shot. It came from the side, so indeed, off the trail."

"They have recovered the bullet?"

"Yes."

"Give me the details. I know bullet wounds are pretty horrendous." Her medical training hadn't included gunshot wounds, but she'd seen a couple of minor hunting accident in Agate Creek. Her scientific mind always wanted to learn more.

He shook his head. "It hit from the side, shattered the elbow, the ribs and penetrated the chest, hit the spine and stopped. Even high velocity bullets stop when they hit large bones. The shooter didn't come down from the sky, so there'll be some kind of tracks in the snow. A snowfall follows contours. It doesn't fill depressions."

A brief sadness passed over her face. "Of course. Could you use a drone?"

"Ah, our dream. Byron and I are planning to buy one out of our personal funds. The department is too short of money right now to supply us with one. You're right. It'll be invaluable to track down poachers, see animal tracks or human prints for that matter."

"Send them the bill." They chuckled. "Thanks for coming to tell me, and good luck in your search."

After Conrad left, she leaned her forehead against the window. Why wasn't she feeling more than a passing sadness at the death of her husband? Sad, because a human life shouldn't be taken willfully, but nothing came from deep within her heart. The only rising emotion she experienced was anger. Anger that someone would willfully kill another person. *I'll find the bastard and make him pay!* Surprised at her surge of ire, she gathered her bag and set off for the clinic in Donek.

By the end of the day, what with dealing with vaccinations, weight management for obese pets, and a cat owner whose scratch was infected, she was ready to let Erin, her able technician, close the clinic. Finally, Brooke was able to drive home.

A profound fatigue fell onto her shoulders while she put her bag in its place and a box of antibiotics in the fridge. The Canadian Inuit dogs' howls drew a strained smile. "Okay, pups, I'm making your dinner." She glanced out the window. A dog transporter had just driven in.

Before she had time to grab her coat, a knock sounded, and the door opened.

"Dexter! You're back." *What an inane welcome!*

"I've got something for you——"

He didn't finish his sentence. She flew outside hugging the transporter where familiar noses were pushing through breathing holes.

"My huskies! Oh, babies, you're home again!" Tears in her eyes, she turned to Dexter. "How?"

"A long story, but in short, Jimmy sent me a message. That was when we were having dinner at Antoinette's and told you I had to leave on business. I didn't want to tell you about locating the kennel just in case it didn't turn out to be the right one. Jimmy and I drove to the place."

"But they had been bought and paid for."

"There was the problem of the four that had escaped. The musher had called the Mounties, believing they had been stolen. We had to explain over again, but the evidence was there, broken collars still lying in the snow. That's why it took so long."

"First time those breakaway collars have proven their worth."

He tilted his head, waiting for an explanation.

"Breakaway collars will separate under abnormal pressure, like being caught on an obstacle or the dog lunging forward with great strength."

"High tech! They must be expensive. He knew about this type of collar. Anyway, when he admitted that he had no bill of sale and no health certificates for the dogs, the Mountie suggested we negotiate. It was obvious the dogs were sold without the consent of the rightful owner. They were stolen property."

"Never thought of that."

"The officers gave him a lecture about buying without papers. As a goodwill gesture, I told him to keep the collars and added a few bucks. He already had ten dogs and had hoped to build a team to race. When I told him those had been discarded because of injuries that made them unable to run a race, he finally parted with them. He said something about if they didn't race, he could always keep them for breeding. That is until Jimmy informed him they were spayed and neutered. They are, aren't they?"

"Yes, they are! Thank you! Thank you!" She threw her arms around his neck and kissed him. Then jumped back, reddening. "Sorry, I'm so happy."

"You can thank me like that any time you like."

They unloaded the huskies and led them to their pen. "Now I am really in your debt." She didn't like the prospect, but she'd deal with that later.

After all the dogs had been fed and petted, Brooke invited Dexter to dinner. "It's only a stew."

"That's an offer I can't refuse. Fast-food restaurants don't offer what I call meals."

Over her homemade tisane, she broached the subject of finance. "How much do I owe you? Would you accept monthly small amounts?"

"You owe me nothing."

She bristled. "That's not how I work. How much?"

He let out an exaggerated sigh. "It was only a few bills. I'll give you an invoice only if you agree to the terms of repayment."

"Which are?"

"That all the other creditors get paid first."

Arms lifted in defeat, she stood. "By the way, the RCMP want to talk to you."

Dexter screwed up his face. "What for?"

"Of course, you don't know. Seth Lammers, my now ex-husband, was found dead on the trail with a broken neck and a bullet in his chest."

Eyebrows raised, Dexter remained silent for a moment. "When?"

"I'm losing track of time. I came back on the Thursday's bus, learned the news on arrival. It was the day before that."

"Where did this happen? Any suspects?"

"Out near Tootook Lake. As for suspects, I'm Number One."

"You? It can't be. You were in Whitehorse with me."

She sighed. "That's what I told the investigator, but it hasn't stopped them pointing fingers. He wanted to speak to you when you got back. Here's his card."

"I better phone to let him know."

"It's evening. Good luck with cell phone coverage." She poured another cup of tisane. "You better use the radio. Just remember, everybody will be listening."

"Of course, all the Donek kids are on the internet sucking up the bandwidth, what little there is of it." He helped himself to more tisane and another biscuit. "I don't understand why they can't build a relay tower."

"That's what I have been pushing for, but it'll never happen."

Dexter stood up. "I do keep some business connections. I'll make that tower happen, if it's the last thing I do. I'll go home and phone."

"The internet is probably better at three a.m."

He laughed and pulled a phone from his pocket. "Satellite. I have to go to Donek. I'll call in on my way back. Do you need anything?"

A head shake and a grimace were her reply.

After doing the dishes and going over her accounts once more, Brooke squared her shoulders. "I won't let it pull me down into a dark abyss. I'll survive. It's only money. The dogs are alright." Glad there was no one to hear her talk aloud, she put the books away. Just then, Dexter's Jeep pulled into the yard. He walked in carrying a small box of groceries.

"I heard that chocolate cake was your favorite."

The sound that came from her throat was half way between a wail and a whoop.

"Glad to hear your appreciation. Let's make coffee."

"Sorry, I don't have any."

With a wink, he pulled a packet of coffee from the box.

Chapter Six

Routine wasn't a feature of Brooke's life. The highlight of her day was the couple who came to adopt one of the huskies. They already had adopted a rescue and wanted a companion for it. There were just a few howls. The rescued huskies had all come from different places and hadn't formed a pack. They were just good neighbors to one another. Before starting her dinner, she took the remaining huskies for an easy sled ride, much to the protesting dismay of the Inuit dogs. They always considered that it was their right to go, too, although Alex had earlier taken them out on the small sled two at a time.

In the morning, she was preparing to go to the clinic in Donek when a SUV pulled into the yard. A man carrying a child and a woman came to her door. Brooke had long since got used to taking care of the scrapes and bruises of the local children. She ushered them into her living room.

"Sorry to disturb you, Ms. Porter. I am Roy Johnson, from Fletcher Creek. We're very concerned about our son, Ethan."

Brooke's eyes went back to the pale, lethargic boy in his father's arms.

"Roy went to Donek, but the nurse practitioner isn't..."

At the sound of the voice, Brooke turned to Mrs. Johnson with a frown. She knew that melodious voice. High school choir. For a few seconds, the silence stretched.

"Mélanie?"

"Yes, Brooke. It's me."

She motioned the couple to sit in the corner she called her home clinic. "What's the problem with Janice Miller?"

Mélanie took a big breath. "She said Ethan had the flu and is just a bit anemic and to give him vitamins and good food. His teacher, Miss Peters, said he has deteriorated and is so tired all the time that maybe we should take him to the doctor in Whitehorse. His flu isn't going away."

Brooke bristled. "You realize I'm not a doctor. I'm not licensed to treat anything other than animals."

"I know, but I'd like your opinion. After all, there can't be much difference between doctoring dogs and children."

Teeth gritted, Brooke made an effort to remain impassive while images came back, haunting her mind. *I can't. I can't.* "Lay him on the sofa. I can listen to his heart and take his temperature. That's all."

The temperature was elevated. "Does he often have a fever?"

Mélanie bit her lip. "I didn't think to check. But sometimes he feels hot."

"Nosebleeds?"

"A few times, and I think twice in the last two weeks," Roy said.

With gentle hands, Brooke opened the boy's shirt and, after warming her stethoscope in her hand, she listened to his heart. She took her time when she detected one beat out of tune with the rest. At the same time, she was aware of the parents' mounting anxiety. When a second beat faintly registered in her ears, she knew the child had a problem other than a persistent flu or anemia. As she palpated his neck, her mind ran over her old medical textbook. Swollen lymph glands. She checked his armpit, knowing already she'd find swollen lymph glands.

No, she wasn't a doctor. She had no right to tell the parents that she recognized the signs of what could well be Acute Lymphoblastic Leukemia. The symptoms were all there, including the diagnosis of anemia from a health care professional. But, there was something she could do in the immediate. She took a bag of plasma serum and began a perfusion under the alarmed eyes of the parents. Legally, she wasn't allowed to do this, and no need to tell them it was serum from dogs. She remembered how a colleague had saved a child's life with it. It was a struggle to find a vein in the dehydrated child, but after a couple of attempts, she was successful.

The tension in the room rose to unbearable. "Ethan is very weak and dehydrated. This serum will give him enough strength for the trip to the capital."

"What... what..." Roy was stuttering and Mélanie let tears run down her face.

"Do you have an emergency bag in your vehicle?"

Alarm spread over his face. "Yes. What... What is wrong?"

As Brooke was not answering, Mélanie straightened. "Tell me! I know you went into medicine. Tell me!"

The anguish in her voice shattered Brooke's heart. It took her a lot of efforts to speak. "I changed to veterinary. I am not a licensed physician. That's why you have to take your child to Whitehorse without delay. Give him sips of water, keep him warm and go straight to the emergency at the hospital."

Roy rushed out to warm up the vehicle.

Tears ran down Mélanie's face. "You know it. Tell me what's wrong, please, tell me."

Brooke closed her eyes, the anguish in the mother's voice tearing at her heart. "I wish I could. I hear an uneven beat in his heart and he has swollen lymph glands." That she could tell. "It has to be attended to in a hospital."

"He is going to die."

"No. You take him to the hospital and remain calm, cheerful and positive. Yes, positive, so he can feel your love and support. Do you have food for the road?" She was removing the empty serum bag and needle.

Roy had come back in carrying a blanket. "Just the emergency rations."

"I'm glad you do have an emergency pack. But take these." While Mélanie dressed Ethan, Brooke hurriedly packed several of the old-fashioned biscuits she had made the night before and the boiled eggs she had intended for her lunch. In the fridge, she had a slice of elk meat already cooked. She cut slices of the last of her bread and made sandwiches.

Mélanie had wrapped her son in the blanket and talked softly to him. Roy took the package and reached for his wallet.

"This isn't veterinary care, so there's no charge. You'll come back to tell me how it went. Just go for now. Don't waste time, but drive safely. The road conditions are unpredictable in winter."

Jaw clenched, Roy nodded. After their vehicle had departed, Brooke collapsed on the sofa. Since she had come back and built up the vet clinic, she had believed the nightmares were over. This had just started them over. She shook herself. No, it was different. There was no nurse handing her the wrong medication. Medication she hadn't checked before injecting it into the baby when she was an intern in the pediatric ward. She had requested atropine to sustain the child's heart. Why, oh why, had she not checked the label? The vial contained potassium chloride. Brooke shuddered as the image of the little body convulsing still grew larger and larger before exploding in her head. Despite the diligent effort of the resuscitating team, the life that had barely begun was extinguished forever.

There was one thing she could do, and that was to phone to warn the General Hospital in the capital. Not trusting the internet to cut off in the middle of the call, she drove to Donek at breakneck speed by the shortcut over the frozen creek.

As she told the hospital receptionist to expect a child in a serious condition, the woman asked if she wanted to speak to a doctor. Brooke couldn't say no.

"What serious condition do you mean?"

"Sorry, Dr. Fischer, I am a veterinarian, not a medical doctor. All I know is the child needs urgent attention."

"You've taken the trouble to warn us. You must suspect something. It'd help to have your input."

"What if I'm wrong?"

He chuckled drily. "Then I'll remember you are only a vet."

"Alright. He has a fever, and according to the mother, it's recurring. He also has an irregular heartbeat, swollen lymph gland and nosebleeds. He is weak and tired to the point of being lethargic."

"Anemia?"

"Acute lymphoblastic leukemia?"

"I'm impressed. You described the symptoms accurately. You're most likely right. Have they seen a doctor?"

"This is Agate Creek. There's no doctor in our neck of the woods. The local nurse practitioner diagnosed anemia, but that's almost always the first diagnosis until tests are conducted."

"My! You're knowledgeable. True, anemia is the first handy diagnosis. Thank you for talking to me."

"By the way, I gave him a perfusion of serum of plasma... dog plasma."

There was a throaty sound on the line. "Sounds like the right decision. I heard some case when dog serum of plasma had been used to save a life. I didn't expect to ever see it, though. I'll prep for his arrival. I suppose you'd like to know the results?"

"Yes, please."

"I'll phone you."

"My home number is at the mercy of a freak internet connection, but I have an answering machine at my Donek clinic."

She gave him both numbers and leaned back in her chair. Thoughts raced through her mind. What if I'm wrong? No, I'm sure I made the right diagnosis. It's not... The memory clouded her vision. She hit the desk with her fists. "No, no..."

Her assistant half-opened the door. "Psst! Brooke, got some clients waiting."

When she arrived home that evening, Jimmy and Dexter were talking in the yard. Jimmy told her he had fed and exercised the dogs.

"And he gave me a lesson in dog sledding," Dexter said. "And by the way, I gave your rifle to the RCMP."

"Will I get it back? It's needed in the spring to scare off the hungry grizz that are roaming, looking for food."

"You will. They only want to verify it wasn't the one involved in the homicide."

"That's reassuring." She couldn't hide the sarcasm in her voice. "How will they know it isn't the rifle that did the killing?"

"Easy. It hasn't been fired in months."

Her shoulders rose up to her ears and her hands opened in a hopeless gesture. "More like a year or two. How can one tell it's not been fired?"

A half-smile hovered on his lips. "Dust in the barrel."

"Bang goes my housewife's reputation."

"Apart from that, they've recovered the fatal bullet. Ballistics will eliminate your Marlin."

They laughed heartedly. Jimmy went home, but Dexter lingered.

Brooke teased him. "Waiting for an invitation to supper?"

"I have a fresh fish to contribute." His smile disarmed her.

"Sure, bring it in."

He picked up the cooler in his truck and followed her in.

"Look at that! An Arctic grayling! You didn't catch it yourself, did you?"

"Alas no. I don't have time to fish. I talked to a fellow who was ice-fishing. It always intrigued me how someone could sit for hours in the cold to catch some fish. He was jigging. That too was new to me."

"I've seen it done. Lightly shake the line up and down."

He smiled. "That's what the guy said. Not any old shake, just the right one."

Brooke had to laugh. "Excellent advice."

While talking, she was expertly fileting the grayling. "Please grind up some breadcrumbs with the manual mill on the shelf. One slice should be enough."

They worked in silence. Once the breaded fish filets were sizzling in a pan on the stove, and yesterday's baked potatoes were warming in the oven, Brooke rolled her aching shoulders.

"Allow me." Dexter moved behind her to massage her shoulders.

She liked the feel of his warm hands. It awoke sensations long dormant in her. For a moment, she wondered whether he was going to kiss her. Just as well she had her back to him, because he would have read that she was willing to taste a kiss from his well-formed lips. The temptation to turn round grew in intensity. The timer pinged all too soon.

They were doing the dishes when there was a knock at the door. Inspector Whitford stood on the threshold. "Mr. Weiman? I was told I could find you here."

"Good evening, inspector. I have already taken the rifle to the Royal Canadian Mounted Police detachment."

"So I heard. I need to ask a few questions about your whereabouts in the last seven days."

"Certainly. If you like to follow me to my cabin."

"You have a brand new truck with dog boxes, but you don't have any dogs."

"Not yet. Please, follow me."

"Where did you go on the night of the fifth?"

"I'll give you a detailed account of my movements. As I just said, follow me to my cabin. Ms. Porter needs to rest."

His bearing, his voice, the way he articulated his words, struck Brooke that this was a man used to being in charge of men. The inspector must have felt it too. He meekly turned and stepped after Dexter.

Brooke allowed herself a quiet laugh. Who exactly was Dexter Weiman? He had bought the big cabin in the woods for cash, as far as anyone knew. He was absent several days at a time without telling anyone where he was going. In the north country, people always let a neighbor know of their destination. It was an unspoken rule of safety in a region with a harsh climate. Satellite phones were very expensive to own and operate, yet he had one. He also had a fancy Jeep, a Grand Wagoneer, no less, and now an almost new truck with a transporter to make him blend in. Even second hand, they weren't cheap. Come to think of it, his clothes, though not flashy, were above average quality compared to what dog mushers usually wore. That was not surprising. Mushers were cash poor. All their money was sunk into dog care and race fees. In Donek, there were a few well-off people who dressed expensively, yet not quite like Dexter. Or rather, the difference was not so much in the price of clothes but in his bearing. He could wear cheap garments and still look in charge. Yes, that was it. The man had that air of people who had always been in charge of situations.

A stress headache was threatening. She went out to check on the dogs, talking to them and promising the last two rescued Alaskan huskies that they would be adopted together or they would stay with her appeased her tormented mind.

***

Brooke contemplated her shopping list and crossed out half of it. Dried beans and lentils were nutritious, with a load of protein, carbs and minerals. She had plenty of herbs and still enough spices to make them into delicious meals. And most essential, they were cheap. Add to that the odd rabbit or cut of moose meat, or the pickles and other home preserves she frequently accepted in payment for her services, life was still good.

The bean chili she had put on the stove simmered, releasing a tangy aroma. A glance at her accounts book depressed her, but she fought off the impending gloom. Once that every dog, cat and parrot in the area had been vaccinated, dewormed and neutered or spayed, there wouldn't be too much ongoing revenue. The now familiar knock on the door pulled her out of her reverie.

"Dexter, did you smell my bean chili?"

He laughed. "No, but now that I'm here, I can say it smells mouthwatering. Am I too late with moose steaks?"

Emotions roiled inside her. She was so afraid to misread his attentions. Did he by any chance bring her steaks knowing she wouldn't buy any because of her financial predicament?

As the steaks finished grilling, she transferred the bean chili into a serving dish and put the bread she'd baked late last night on the table.

After coffee, he took his leave but lingered by the door. Brooke smiled. "Thanks for bringing the steaks. It was pleasant sharing supper with you."

His hands snaked around her, pulling her against his solid frame. "I enjoyed every moment. Can we do it again?"

"Any time loneliness descends on you."

A gentle kiss touched her lips. She sighed and let herself go against him. The brief kiss lit a fire in her. There would be more to come, she was sure. When she thought about it, she liked the idea.

CHAPTER SEVEN

In the morning, just as Brooke was preparing to head to the clinic, the phone rang. She hurried to it before the internet might cut off.

"Brooke, Dr. Fischer here. You made an amazingly accurate diagnosis. We have a problem, though. To save the little tyke's life, we need to do a marrow transplant."

"With a compatible donor. How can I help?"

"Mrs. Johnson would like to talk to you."

The phone began to cut out. Brooke had only time to hear Mélanie plead for her to come to the hospital. Aghast, Brooke stared at the dead phone in her hand. Go to the hospital? But she was in no way related to Mélanie's family. The woman's parents had moved from Montreal to Donek when Mélanie was a baby. Her father, a doctor and a keen musher, had ambitions that could best be achieved in a community dedicated to sled dogs. It all came crashing down when the teenage Mélanie became pregnant and ran away from home during a blizzard. The whole town searched for her. It added to the scandal when it was revealed her boyfriend had stolen money from his parents' house and gone away with her. Mrs. Dubois' daughter's sense of the dramatic cost the town much anguish, not to mention expense. What didn't have an apparent cost were the rumors, secrets behind the closed doors of the doctor's house. It was too much to take in and Mrs. Dubois fell victim to a stroke. After her death, the doctor packed up and left.

Brooke checked her agenda. Nothing more serious than dispensing deworming pills, which Erin could do. Another look at her useless phone irritated Brooke. She got on the radio, calling to any Donek resident who might be monitoring the waves. Glenn came on and reassured her he was phoning Erin. Her heart filled with warmth at the kindness of people and dressed for the long trip, grabbed her thermos and the sandwiches she'd made for her lunch and headed out.

Her truck engine protested loudly while Brooke shivered. "Come on! Start!" Her frustration was mounting beyond her usual patience when she saw Dexter's Jeep pull into the yard.

"Trouble?"

"Not half. I plugged the block heater in last night, but the plug must have fallen out. I think I tripped over the wire and didn't check back."

"I'll give you a ride."

"Thanks, but I'm on my way to Whitehorse."

"Then, I'll drive you to Whitehorse. You can use my phone to talk to your assistant. It sounds like an emergency."

Brooke jumped down and threw her arms around his neck. "Thanks." She reddened, and not from the cold.

"Mmm... I could get used to being thanked."

With a laugh, he picked up her bag and lunch from her truck while she called Erin on his satellite phone to apologize for leaving without notice. Her assistant confirmed that she had received the message from Glenn and not to worry, everything would be taken care of and if there were an emergency, she'd call Jimmy.

Moments later, Brooke and Dexter were on their way.

"Where to in Whitehorse?"

"The hospital." At his brief enquiring look, she elaborated. "I sent parents with a sick child to the hospital. The boy needs a marrow transplant, and the mother believes I can help find a donor or something like that. The phone cut off before we could talk."

His hand found hers and squeezed it. "Do you always put people in need ahead of yourself?"

She cocked her head. "Wouldn't you if the life of a five-year-old was in the balance?"

"That's why I'm driving you. I don't know the story, but the vibes you're giving out speak of the urgency."

Thankful that the good weather was holding, Brooke told him about the visit with Ethan and Mélanie's morning frantic phone call. Dexter handed her the phone again and told her to phone the hospital to say they were on their way and could she talk to Ethan's mother. A distraught Roy came on the phone to say that Mélanie was in crisis and a doctor was attending to her.

Brooke reassured him she'd soon be at the hospital. She didn't tell him she hadn't a clue how she could help, but she'd try, anyway. Daylight made a short appearance while she shared her sandwiches with Dexter, as they ate without stopping.

In Whitehorse, Dexter let her out at the hospital. "Your phone will work here, so call me when you need picking up." He tucked a brown, errant lock under her tuque and lightly touched his lips to hers.

The fleeting kiss lightened her anxiety. She strode into the hospital lobby. A tear-faced, wobbling Mélanie jumped out of a chair, almost colliding with Brooke.

"I'm sorry."

"Calm down, please. I'm here to see if I can help." She led Mélanie back to a chair and sat beside her.

"The doctor said it's cancer." A new fit of tears shook her. "We have to find someone closely related for a marrow transplant. I'm not a match. I'm his mother and I'm not a match!" She took a long breath. "I was fifteen when I first got pregnant. I went to my grandmother in Montreal and had the baby adopted. I must find the baby."

It wasn't a big shock for Brooke. "How old would the child be now? Fifteen?"

"Fourteen. I didn't want to know anything about it."

Although she suspected the answer, Brooke had to ask. "Who is the father?"

"You can't involve him."

"Mélanie!" She was rapidly losing patience. Eyes closed, she took a deep inhalation. "The rumor had it that Garth Devriendt was the father."

Head down, Mélanie said "yes" in a low voice.

"He's back in Donek, managing the hotel. He's married with a fourteen-year-old daughter." The coincidence appeared too enormous to Brooke. Garth's daughter? Mélanie's daughter? It couldn't be. For the moment, it was best to say nothing. "Either one could be a match. I'll need to find out more."

"Dr. Fischer and Dr. Lewis asked to see you."

"I know the way. Pull yourself together, then come up."

Mélanie caught Brooke's arm. "Please don't tell Roy about my having had a baby."

"That might be difficult if we are to try to find that baby."

"Our marriage is very shaky. My fault, I know. We're only together because of Ethan." Mélanie's mental state was degrading. Brooke signaled to a nurse hovering nearby and repressed a sigh. "It was very obvious to me that Roy loves his son. Was he not registered for the Yukon Quest?"

"He was."

"Yes. I microchipped his dogs. At the time, I didn't know he was your husband. And he's missing training. That shows me he'll do what is best for his boy." Brooke turned and went to the elevators. The nurse took over with Mélanie.

At the pediatric ward reception, she encountered Dr. Fischer leaning on the counter and talking to another doctor. Dr. Lewis she presumed and approached.

"Ah, Brooke, let me introduce——"

"Eileen!"

"Brooke!"

"Okay, I think you've met," Dr. Fischer said. "I'm David."

The two women hugged, ignoring him.

"It's been a long time. So you became a vet. Why don't you come back to medicine? You don't seem to have lost your touch."

With a strained smile, Brooke shook her head. "I'm a vet and love it."

"I think you'd make a terrific doctor, if I may say so," David Fischer said. "Your diagnosis and prompt action with the dog serum saved this little boy's life... for the moment."

The turmoil of emotions threatened to drown Brooke. She steeled herself. "You're looking for a marrow match. How do I come in?"

The pediatrician held her elbow and directed her to her office. "We started chemo. It gives us a few more days to find a donor."

David Fisher followed. "Mrs. Johnson is far too distraught to be of any help, but she said you could."

"A complicated story. Ethan's mother had a baby when she was a teenager. We have to try to trace it. She or he would be about fourteen now," Brooke said.

"And she doesn't want her husband to know about it," Eileen replied.

"I don't see how she can avoid it. She left Donek and went to Montreal to her grandmother's, according to the gossip."

David pulled the computer toward him. "Can you ask her where she gave birth, what day and time, and who made the arrangements for the adoption?" He scrolled to a protected website and entered his password.

"I know who the father is. He has a daughter, too." She refrained from mentioning her suspicions. She wanted to make sure.

"I'll go and talk to Mélanie again. She must be calmer now," said Eileen.

David handed Brooke his phone. "Call the father. We're asking volunteers to try for a match."

A feeling of doom invaded Brooke, like being in the eye of a hurricane. She punched in the Donek hotel number.

"May I speak to Garth, please? Tell him Brooke is calling." She drummed her fingers on the desk.

A man's voice came on the line. "Brooke, what's going on?"

"Thanks for taking my call. Can you talk privately?"

"I'm in my office. Privately?"

"I'm at the Whitehorse hospital. Mélanie's five-year-old son has leukemia and is desperately needing a marrow transplant. We are trying to find the child that Mélanie gave up for adoption in the chance that it could be a match. Do you know anything about the adoption arrangements?"

There was a stony silence. "I know nothing."

"Yes, you do." Brooke asked forgiveness for the lie, or half-lie or no lie at all, she was about to articulate. "You followed Mélanie to Montreal."

The sound of the phone being disconnected resonated in her ears. He knew! She crumpled into the armchair, but promptly straightened again. "He hung up."

"Not cooperative, that fellow." David shook his head. "He does have a kid, you said?"

Lost in a turmoil of thoughts, Brooke didn't hear him, but her subconscious registered the words. She jerked upright. "It'd be too much of a coincidence. It can't be. Of course, he doesn't want his wife to know. But that would mean Donna, the wife, may not be the mother."

"Would you, please, explain what's going through your mind?" Dr. Lewis asked.

Brook started. "I think I'm going crazy. Garth Devriendt is the father of Mélanie's baby. He recently came back to Donek with a wife and fourteen-year-old daughter." An expectant silence settled for a minute. "Garth was sixteen at the time. I was already in university, but according to the gossip, when Mélanie ran off in the middle of the storm, he left his home, too, telling his mother Mélanie was about to commit suicide. Every able body in town looked for her in the middle of the blizzard. The town's volunteer search and rescue was alerted. They all thought Garth was also trying to rescue her. It was known they were constantly seen together. They didn't find her and a rescuer almost lost his life. When the storm abated, Garth had also disappeared. His father was the mayor at the time and was raving mad. He halted the search. Garth didn't come back to finish high school. I don't know what had happened in their house, whether he had thrown him out or told him to go and shoulder his responsibilities. I suspect Garth knew where Mélanie was going. Probably had agreed to meet beforehand."

With his chin in his hand, David was frowning. "What could he do at sixteen?"

"He could have made sure his name was on the birth certificate," Eileen said.

Brooke nodded. "I imagine the grandmother helped somehow. Unfortunately, she passed away."

"Do you really think the fourteen-year-old could be Mélanie's?" David asked.

"If Garth looked mature enough when he went to put his name on the birth certificate, he could have been able to take the baby," Eileen said. "Especially with the grandmother coming along to guarantee a home and proper care for the baby."

A shake of the head from Brooke showed the suggestion wasn't plausible. "Mélanie said she didn't even know whether it was a boy or a girl. The baby was taken away immediately."

"This could be true, or what if Mélanie is lying?" David said.

The two women raised their eyebrows. They had thought of it, too.

"I'll go and wring her neck," Brooke said.

She stood and strode out. She found Mélanie in her son's room, watching him through the plastic curtain that isolated him and his fragile immune system. Brooke signaled for her to come out. Roy was snoozing in an easy chair.

"If you want to save your son's life by finding the baby you gave up, you have to be completely truthful and give me all the answers. Come to the doctor's office." While talking, Brooke was gently leading Mélanie. "Where and what date was your baby born?"

The young woman opened her bag and extracted a wrinkled paper. "The nurse gave it to me, saying that I had to keep it for legal purposes."

Brooke's eyes rounded.

"It shows Garth as the father?"

"He told me to agree, otherwise he'd go back home and tell everything."

"I'm not interested in the rest, just what happened after the birth."

"I lied. I said I didn't know, but I had a baby girl. My grandmother took her away."

"Garth knew?"

Mélanie wiped her tearing eyes. "He was staying with her. He worked in a hotel and paid my room and board to a foster home social services had found for me. He was with me when the baby was born. I was a wreck. I didn't want the baby. I never saw her. Grandma sent me to a boarding school in Ontario. As an orphan. That's what my grandmother said I had become. I stayed with a family during all the holidays. They were good to me, not like my parents." She shuddered.

For a moment, Brooke regretted not having paid more attention to the gossip. there was a lot that remained unsaid. "So, Garth and your grandmother raised the baby. Correct?"

"I presume so. Grandma could have had her adopted. I don't know. I never went back. I don't know where Garth is. He never tried to contact me. I didn't either. The Kershaws, my foster parents, paid for me to go to Dalhousie University. They introduced me to Roy. I didn't know he was a dog sledding racer from Lac Saint-Jean in Quebec, but I was happy to be around dogs again, and when I finished my degree in accounting we were married. All was well until two years ago, when he had the opportunity to move to Fletcher Creek and train for the big races, like the Yukon Quest. We had rows, because I didn't want to move. It was too close to Donek for comfort."

Brooke squeezed her shoulder. "Go back to Roy and Ethan. I'll keep the note while I try to sort things out. Be reassured, we'll do whatever is needed to save your son's life."

In the doctor's office, Brooke smoothed the paper. "The date, time and location of the birth is here. I'm going back to Donek to confront Garth in person. Vicky, his daughter, is fourteen. If my math is correct, since he was two years behind me in high school, he fathered her when he was sixteen. So far, it all fits." And if it did, a lot of people were going to be hurt.

"Good luck!" the two doctors said in unison.

A quick glance around the hospital lobby and Brooke spotted Dexter. He had seen her.

"Can we go back to Donek, please?"

He frowned. "We'll go first thing in the morning."

"What about right now?"

"It's that urgent? We should eat first. I can't drive on granola bars."

Shoulders slumped, she sighed. "You're right. We'd arrive after midnight too."

Briefly, she appraised him about the situation. "If he refuses to see me, I don't know what else we can do. He hung up on me."

"Then maybe I'd talk to him, man to man."

"You would, although it isn't your problem?"

"You said a five-year-old child's life is in the balance. I'll make sure the scales tip on our side."

"Thank you." She was saying that word rather a lot these days.

The Jeep pulled into the parking of the Raven Inn. "I've booked the last couple of rooms. With all the events happening in Whitehorse, the hotels are pretty full."

"The Alcan international snowmobile rally and the Carbon Hill sled dog race do attract a lot of people."

"Not to mention the exceptional display of northern lights this year, which attracts many tourists from more southern countries."

The hostess showed them to their rooms. "This is an apartment suite. You can lock the communicating door."

They thanked her and examined the suite.

"Which side do you want?" Dexter asked. "The bedroom is small, but has the bathroom."

"Fine with me. If you don't mind sleeping on the sofa bed in this lovely sitting room."

He dropped their bags onto the stand. "Let's go to the restaurant downstairs."

"I'm ravenous. How early can we leave in the morning?"

"We can set off before dawn if you like."

"Dawn is relative. It doesn't get light until mid-morning."

"We can leave at four or five, then."

A smile spread over her face. "We'll make breakfast here, since we have a kitchenette."

Dexter laughed and motioned her into the elevator.

"Five, after breakfast?"

"It's a deal."

They were shown to a table. The conversation came back to what Brooke called *her problem.*

"In fact, if you had Vicky's birthday, it'd confirm your suspicions."

"No point in asking the school. They wouldn't release it. Privacy concerns and all that."

A waiter brought two steaming plates and a takeout bag of breakfast items. Dexter placed his hand over Brooke's, his thumb gently caressing her smooth skin. Shivers ran down her spine. She tried to recall when was the last time a current of pleasure ran through her.

"Maybe your friend Ron could look it up," he said.

"The RCMP doesn't have the power to do that instantly. Fletcher Creek is a small detachment. Only two officers."

"It wouldn't hurt to ask. A child's life is at stake."

Brooke dug into the chocolate mousse. "As you said, a child's life is at stake. We don't have time to wait for people to go through official channels."

In the crowded elevator, Dexter's arm encircled her waist. She trembled under his touch. Her heart beat faster. Back in the suite, they stood by the communicating door.

"Goodnight," Dexter whispered. He pulled her close and his lips left a butterfly kiss on her forehead.

Her heart pounded against her ribs as she struggled to find words to stop the inevitable. She could no more push him away than douse the wave of heat that rolled over her. When his lips took hers, she was lost.

Chapter Eight

The day was sweeping away the last grayness of the sky when Dexter pulled up in front of the Donek Hotel. Brooke alighted from the vehicle. Her mind rehearsing the words she'd use to convince Garth to talk. She didn't stop to speak to the woman at the reception desk but marched straight to Garth's office under her bemused look. The clerk was probably thinking nothing had changed and women were still running after him.

Without wasting time, Brooke knocked and entered the room.

"Brooke!"

"I don't have much time. When is Vicky's birthday?"

"Get out of here!"

"Actually, it doesn't matter. We can get the exact date by other means. What is important is that Vicky is your and Mélanie's child and that Mélanie's five-year-old son is her half-brother who needs a marrow transplant to save his life. Parents are never a match, but siblings very often are. Now, do you want to be responsible for the death of an innocent child?"

Garth collapsed in his office chair and cradled his head in his hands.

Brooke's patience grew thin. "Well?"

He lifted his head. "Vicky doesn't know Donna isn't her biological mother."

"She needs to be told."

"She'll be devastated. My wife came into our lives when Vicky was two. As a toddler, she never bonded very strongly with Donna. I swore never to tell my daughter. Too much hurt is going to happen."

Brooke sighed. "This is not the moment for maudlin sentiments. First, tell your daughter on her own."

"Is there not another way round this? Like an appeal in the media. I'd encouraged her to volunteer."

"Garth! The situation doesn't leave enough time for that. And no matter what, the truth needs to be told. Secrets have a way of blowing up in the participants' faces."

"I didn't want to come back. My father sent the ad for the hotel manager to me. Donna saw it. He begged me to come home. Both my wife and daughter pressured me. What an opportunity for dog sledding for my daughter and being close to the grandparents."

"Great. But now you've come. Tell them the truth."

Garth slowly drew both hands over his face. "She's in school right now."

Brooke's tone hardened. "That's precisely two blocks west, turn right."

"Shut up!"

"Would you prefer me to go and do it?"

He deflated like a party balloon. "It's almost lunch time. I'll get her. Please, stay. We'll have lunch in the private dining room. She thinks the world of you. It could help."

"Agreed."

He struggled into his parka while Brooke paused in the lobby to tell Dexter to grab some lunch for himself. She took a seat in the cozy private dining room. Minutes later, Vicky bounded into the room.

"Isn't this marvelous? Dad's taken me out of school just so I could come and have lunch with you."

She began to launch into dog talk. Brooke smiled with indulgence. A waitress pushed a trolley laden with salad and cold meats, as well as a mouthwatering chocolate cake. After inquiring whether they needed anything else, she promptly served and left. They ate while Vicky still talked between mouthfuls.

Before Garth reached for the dessert, he took his daughter's hand in his. "Sweetheart, we have got something to tell you."

The seriousness of his tone halted Vicky in mid-sentence.

"I have a secret I kept from you. When I was a teenager, I had a love affair with another teenager and you were conceived."

Vicky's head swung a questioning face to Brooke.

"No, not me."

"Mama?"

Uncomfortable, Garth squirmed in his chair.

Brooke took a deep breath. "Your biological mother couldn't keep you, but her grandmother, your great-grandmother, took you to raise with your father's help. Now, she has married a good man and you are half-sister to a five-year-old boy."

The young girl leaned back against her chair, face screwed to try to make sense of the bombshell. After a moment, she turned to Brooke. "So my mo... my biological mother has been found and I have a brother. Does Mom know?"

Eyes down, Garth shook his head. "She'd have been so hurt."

"Your father thought it was best if you grew up before telling you——"

"That's stupid!"

"Why this has come to a head now is that your half-brother has a serious disease, leukemia. We're looking for a bone marrow match and you are likely to be one."

Vicky grabbed her head in her hands, closed her eyes and let out a huge breath. She rocked against the backrest of her chair. A moment later, she stood so suddenly the glasses fell and spilled water over the tablecloth. "What are we waiting for? We must go to the hospital."

"First, we tell your mother, then I'll drive you," Garth said. His voice sounded unsure and almost wobbly.

Her face set hard, Vicky shook her head, a new assertiveness empowering her. "You tell my mother. It's your mess. Brooke will drive me."

"You need a change of clothes," Brooke said.

"Okay, let's go home."

Brooke eyed the chocolate cake regretfully. The girl caught her look and grabbed the cake.

"We'll eat it on the way."

In the lobby, a waiting Dexter stepped forward. "Happy to meet you, Vicky."

"Are you driving Brooke?"

He smiled. "I am."

"Good! I'm going with you. Here's the cake."

He glanced at Brooke and Garth. "I'll be happy to be your driver."

His face drained of color, Garth nodded and hurried to his office to get his coat. Outside, Dexter led the way to his Jeep.

"Cool truck!" Vicky carefully took back the cake. Dexter pulled the tablet in the back and set the cake on it with his pocketknife next to it. Vicky and Brooke settled on the soft leather seat in the back.

Chapter Nine

At the house, Donna was sitting with a sandwich and a coffee. She stood when her daughter burst into the kitchen and threw her arms around her neck.

"I have a brother. He needs me. I'll pack some clothes." In a whirlwind, she reached the stairs. "You are not my mother, but it's alright, I love you."

Pale and about to faint, Donna tottered. Brooke caught her and helped her sit down, then succinctly explained the events of the last few days. Hurried steps on the stairs announced Vicky's return. She bent over and kissed her mother. "Love you, mama. Dad is arriving. He'll explain. I must go." Still moving like lightning, she grabbed spoons from a drawer, a handful of paper napkins and rushed to the door.

"Where to?" Her mother spoke with anguish.

"Whitehorse hospital. Don't worry, I'll be there," Brooke said.

As Garth entered the kitchen, Vicky, without a glance at her father, stepped out.

Dexter held the passenger's door opened.

"Ladies, please sit in my mobile restaurant. Dessert is served." He caught Brooke's eyes and nodded. She sat next to Vicky.

Brooke had already punched in Dr. Fischer's number into her phone and told him they were on their way with a possible donor for Ethan. His half-sister.

In the back with Vicky, Brooke explained about blood types while they passed small pieces of cake over the backrest to their driver.

"So if I am type O, I can give my brother my marrow?"

"Only if he is also type O."

"I thought type O was universal."

"It is, but for a successful transplant, both the donor and the recipient must be of the same type."

"Gash! This biology stuff gets more and more interesting."

Darkness had fallen when they arrived at the hospital. Vicky submitted to the blood test and grew impatient. "What's taking them so long?"

With his arm around Brooke's waist, Dexter asked Vicky questions about dogs and sledding to distract her from worrying while they waited for the results.

The door burst open and Eileen rushed in waving a paper. "It's a match!"

After a round of hugging, Vicky was wrapped in a gown and masked before being led to her half-brother's room. She stopped in awe. "My brother," she whispered.

With her biggest smile, she stepped up to the bed. "Hello, little brother. I've brought you something." Persuaded it wouldn't endanger her brother, she retrieved a well-worn stuffed dog she had smuggled under sweat shirt. "My great-grandmother gave it to me when I was a little girl. It is magic, so now you must have it." She lifted the plastic curtain.

Ethan's face illuminated. He took the plush dog and pulled it against him. "I'll call it Moomoo. You are my sister? How come I don't know you?"

A frown marred Vicky's forehead. "That's because my father and your mother divorced."

"Okay. Are you going to stay here?"

"I can't stay in the hospital, but I'll come and see you often. First, I'll give you some of my bone marrow for you to get better."

"You're nice."

Sleep and fatigue overcame the little boy. With tenderness oozing from her body, Vicky tiptoed out. In the hallway, Mélanie was clutching Roy's arm.

Vicky pulled her mask off and went up to her. "So, you're the one who abandoned me."

Mélanie bent her head, tears streaming down her face.

Vicky placed her hand on her biological mother's arm. "But it's okay that you did because I have the greatest-of-all-times mother."

"I'm sorry——"

"Chill, will you! I'm not interested in you. I just want to help my little brother."

Dr. Fischer and Eileen had joined them. "Now we need to get you ready. Vicky, we'll keep you overnight. You can go home in the morning if all is well. Young Ethan here is staying with us for three months."

Vicky's eyes widened. "Three months, phew! I'll come every weekend, I promise."

"I heard you're a keen musher, is that right?"

"You bet!"

"You're not going to like me, but you'll have to stop mushing and phys. ed. for the next three or four weeks. That's about the time it'll take for your own marrow to regrow the cells you'll give to Ethan."

After a moment of hesitation, the young girl smiled. "No problem."

Roy Johnson approached her. "I don't know how to thank you. I'll be eternally grateful to you."

"It's just normal. He's my brother." Her face grew somber. She was suddenly unsure of herself.

The doctor smiled at Vicky. "Come along, now."

"We'll pick you up in the morning after breakfast," Brooke said. "Did you want me to stay with you?"

"Thanks, but no, it's okay." She was putting on a brave face.

Dr. Lewis hurried to join them. "I'll be here with you." Eileen offered her hand to Vicky who took it, her assurance springing back.

In the elevator, Dexter took Brooke's hand. "I booked the same suite."

CHAPTER TEN

After school, as she had been doing for the previous two weeks, Vicky slipped into the Donek clinic and went straight to a dog recovery cage. The howling dog sat down. She crooned to him and let him have a treat.

"Time isn't passing fast enough, is it?" Brooke said.

A big sigh escaped Vicky. "I'm not feeling tired anymore. My mom won't let me do anything. She feeds and cleans the dogs and exercises them. All I do is pet them. Are you going to Whitehorse tomorrow? I saw Mr. Weiman's black Jeep."

Brooke chuckled. "Yes, he's back. Don't you like my truck?"

"I like his better."

They laughed. "Who's picking you up today?"

"No one. My dad has to supervise some meeting."

"I'll take you home."

"I told him I want triple chocolate brownies for the trip tomorrow. And his French chef will make a nice takeout for us."

"Great. We'll stop at the picnic site near Haines Junction to eat." Although it really was none of her business, Brooke had a burning question she had to ask. "Have you forgiven your father?"

"No, well, yes. It's different now. Before, I was just a little girl admiring him. Now I have aged ten years, and we are two adult friends. Does that make sense?"

Brooke had to smile. "Yes, it does. I guess it was a lot to absorb all in one go."

"It was. But I wish they could've told me. 's not fair. Adopted children are told when they are little. They get used to it."

"It was different for you because you have your father. It isn't quite the same as being adopted by strangers."

Vicky shrugged. "It's still not right."

On the way home, and after a long silence, Vicky sat up straighter. "Is it difficult to become a doctor? I see what they do at the hospital. I'm so impressed. I'd like to help them. Ethan goes in the children's room now and I like reading stories to the kids." She paused. "Some have cancer. I wish I could cure them."

A wave of anguish swept over Brooke. She closed her eyes for a second. "It's just hard work. You have to like the sciences and math."

"I do. I'm good at them. I signed on for the same biology course as Alex."

"You'll do well." Brooke hadn't realized the two teenagers were close friends.

Vicky was talking over some of the new things she'd learned that day and asking her mentor to clarify them for her. Brooke dropped Vicky at home on the Point and got back on the road. She wondered whether Dexter would come to her. She didn't have long to wait to find out. His Jeep was already parked in her yard. He and Alex had just finished taking care of the dogs. It was time to pay Alex, but he forestalled her.

"No need to pay me for doing what I love doing. I'd rather you helped me with my biology assignment. I brought it with me."

Not sure whether he was being considerate or really needed help, she nodded. "Come in, then. Vicky also signed up for that course."

"She did. I know."

"You can share your notes with her."

"Of course, we already do."

"I'll make dinner," Dexter said.

"Thanks! I put lentils to cook in the InstaPot™ this morning."

"Got it."

Alex sat next to Brooke and pulled his notebook out. "It's an advanced course online, but I don't have the textbook nor does Vicky."

"They're beyond expensive." She examined the assignment and the description of the course. "I have a textbook that you could use. It's not the one specified here, but it will cover everything you need for that course. You'll just have to dig for the info you need." She led him to the bookcase at the back of the living room.

"Wow! You got lots of books."

"Any time you want one, you can borrow one."

"Cool. Tomorrow, I'll come in the morning to take care of the dogs. It's okay for me to sleep here again? Jimmy's off to a race. I'll put Midnight on the kick sled. He is very eager. Can he go in the pen with the two Alaskan huskies?"

"Sure. They're sweet and gentle females. We'll be back on Sunday evening. Help yourself to the food in the fridge and there'll be homemade bread too."

"Don't worry. My mom said she'd bring me supper."

A pang of sadness mixed with gratefulness hit Brooke. People were finding little ways to help, like the musher who brought a dressed rabbit, insisting it was an overdue interest on the credit she'd extended to him. Or the woman who wanted a check up for her perfectly healthy poodle, and, after paying, pressed a big jar of pickled eggs on her with the flimsy excuse that she had made so many, her husband didn't want to see another one. And Dexter. She still was hesitant about him. Every evening he wasn't away on business, he would come bearing fish or meat, and cooked... and spend the night.

An hour later, a happy teenager snowshoed home with a hefty textbook strapped to his backpack.

CHAPTER ELEVEN

Dexter shook off his skis and propped them in the rack outside Agate Creek grocery-and-everything-else store.

"Mr. Weiman, are you training for the skijoring Loppet next weekend?"

"I've never skijored and I don't have a dog."

"No problem. You should ask Dr. Porter to lend you one of her big Inuit dogs. They go like the wind."

Dexter laughed. "That *is* the problem. They go like the wind, but I don't. I'd end up flat on my face."

"Of course not. We've seen you ski and you're really good."

"You're too generous. I like snowshoes better."

Tom laughed. "There's a race the weekend after next."

"And you've probably already signed me up."

"Of course. What do you need today? I saved you half a dozen of brown eggs. The truck came in from Whitehorse."

"I'll take them. Did... Did Dr. Porter buy anything?"

"She came in for flour. I pretended we were very low, so I sold her just one pound. Do you want to take her a ten-pound bag? No charge."

"Thanks, but I can pay. You've already given her a lot of staples. If Brooke asks, what do I tell her?"

Tom twisted his chin in his hand. "Something like there was an error in the supplies? So it's a bonus?"

"Good enough."

Dexter paid for the purchases. Tom helped him secure them in his backpack.

On the way to Brooke's house, Dexter's ruminations took a somber turn. *I didn't mean to become so attached to Brooke Porter. I'm a fool. The fact I'm winning her affection to obtain information makes me sick. We got Cipola for the drugs, but there's still that missing link. The darn man isn't talking. Wasn't his department, he said. But he knows about the diamond syndicate. I know he does.*

He dropped his backpack by the door to take Brooke in his arms and kissed her soundly. "I could get used to this kind of welcome."

She brushed him off. "Homemade baked beans for supper."

"How about an omelet as well? I brought some eggs. And here is some flour for you." He hefted the bag on the counter.

"Oh! But Tom said he didn't have any."

"The truck came up just before I got to the store."

Her mind raced with figures. "Ten pounds. How much do I owe you?"

"I'm only the delivery boy."

"I'll see Tom tomorrow."

He lifted an errant curl off her forehead. "I wouldn't if I were you."

She whipped two eggs. "Why not?"

"Some delivery mix-up on the part of the supplier. This bag must be compensation." Dexter strove to sound casual while setting the table. Lies, lies. It was becoming too much.

They talked about everything and nothing. "I'm intrigued by the mushing life in the area, how do people do it."

"I'm not sure I follow your thread."

"For example, how did... do you mind if I talk about your late husband?"

"Not one bit. Don't think I'm heartless. I grieve that a human life was lost, but he and I were finished a long time ago. It should never have started, but it did. We lived in the same house but couldn't be more remote. He spent most of his time training, anyway."

"He had expensive tastes. How did he manage it?"

"I was too busy to keep a close eye on the accounts. He took it all, as everyone knows now."

Dexter raised his eyebrows while pulling a face. "That was not enough for all he acquired and staying in five-star hotels on his way to races."

Her mouth inelegantly open, she frowned. "What do you mean?"

"There's a rumor in some circles that he was part of a shady business organization."

Stunned, she stared at Dexter. "What sort of shady business? Around here you can't scratch your ear without the whole village knowing about it."

"It probably was farther away."

"Like that earlier business with Ingrid what's-her-name in Wolf Hollow?"

"I presume so."

Brook shrugged. "I heard no such gossip."

"I know you have nothing to do with it. Did he ever say something or even behave in a way that was out of the routine?"

The frown on her forehead deepened. "He led his life. I had mine. He slept in the annex at the back. We converted it into a one-bedroom studio suite, complete with its own bathroom. It even has a door to the outside."

"You're both from Agate Creek?"

"I am. He was from somewhere down east."

"What about his friends?"

"I haven't a clue. Why are you so interested in him? He's dead now."

Dexter took a sip of coffee to try to think of an adequate response. He didn't want to tell her why. "The rumor is that his accomplice killed him."

Brooke pulled back to look at Dexter. "Just a moment. Who are you, exactly? You're asking questions like a cop."

He sighed. "That's because I'm an inspector with the Drug Enforcement Agency, DEA for short." At her blank look, he added, "Drugs and other illegal substances." A heavy silence fell between them. Dexter began to fear her reaction.

Light dawned on Brooke. "You rat! You cozied up to me to get information!" In a swift movement, she stood, grabbed the bag of flour from the counter and threw it at his chest, followed by the egg box. "Get out! Don't come back!"

"Please listen. My loving you has nothing to do with my job."

"Get out! You lied to me. I've no time for liars. They ruined my life. Never again! Out! Now!"

He hadn't moved fast enough to avoid the coffee pot hitting his shoulder. The sound of breaking china against the door reached his ears. Desperation washed over him. For the first time, he understood the meaning of a broken heart. Not just his heart, love encompassed his whole being and now it was reduced to nothing.

***

Brooke dropped wearily onto the sofa, catching her face in her hands, "loving you" circling at full speed in her mind. Blackness surrounded her. Why was it she fell prey to liars and cheats? The nurse who handed her the wrong medication lied over and over in court, saying that Dr. Porter had asked for potassium, not atropine. Luke Petrov had lied to her when he professed eternal love and ran the moment the fatal mistake landed her in court. Seth had lied to her when he insisted they move to Agate Creek, her home town, for the mushing and racing, despite her objections that there wouldn't be enough income to sustain a veterinary practice. As it turned out, his insistence had nothing to do with his dog sledding but everything to do with the web of illegal activity he was engaged in as she had just learned. Now, Dexter's betrayal put hurt on top of other hurt. Cautious with her feelings, she had finally reached the point when she trusted him. Trusted his love.

The stove had long gone out. The broken china still lay on the floor in the midst of the brown mess of coffee, eggs and the flour that had burst from the split bag. From outside, only Spitzweg's long howl reached Brooke's ears. She had promised herself to take him and his Inuit companions for a night ride with Dexter, and outing time had long passed. As if they knew, the pack was protesting. She grabbed the broom and cleared the door by pushing the debris to the side. On the porch, she unhooked the harnesses and went out.

A short while later, the Inuit dog family, hitched up to the big sled, was galloping down a trail. On they ran. Standing on the runners, Brooke concentrated on the dogs and the trail ahead. Two or three hours later, she didn't know how long, as she hadn't even looked at her watch, she called the team to stop. Her emergency bag contained tasty treats, which she distributed to the dogs while she thawed snow on the primus camp stove. After eating a snack and drinking a steaming mug of hot chocolate, she watered the dogs and gave each one a piece of hard fat, after which they curled up in the snow, their bushy tails protecting their noses. Brooke leaned against the sled and contemplated the myriad scintillating stars spread across the darkened heavens. The green veils of the aurora borealis danced in the northern sky before gradually fading away. It was as if Nature was telling her it was time to go home.

The night hurried away to let the reds and golds of the pre-dawn paint the sky with beauty. Brooke switched off her headlamp and absorbed the cascading richness of the light.

"Julot, Nana, haw!"

As one, the team turned left, trotting toward home. She was going to be late for the surgery scheduled at the Donek clinic. Without hesitation, she urged her team onto the trail going straight to the town across the lake. Once her team was picketed and watered in the snow-filled picnic park nearby, she walked the short way to the clinic.

As usual, Erin had prepared everything. Her assistant gasped when she caught sight of Brooke. She promptly seized a hairbrush and pushed her boss into the bathroom. "Excuse me, but you look as if you crawled out of a barn. Here, take this." She handed Brooke the hairbrush.

Moments later, Brooke emerged, once more the poised professional. Her private persona left somewhere on a snowy trail.

Chapter Twelve

On Sunday morning, Brooke was watering her dogs when Jimmy arrived with his team.

"Jimmy! Aren't you supposed to be on the Yukon Quest starting line?"

"Not the Quest. I'm doing the Iditarod this year. Are you ready for the skijoring Loppet?"

She shook her head. "Not this time. I have work to do."

"But you're the judge for the junior race."

"Argh! I suppose I am."

"Climb in. I'll give you a ride."

"Wait a sec. I'll get my first aid bag."

A deep laugh accompanied Jimmy's next words. "The dogs won't need it, but the skiers might."

The competition was held in the park, where four well-groomed trails crisscrossed a wide clearing. The adults were to skijor either a five-mile or a three-mile loop. Brooke volunteered to hold the eager dogs while the timekeeper counted the seconds. Not far from her post, she spotted Dexter standing immobile, watching her. She turned her head and concentrated on the next competitor. When it was number eighteen, she excused herself to go and attend to a skier who appeared to be limping. Dexter was number twenty-one.

The limping skier had nothing more than a bruised knee. As Brooked reassured him, the marshal's whistle sounded the alert. The skijorer about to depart turned round. The whistle meant an accident on the trail.

"Dr. Porter!" Simon was running toward her with an out-of-breath skier. "Two skiers collided about two and a half miles along the five-mile." The young woman skier puffed and coughed, trying to breathe and speak at the same time. "It's not a racer. A woman was going the wrong way on the downhill. The guy behind me stayed with them."

While she talked, Simon had undone his own skis and handed them to Brooke. Most people in Agate, who used their skis to get around, had universal bindings fitted on their skis. She tightened the buckles over her boots. A volunteer freed the straps of her veterinary bag and helped her shoulder it. Two other volunteers had already put on their skis and waited for her to start.

Knowing the trail would be free of competitors, they put on the maximum speed. A dog barking signaled they were approaching. Brooke took in the scene in one glance, recognizing Zach, the young man who had opened a gym in Donek. He was sitting with his head on one folded knee. The unknown skier, a woman, judging by her pink outfit, lay sprawled at an awkward angle. Brooke went to her. A broken leg was likely judging by the fate of one ski in pieces by a tree. The competitor who stayed behind had removed the other ski from her foot.

"Can you hear me?"

The woman's glazed eyes tried to focus on Brooke.

"Does your head hurt?" She couldn't understand the feeble, garbled words the woman said. Why didn't cross-country skiers wear helmets? Her professional fingers began palpating the woman's body. No wound to the head, but a possible concussion. The patient emitted a grunt when she touched the right arm. Fortunately, she wore a thermal fleece outfit that hugged her body. The young woman slipped in and out of consciousness. Brooke continued her examination and found an open fracture of the forearm. She had to finish examining her before attempting to immobilize the break. There were no painful reactions from the patient when she palpated the torso and the abdomen except for a small gasp.

She moved to the leg, bent the wrong way, with a telltale swelling. "Shit! The femur!" She checked the other leg and found no cause for concern there. She pulled a survival blanket from her kit and debated what to do next. A doubt crept into her mind. "Zach?"

"Yes."

"What are your injuries?"

"Sprained ankle and bloody sore side from head to toe. Nothing broken." He swiveled on his behind toward Brooke. "I saw her top the crest and launch downhill like a crazy person. She never saw me. I turned sideways, got Ruby and Rusty out of the way into the bush, but couldn't move fast enough and she couldn't stop. Just screamed."

With femur break, pelvic break went round in Brooke's head. "Someone has to go and call the Star helicopter. It's serious and I don't know about her head."

"It collided with mine, with my helmet rather, so it was a hard knock."

"I don't like that, but I have to line up the femur and hope the bleeding will slow down. It's going to hurt." After a moment of hesitation, Brooke took a syringe and a small vial of morphine. *Totally illegal, I know, but femur and pelvic injuries have to be the most excruciating. It'll be a while before we get the helico. One cc will only take the edge of the pain, but better than nothing when I pull on the broken bones.* With sure and rapid gestures, she injected the drug.

"Can I help?"

Alex had arrived. His intelligent and concerned air comforted Brooke.

"You can. Alex, I know your strength. Put your hand around the lady's hips, like this." She guided his hands. "Hold tight when I pull so there is no movement, except mine."

"Got it."

Brooke changed position and delicately inserted her hands under the broken femur and brought back the leg parallel to the other. The patient screamed before falling into unconsciousness. Beads of sweat ran from Alex's forehead, but he smiled. Setting the open fracture on the forearm was somewhat easier.

But I shouldn't be doing this.

"I called the chopper."

Brooke looked up at Dexter's voice, sounding strangely intimate to her ears. Of course, he was participating and had followed her. "Bless the satellite phones. But we have to get her to the clearing, if we can, to save the paramedics hours of trudging up here."

"There's an old canvas stretcher at the fire hall," Zach said.

"No good. We need a slim but rigid board."

"I'll get Simon to go to his lumber store and cut a piece of plywood. Will that do?" Dexter's voice was anxious.

"Yes. And blankets!"

"Ask Henry. He's got a snowmobile. He'll help," Zach said.

Dexter was off at top speed down the hill.

The competitor who had been behind Zach said. "I could take your dogs back to the holding area, Zach."

"Thank you, John. It'll help. I can manage my ankle, but not the dogs."

Brooke took a bandage and kneeled in front of Zach, who had built a snow hill on top of his ankle. "Right, first aid is ice." She applied the bandage and returned to her patient.

Since Bill and Ray, the other volunteers who'd come along with Dexter, had been helping to keep spirited dogs in the holding area and not moving much, they were wearing jackets. They took their jackets off and laid them over the injured woman over the gold survival blanket. The frozen ground was sucking the woman's body heat. Two other volunteers climbing up the slope approached cautiously.

"Anything we can do?"

"Hang around. We'll need manpower to carry the board when the guys come back."

"Henry will probably come up with his snowmobile and toboggan trailer." Zach said. "Would it help?"

"We'll see if we can prevent undue movement."

Her patient wasn't conscious enough to even give her name. Soon, Dexter and several other skiers returned, empty-handed.

"I had a communication from the SAR's medics. They will hover over the trail and will winch down. ETA…" He looked at his watch. "Thirty more minutes."

"Why the Search and Rescue?"

"The Star in Whitehorse contacted them. They were close by."

John unrolled the blanket from his torso. "I had one in my truck. Got a bit of dog hair on it."

Someone put a short blanket in Brooke's hand. "To put under her head," Taylor said. "I shook the dog hair out."

Chuckles greeted her words. The patient moaned. The morphine had taken effect and although still in pain, it was not longer so acute. Brooke reassured her in a calm voice that help was on the way and she'd soon be in expert hands. The volunteers took turn speaking to her to keep her conscious and calm.

Preceded by the typical clatter of the rotors, the yellow and red SAR helicopter arrived and hovered overhead at tree-height. The friends on the ground felt the wash. A paramedic was winched down. Brooke watched as Dexter helped the paramedic unbuckle and send the winch back up.

"I'm Ari. We were on a training exercise in the Arch Mountain area, less than an hour's flight time away."

The winch was coming down again with a Stokes basket and another paramedic.

While talking, Ari crouched to inspect the patient.

Brooke leaned over. "Open fracture of the right forearm and I suspect a closed femoral shaft fracture. I straightened the leg. The pelvis is sensitive on the right side."

Rob, the second paramedic was on the ground. They examined the woman and talked to her. She made valiant efforts to answer their questions between two bouts of consciousness.

While inserting a cervical collar onto the patient and an oxygen bag, Ari turned to Brooke. "Good job, Ms..?"

"Brooke."

"Nice to meet you, Brooke. Is this bag your first aid kit?" He moved it out of the way.

"Yes."

"Nice looking bag."

While talking, they secured the arm in a splint as well as the thigh. Ari and Rob now directed the men on how to lift the patient to put her onto the inflatable stretcher. "Brooke, push the stretcher under while we hold her up." It took just two seconds to perform the task. He released the valve to inflate the stretcher to take the shape of the body.

It all went smoothly. Now that the patient was immobilized, they lifted her into the Stokes basket. The winch came down. Rob tightened the straps and buckled his harness, checking the lines of the stretcher before giving the signal to winch them up.

Ari kept his eyes on the swinging basket going up while kept on talking. "I think you diagnosed the femoral shaft break pretty accurately. That's beyond mere first aid. What do you do for a living?"

"I'm a vet."

"A vet, you should be a doctor."

She winced. "Animals need care, too."

He glanced at her. "I know. We rescue them too."

The winch was coming down. Ari said goodbye. The little group watched him disappear inside the chopper.

"Well, folks," Simon said. "Let's go back and finish that race. I need someone to go and check what happened at the fork in the trail. Our guys have a barrier there to prevent tourists from coming onto this trail."

Two volunteers set off. The rest turned back

At the staging area, people crowded around the returning skiers, demanding to know everything. Simon couldn't get away from the people until Dexter stepped in and soon put order to the chaos, so the race could resume.

When it was the children's turn, the best skiers posted themselves along the one-mile course ready to help should a child be in trouble. From the corner of her eye, Brooke saw Dexter catch up with the seven-year-old that had just departed from the start line, but fell on his back less than a hundred yards down the trail, while his placid dog sat down to lick his paws.

"Poor kid, he's finished so soon. He'll be so disappointed," Tricia, the marshal, said.

"No, he's continuing. Look!"

Dexter scooped up the child, brushed him down and put him back on his skis. Apparently, the child wasn't hurt.

"What's Weiman doing?" Brooke squinted to see better.

"He's skiing with the kid, but not touching him."

"It's permitted under our rules."

"That's a good man, Brooke!"

"He's all yours," Brooke replied.

"Good looking too. He's sweet on you, so I won't throw my hat in the ring."

"Go ahead, throw all the hats you want. I'm not interested in him."

"We thought you were. He's been driving you——"

"Next!" the timekeeper shouted.

Finally, the last competitor was back and everybody retired to the covered shelter where prizes had been laid out on the picnic tables, next to snacks and beverages. Every competing child received a prize, and Brooke found the right words for each. A couple of the more competitive boys wanted to know whether they had won. She had to explain that in the junior category, the competition was against oneself.

"Did you do better than last year?"

"Only by thirty seconds. But I'm better than Bobby. I beat him by twenty seconds. So I win."

Bobby made a face at his friend. "But I did better by one minute over last year. So I win."

"In fact, yes, you both win and you each get a Crankity Brainteaser."

A whoop of joy made smiling heads turn toward the prize table, winning the race forgotten.

Aware of Dexter's eyes on her, Brooke moved farther away, vainly hoping to see someone going back to Agate Creek. Like most of the population around, Ian Campbell had come to watch. He'd pass her house on his way home, but he was the last person she'd ask for a ride. Tom and his wife, Bev, were serving the last of the food and drinks. A few hurried steps took Brooke to their side to help.

"Can I hitch a ride when we've finished here?"

"Of course. Isn't Mr. Weiman taking you back?" Bev asked.

"I came with Jimmy, but he has to take Savanah and the little ones home."

"You're most welcome."

While she helped pack and clean up, Brooke vowed to go to Whitehorse the following weekend to see Ethan and skip the snowshoeing race. She'd give a ride to Vicky, knowing that Garth would be relieved not to have to meet Mélanie again. The first meeting, arranged by Vicky, had been strained, but polite. Her daughter had made peace with her biological mother and stayed with her overnight in a rented furnished apartment while Roy traveled back and forth. Although Brooke had been cordially invited to stay, she declined. Mother and daughter were learning about each other and needed privacy.

CHAPTER THIRTEEN

Feet dragging, Dexter closed the door of his chalet, just as his satellite telephone buzzed. "Yes, I'm home."

—— What have you learned from the widow Lammers?

"Not Lammers. Her name is Dr. Porter. She kept her maiden name. She is totally unaware of her late husband's activities. They were estranged."

—— Surely, she must have heard or seen something.

"She never did. Nor did any of the village folk. Since I wasn't getting any luck with Brooke, I told her about her late husband being involved in illegal activities in the hope the shock would elicit something or that I'd see a hidden reaction, or best no reaction at all. Complete surprise to her, and she wasn't faking it. Have you made progress about the missing months of his life?"

—— Not one iota. Seth Lammers rented a team of dogs, registered for the Yukon Quest starting in Fairbanks, ran it a bit, scratched at Scroggie Creek and returned to Dawson City, where we completely lost track of him. He disappeared into thin air.

"Only to reappear nine months later in Agate Creek, with money to burn."

—— But he financially ruined his wife. What's going on? There is no clue linking him with the Cipola case so far. Cipola denies knowing Lammers.

"That may be true. Cipola only smuggled drugs, which are voluminous and not so easy to hide. Lammers was involved in smuggling raw diamonds, less bulky and easier to hide. They may not have worked for the same boss."

—— The man we caught at the airport was carrying a single finished diamond, a sample possibly.

"With a Canadian logo on it, of course."

—— Of course. The experts are trying to determine who cut it.

"There aren't that many lapidary artisans in Canada. Probably an illegal one. And that's another point. We don't know whether he's dealing in cut or in raw diamonds."

—— HQ doesn't think the missing link is in your corner, despite the Cipola case. Too far away, too cold.

"Precisely why someone could smuggle a large quantity of small stuff undetected."

—— Damn those blood diamonds! How did your dead body launder the money?

"I'm sure he had to have an accomplice. Something didn't go right, and he ended up dead. Let's start with the premise that he was part of a larger syndicate, and he has to have been if it involves smuggling diamonds or other precious gems. He became dissatisfied and tried to go solo or bypass a link. Though, no matter what, he'd still have to recruit someone. I should concentrate on finding that someone."

—— Or the *someone* recruited him?

"That's a possibility."

—— What I don't understand is the dog sledding.

"Would you suspect a guy whose life is spent freezing his balls off on the back of a sled?"

—— No. Maybe you've got something there.

"Lammers was a keen musher, entered the big races. Must have seen it as a way to satisfy his passion. One of those races crosses the international border. It didn't leave him much time to run around organizing collections and distributions. So he had to have a partner. He can't have been just a mule. They don't get enough of a cut for expensive tastes."

—— But if he was an underboss, all he needed was a phone.

"I met him a few times. A big, brash talker. Nothing discreet about that guy, unless he was an award-winning actor."

—— Okay, go back to start.

"This is not monopoly.

—— Lighten up, Dex. Did you develop a relationship with Ms. Porter?

"When she discovered I was a cop, I was on the receiving end of flour, coffee, eggs, china before I made it out the door."

—— You're smitten, aren't you? You can't afford to be. This is a job.

"Playing with people's affections is despicable."

—— It happens in our line of work. Don't forget we work for the greater good. Have you searched her house?

"No need, I thought. Brooke had no qualms about ordering me to get this or that, including in her office corner or the clinic when she needed help."

—— You surprise me. You're an expert about searching ladies' dwellings.

"Don't remind me."

—— How are your investments doing?

"Thanks for the tips, Max. I'm now VP on the board of the Urban Development Alternative Company."

—— Don't retire from the Force too soon. We need you. I'm off to read up more on diamond and precious gem smuggling now.

"By the way, Dr. Porter doesn't own any jewelry." Tired and dispirited, Dexter switched off the phone and leaned back into the armchair. He had never meant to fall in love. He hadn't wanted her to fall in love. What would she have done if he had asked her for her cooperation right from the beginning? Her husband's death complicated everything. While he was alive, it was easy to be the friendly neighbor and repress those surges of affection for her, a married woman. Sometimes a genuine friendship could achieve the same results. Friendship he understood. Love he didn't.

After hours of worthless meditation, he stood up to relight the stove, then proceeded to clean his jacket of the now dried mess of the projectiles he had been bombarded with. The stains resisted. He'd have to take the jacket to the dry cleaners in Whitehorse. With a sigh, he opened a can of beans. It wasn't good for the mental state to go to bed hungry. Also, he too intended to do more research into the smuggling of diamonds and precious stones. He thought he knew everything about smuggling, but obviously not. The proximity of the U.S. border was a factor, but who, why, how in these desolate parts of the territory, where the internet was unreliable or non-existent? Blood diamonds, mined in Africa, or the States. Mexico? No, their diamond mines had closed decades ago. Those blood diamonds were sold to European dealers with forged certification. It didn't make sense. Unless... suddenly, the picture became clearer.

Chapter Fourteen

Although Brooke was not hungry, she cut a slice of bread and dipped it into her lukewarm coffee cup. Before she might have thrown it away and made a fresh cup. Her self-imposed austerity regime precluded such a waste. The homemade raisin bread was a gift from a dog owner who had wanted her Bichon's toe nails clipped and had come all the way to Agate for it. A job Erin normally did at the clinic. Parka and tuque on, she picked up her bag and looked forward to her day at the clinic. She almost bumped into the visitor standing on her porch.

"Good morning, Inspector Whitford. Nice of you to bring my Marlin back." Brooke extended her hand to take the rifle.

"I have to put it into your gun cabinet myself."

Taken aback, she stared for a couple of seconds. "Oh, I see. Just in case I turned it against you, even though it's not loaded."

"It's regulations."

Brooke pointed to the cabinet. "It's open." She reached into her desk drawer and pulled out the key.

"Here, you can lock it too."

"Where do you normally keep the key?"

As if anyone around here bothered with rules about keys since no one locks their doors! She didn't have a special secure place. She improvised. "In the fridge behind the antibiotics. The fridge key remains in my bag."

"Here's the trigger lock key. But by law, you must keep the keys in a safe."

"This is Agate, inspector, not the Chicago slums."

"Firearm regulations are in place for a purpose."

She snorted. "If someone decided to steal my rifle for nefarious purposes, they wouldn't bother looking for the keys. They'd haul the whole cabinet away."

He had the good grace to look chastened as he took his leave. She waited until his car turned round to get on the road. What a sad affair it really was. Deceived, cheated she had been. *Stupid, I was so stupid not to see through the scams.*

The knock on the door pulled her out of her misery.

"Inspector Weiman. I'm not sure I want to see you."

"Brooke, we need to talk."

"We've got nothing to say to each other." She pushed the door closed, but he already had his foot inside. "Unless you're here as the inspector to ask official questions, get out."

"I do have formal questions."

She put her weight against the door to prevent it from opening wider, all the time knowing that a shove from him and she'd land on her backside. "What's the first one?"

"Won't you let me in?"

"By law, I don't have to."

"Brooke, we know each other and you know I won't go against your wishes."

"My wishes are you stay outside."

He sighed with some exaggeration. "Fine. But you're losing all your heat."

Her anger rose a notch. He was right. She opened the door and slammed it behind him, but didn't invite him any farther. "Questions? Make it fast. I'm on my way to work."

"Do you own another rifle?"

"That question has already been answered to Inspector Whitford who actually was here two minutes ago. Or are you people not sharing information?"

Dexter looked into her eyes, pleading. It almost undid her. He inclined his head.

"We do, but sometime things get overlooked. Whitford is in criminal investigation. I'm Drug Enforcement Administration and international organized crime."

Brooke snorted. "Organized crime in Agate Creek? What a joke."

"You'd be surprised and if we can sit down, I'll explain it to you."

Reluctantly, she moved to let him pass. He sat on the sofa, she in the armchair.

"Think of a chain and its multiple links. One of those has been traced in this area."

"I thought that was all over with that other case, near Donek."

"That one is over, yes, but it led to another, and we have good reasons to think they are tied, but this one doesn't involve drugs."

"So, what are you investigating?"

"A hunch."

"Do you toss coins in your job?"

He winced. For a split second, Brooke was almost sorry to be so hard on him.

"In your work, you're bound by confidentiality. So am I in mine. Yet I'm going to reveal to you my suspicions under that confidentiality rule."

"I'll make sure to forget all of it the moment you leave this room. I want nothing to do with it."

"We're strongly suspecting a diamond and precious gem smuggling operation."

"Not in Agate Creek, surely? Most people couldn't find the place on a map."

"Well, it happens. There are still conflicts in parts of Africa. For some people, mining diamonds is an illegal source of cash. For others, it's their only way to buy food. The investigation in your... in Seth Lammers' death uncovered a lifestyle of his that you were seemingly unaware of."

"That's for sure, I don't understand. He was so strapped for cash he took all I had, and I'm about to lose my house."

"Your lawyer is working hard to prevent that. We're doing our best to help."

Head turned away, she whispered her thanks with a tight throat. "Tell me how I can help."

"Do you know the people he associated with?"

"He knew everyone in Agate, and half of Donek. Besides that, he knew every racing musher and dog breeder on both sides of the Yukon-Alaska border and down to the other side of Fletcher Creek. When he was here, he'd talk to anyone who came through. Some friendly, others less so. On the whole, despite his chummy nature, I think few people really liked him."

"Can you think of anyone in particular he had words with?"

"Ian Campbell, Jimmy Redhead, Bill and Ed, Jerome Renard, a newcomer to Fletcher Creek, Victor Ayupaq. He's a member of the First Canadian Rangers Patrol Group. That's who I can think off the top of my head. I'd think he had words with every racer in the area."

Dexter had noted the names as she spoke. "We'll talk to them and follow any lead. Words with Victor, a patrol ranger... that's interesting."

"Because of the border? Are you thinking he had an accomplice? So who would that be?"

"That's who I'm looking for. If he was indeed trafficking in diamonds, he would have to have hidden them somewhere. Can you think of where he could hide gems?"

"You can search his rooms. I've never been in, nor has anybody else as far as I know, at least not while I was here."

"Thank you."

He stood and followed her to the door of the suite. She pushed it open and stepped back. The whole affair seemed unreal to her. Without thinking, she made coffee and sighed. There wasn't much left. Her phone ringing surprised her. The Donek clinic. Of course, she was now very late. Erin reassured her that she had everything under control.

"Only Mrs. Courtenay and her pug. He has lost more weight, but is still five pounds above where he should be. Does she keep him on the same diet or do you want to make a change?"

"She can increase the food by one tablespoon to slow the weight loss over the next six months."

"By which time the dog will be used to the smaller portions. She swears he gets no treats except a bone on Sundays."

"Apologize for me. At the moment, I have another police inspector searching the premises. I'll come as soon as I can."

"Don't worry. It's all routine and people are buying the dog cookies we baked last week."

Brooke had to smile. The connection faded. She disconnected to put the kettle on the stove. Love in her life was like the phone connection. It worked, then faded away before coming back to life and fading again.

Dexter's return pulled her out of her musings. Her heart fluttered when he made a show of inhaling the coffee aroma.

"I was about to have a cup. How about you?"

"I'd be delighted."

She closed her eyes briefly. Why did he have to have a smile that threatened her sanity? The resolution she had taken... wait, what resolution? She repressed a sigh. The resolution to move forward with her life without him or any other man. She poured two cups.

"I have to go to the clinic after coffee, if you're done here."

"I won't keep you. Do you know this agenda?" He handed her a black agenda.

"No, never seen it. Mmm, leather cover, fancy!"

He nodded. "Fine leather and expensive paper. It looks like an accounting document with figures and what I think are dates and initials."

"Someone on your team will enjoy decrypting all this. I have to go now. Close the door behind you."

"One more thing. Did you have another firearm?"

"They didn't tell you? I do not own another, but Seth did. It was stolen two years ago. It was his prized rifle, silver-inlay on the stock with his engraved initials. He reported it stolen."

"You never wondered about the cost of the rifle?"

"No, why? It was his. Mine is the Marlin that my father gave me when I graduated. He said as a country vet, I'd sometimes be in situations where a gun was indispensable. I have to leave now."

"I'm taking his laptop and a few other things from his rooms. It's quite a little apartment he had there, with electric heat."

"He arranged it a week after we were married and moved here. A month later, he moved in there permanently. Close the door tight. I don't keep the heaters on in there." She shrugged and walked out.

In the evening, Brooke put the rabbit stew to warm up on the stove. There hadn't been any further cozy dinners, and she would ensure there would be no more. The pain crushed her chest. How could she have been so naïve and believe a man's love was genuine? First there was the newly minted doctor two years ahead of her who couldn't drop her fast enough when the tragedy struck. Then Seth... There must be some truth in the saying *never two without three*. What if Dexter had told her right away about his work and his reason to be in Agate? Would it have made a difference? Would they have fallen in love? But maybe he didn't really love her like she loved him. He was undercover and, according to mystery novels, undercover agents get... No, she wouldn't go there.

She hadn't grieved for the man who had been her husband, but she was grieving for her love lost. A whisky jay huddled on a spruce bough attracted her attention. She watched as it left its perch to fly onto the bird table. Fortunately, she had enough seed left to last until spring. There were enough beautiful things in her life as a single woman, beside birds, such as visiting a little boy whose life she helped save, mentoring two young people who planned on careers in veterinary and medicine, and soon flying to her assigned post in the Iditarod dog race. Not to mention the genuine friends that she had around her.

Chapter Fifteen

Several mushers had come to the clinic with dogs they wanted to have assessed prior entering them in the Iditarod sled dog race. Some paid in kind and she now had several arctic hares and graylings in her freezer, enough to feed her dogs as well. At least, she wouldn't starve and this nature bounty would ease the grocery bill for a little while. It wasn't helping pay the bank, though.

Then it was the check-ups and electro-cardiograms for the dogs registered with the Iditarod race. It was also pay day for Erin and, to Brooke's relief, she had just enough to pay her for another month. She was about to close up when the door opened on Garth.

"Sorry, I'm late. Some guests are difficult. I've come to pay Vicky's bill."

A quick look at the computer and Brooke shook her head. "It all up to date."

"No, this is what I owe you for driving my daughter to Whitehorse."

"No need, Garth. I'd go anyway."

He put a check on the counter. "That's for the gas I don't have to use to drive her, and a thank-you for me not having to see Mélanie. Don't argue. My staying home keeps Donna reassured. She fears I could fall for Mélanie again, you know, first love and all that. If only she knew..."

"If only she knew what?"

"Never mind." Garth pulled his tuque down over his ears. "It's all ancient history now. You know it, but I don't want Donna to know. She doesn't need to."

"I don't know what you call the ancient history. If you remember, I kept much to myself. I heard some of the gossip but nothing extraordinary about a boy getting his girl pregnant and them running away together. In a small town like ours, it's still scandalous. Mostly, I think, because people were deprived of a wedding spectacle and being able to watch another child grow up."

Garth leaned his elbows on the counter. "It wasn't like that. Do you remember Mélanie's father?"

"Yes, he was the local doctor when we used to have a doctor."

"He had to leave Montreal because of an accusation of sexual misconduct. It wasn't proven and his license wasn't withdrawn. He chose to come to Donek on the Lake, a place small enough that he could steer clear of publicity. That's what I learned years later. When Mélanie was about twelve, he started abusing her. One summer, my buddies and I were visiting a swimming hole. The others had gone ahead, and I was still looking for my missing shoe when I caught sight of a female jumping fully dressed from a rock. Out of the corner of my eye, I saw that she wasn't coming back up. I dove in and got her out. It was Mélanie. She wanted to die. Then she told me about her father and how he had performed an abortion on her. We were in the same class. I was so shocked. I didn't really understand, and still don't, how a grown man, a doctor at that, could do that to his daughter. I tried to support her. She was adamant that I tell no one."

"Classic response. Some news did filter out, though."

"Rumors have a way of becoming facts. Somehow, she got it into her head that she was the guilty person, that she was dirty."

"Did you not seek counseling, if not for her for yourself?"

Garth looked troubled. "I tried to talk to my father. We argued. He hit me and called Mélanie a slut. Her father was dropping hints of her bad behavior to everybody." He shook his head. "Mélanie wasn't eating. I tried to support her. Since I had saved her life, she was convinced that our love would purify her and her father wouldn't touch her again. So, we made love and her mental state improved. She began to take care of herself again. People remarked on how lovely she now looked. They had us married by the end of school. She found the strength to fight off her father. But one day he got her. She was falling back into depression. We skipped class a couple of times. We had a place in the woods, a dilapidated shack we'd found and repaired a bit. Not long after, she discovered she was pregnant. She was out of her mind, not knowing whether it was my baby or, God help her, her father's from that last encounter. She confronted him and a big row ensued. Her mother, who had been totally unaware of anything the whole time, had a stroke. Mélanie ran away during that blizzard. She'd called me, and I knew she'd be going to our special place. I prepared to leave and join her. Got all my money... and some not mine on my mother's card."

"Had you planned to go away together before?"

"Frankly, no. At sixteen and fifteen, we only talked about it." Seeing Brooke raise one eyebrow, he added, "I was born in January and she in December, same year. We realized that two minors wouldn't have much of a chance to get away, find jobs, a place to live."

"But you knew where to find her and even took money."

"I didn't know what to do beyond going to the abandoned cabin. I was going to give her the money to go to her grandmother's. Then we left together."

"Why didn't she stay with you and her grandmother?"

"Mélanie didn't want to. She was a right mess. She didn't want the baby. She was convinced it was her father. Though I counted for her and was sure it could not be, but her mental state was such that she no longer believe me or anybody. Social services intervened and placed her in a school for pregnant teenagers. There she had professional counseling."

"She told me her grandmother sent her to a private school while you raised your daughter. She'd adopted the idea she was an orphan, did well in school and went on to get a degree in accounting. And got married six years ago."

"I didn't know all that. Grandma, she'd asked me to call her that, died less than two years later. We had a DNA test done. Vicky was really my daughter. I wanted to tell Mélanie, but Grandma and I were told it was better not to contact her, as she had adapted to a new life and was doing very well."

"Misguided concept. You cannot erase events as significant as giving birth, giving life, without some consequences down the road."

"I see that now, but I had graduated. I struggled on my own with Vicky and my job at the hotel. I took online classes in hospitality management."

"Mélanie's father, who went around saying his daughter was a slut, left Agate in the spring after the drama and his wife's death. She hadn't recovered from the stroke. Her husband was suspected of helping her to die. The gossip mill worked overtime."

"People must have known, if not all of it, at least a lot. No one lifted a finger to help Mélanie."

"Except you."

Garth brushed both hands across his face. "What a mess!" He stretched and flexed his shoulders. "Grandma left me her house in her will and some savings. When probate was done, I sold it and invested the funds for Vicky."

"Did you still love Mélanie?"

He shrugged. "I didn't know what love was until I met Donna. And I desperately want to keep all those sordid details from her and Vicky."

Brooke put the check into the cash drawer. "How's your father's health?"

"His heart is functioning at reduced capacity. When I came back, he apologized for not listening."

"He'll be getting better now he got that off his chest."

"I'm so grateful to you, Brooke, for talking to Donna and Vicky. For saving a little boy's life. For what you do for this community. My daughter positively adores you. I won't let you go bankrupt. You'll need guarantors. I'll be there. I know there'll be others too."

His words warmed her heart. "We have a great community, really. Sometimes, errors of judgment end up in drama. Just a word of caution, though. Don't delay telling the whole truth in its sordid details to your wife and daughter before the gossip resurfaces. Vicky is already hearing tidbits from her biological mother."

"You're right."

They parted. Unwilling to rush home, Brooke spent another hour cleaning the clinic and playing with its only permanent resident, a three-legged cat named Bingo.

Chapter Sixteen

Throughout the area, training for the big Iditarod race intensified. The top mushers had sponsors and wanted the best care for their dogs. With the influx of veterinary work, Brooke was able to pay off some of the outstanding bills, having made arrangements with her late husband's creditors. She was relieved when Lara, the locum veterinarian, who had recently graduated, arrived. From time to time, Brooke's vet friend Stephanie would come from Whitehorse to help supervise. Now, fourteen days before the start of the race, mushers lined up with their dogs for their second canine ECG and check-up. The new dogs on teams had had their microchip implanted on the first check-up. Brooke counted once more the deworming medication provided by the Iditarod Trail Committee. She had ordered enough.

Lara was proving extremely competent. Between two teams while Erin was cleaning the examining room, she pulled Brooke aside. "That obnoxious guy Campbell has a team he rented from a kennel in Montana. Is their vet certificate good enough? There's no ECG."

"Let's check out the Montana kennel. Some kennels are on the blacklist."

"It's called…" Lara consulted the papers. "Big Sky Kennel."

"Yes, I know them. The owner is a champion long distance racer. I'll phone tomorrow and find out when Ian Campbell rented the team and if they have done the ECG. Perhaps he left them behind. He wanted to buy his own team. I guess he didn't."

"Here comes our next musher."

"That's Jimmy Redhead. The best dogs of all. Now watch while he takes the dogs down from the transporter."

To Lara's intense surprise, Jimmy's dogs, without leashes, stood two by two on the sidewalk. When the last dog had jumped down, he opened the door of the clinic and his dogs flowed into the waiting room, where they sat down in silence.

"Close your mouth, Lara. The rapport between Jimmy and his dogs is the stuff of legend. It just defies our pedestrian imagination. Back to work now."

"And they're not barking like all those other sled dogs. Amazing."

Finally, the last certificate was signed. Vicky and Alex, who had sat in a corner after he had come back from his duties at Brooke's kennel, sprang into action and helped clean up.

Chapter Seventeen

It was late when Brooke finally pulled into her yard, trusting that Alex had loaded the wood stove with thick logs. A soothing warmth welcomed her and put a smile on her lips.

Her replacement had already made friends. Garth had provided a suite at no cost and Lara had received countless invitations to dinner. The excitement of leaving for the race washed over Brooke. Life did have a silver lining. She went into the pen to pat her Canadian Inuit dogs and give them each a piece of fat. A pang of hunger drove her back into the house.

A shadow of regret passed. If only Dexter had been open and truthful, they might still be together. On the other hand, they'd have met on professional grounds and he wouldn't have pretended to love her. Then she wouldn't have fallen in love. In the nick of time, she stopped herself from slamming the bean casserole on the table. A remnant of her previous anger at her sheer naivety threatened to erase the contentment she felt after a good day's work. The knock on the door made her jump.

"Inspector Weiman."

"Dexter, please."

"Is this an official visit?"

"No, I——"

"Then go. I want to eat my dinner in peace."

He didn't argue. He pushed the door open and closed it behind him. Before Brooke could protest, he had her in his arms and kissed her, drawing an involuntary response from her. A brief instant of lucidity brought her back to reality. She stepped back, chest heaving, breathing labored. Stunned, she gazed into his dark eyes before wrapping her arms around herself, head bent while she recouped her strength. Then she straightened.

There was a moment of tension while their gazes locked, alive with awareness. Gently, he pulled her close. He trailed a butterfly kiss on her forehead, down her nose, to her trembling lips.

Although Brooke pushed him away, he still stood uncomfortably close. "No, Dexter. It's over."

"It isn't over until we have talked."

"You deceived me. That you can't deny. What feelings I had for you have died."

"When I met you, I forgot about my job. You made my heart beat faster. I was finding any excuse to see you, but you were married and I have enough honor not to trespass, even if my likely quarry was your husband."

She didn't want to hear that. Although it cost her, she made an effort. "Have you made any progress on the missing link?"

"Brooke! Don't try to deflect me."

In reality, she could push him away physically, but she could do nothing to quell the wave of heat that engulfed her.

"Then you were free, and my love for you surged even though I tried not to rush you. At the same time, I hated myself because I had a job to do."

Her whole being in turmoil, Brooked leaned her forehead against his coat. Could she trust his words? She knew that if she told him to go, he would. Then he'd become just the inspector. But did she want him to? Slowly, she lifted her head. His mouth descended to imprison hers. His hand sneaked up to pull the scrunchie off and free the glorious mass of auburn curls. There was sweetness in forgiving.

Later, she lifted the lid of the casserole of beans still simmering with a piece of arctic hare and grimaced.

"Let me warm it up for you."

He took over, added some herbs and refried the lot.

She watched his hands handling the skillet like a chef. "Did you want to share? There's enough for two."

"Most definitely. I haven't had supper either."

They ate and talked about the upcoming big race, and dogs of course, until the dishes were done, dried and put away. Brooke sat on the sofa, her bare feet tucked under her.

"Did Seth's laptop and agenda help advance your case?"

"Not much, but it confirms that he was involved in illicit diamonds. His laptop is clean. He never even sent an email from it. But, he bookmarked every site about diamonds in the world. We haven't found his phone yet."

"Step one in the investigation. Was he a mule?"

"We believe he was an organizer."

"So he wouldn't have any diamonds with him?"

"He could have samples to show prospective clients. He could have been a buyer. He could have been laundering money for a syndicate. He could have stolen a whole shipment."

"All that in this neck of the woods?"

"The border is close by, quite unguarded in the mountains. Sled dogs are pretty reliable in difficult terrain."

"I see now why he was so keen to move here and take up dog sledding again."

"Again?"

"He said he used to race in Quebec."

"Interesting. We didn't come up with that information."

"That's what he told me. He definitely knew about sledding. He even had a couple of dogs in Saskatoon. Did you mention something about certification?"

He nodded. "All jewelers must receive a certificate of origin when they buy diamonds. It is vitally important that diamonds for sale to the public are not mined in countries at war, in particular mined by children and trafficked for the benefit of syndicates, drug lords or any other unsavory people, like dictators. That's why eighty-one countries have signed the Kimberley Process Scheme, which seeks to guarantee the legal and ethical source of the diamonds and other precious gems."

"That doesn't stop the illegal trade, though, does it?"

"Alas no. We were looking at Africa where most of the mines are, even Mexico."

"It doesn't have any diamond mines. I looked up diamonds on the clinic's computer."

He smiled. "I should have known."

"What else is there?"

"Mexico used to have mines. What mines they had are now tourist attractions and basically depleted of any worthwhile stones. But that path wasn't entirely wrong. It led to something else, but not for our investigation. I had the idea to look closer to home."

"The diamond mines in the Northwest Territories? That might be the reason behind Seth's unexplained absences?"

"That's pretty good reasoning. You'd make a great investigator."

"Surely, the mining in the North is all legal and above board."

"It is. The gems, however, could be smuggled from anywhere, Utah, for instance, and passed off as originating in Canada."

"Looking perfectly legitimate with a falsified certificate."

"You've got the idea. If only I could find a gem or two in Lammers' belongings, we could identify the provenance of the stones. He really was only a small-time operative. If my hunch is correct, there's got to be much bigger fish above him."

"I'm leaving next week for the Iditarod. I'm one of the official race vets. While I'm away, you can search the premises to your heart's content."

"How about if I stay in your cabin while you are away to prevent your pipes from freezing?"

"What about yours? You'd trek there every day?"

"I have electric heat."

"Lucky you! Thanks, I accept your offer. Alex comes every evening to feed my furry friends and sometimes takes them out, but only two at a time. They are too strong for him. He does weight training, but it takes a bit of time to develop one's upper body muscles."

"I could make time to hitch them up and take them out every morning. Would that work?"

She clapped her hands. "They'll be so happy. Take the big sled, the one Seth bought for the Iditarod race. It's a bit heavier. I saw how you're getting very good at handling the dogs, but you really need to have plenty of weight for them to pull. Add your camping equipment, emergency pack and a couple of the big stones I keep in the shed."

"Will do." He stole a kiss before banking the fire for the night. His eyes asked a mute question. Brooke close her eyes for a second while her heart beat faster. She took his hand and led him to the bedroom.

Chapter Eighteen

After Dexter left early in the morning to attend to his investigation matters, or whatever he was engaged in. If the truth were told, she was no longer sure of many things, and that included almost everything about Dexter Weiman. For the time being, she preferred not to think too deeply about him and whatever relationship existed between them. She was content to enjoy his company and accept his help. Besides, nights in his company were fulfilling.

She contemplated the snowy landscape spread out under the feeble light of the quarter moon. Had she really wanted to take that step last evening and let Dexter back into her life? Everything about him spoke of genuine love. Perhaps it was true. Was she so desperate to be loved that she made herself believe this time round was the real one? Once before, she had believed in true love, but that turned out to be a sham. She'd learned the hard way that there were no guarantees in love. It wasn't like a purchase you could return to the store for a refund if it didn't work out as promised.

What did it do to her? All that warmth in her heart for him was burning her insides. No matter how much she denied it, she couldn't live without him. His gentle strength was addictive. That was it. An addiction or rather an infatuation which she'd get over, eventually. The mind part, she could control. The intimacy made her feel a woman to the fullest. She'd have trouble controlling that aspect. Did that mean she was weak? She sighed. Maybe she should stop psychoanalyzing herself and enjoy the moment. Yes, but she was too practical a person to see herself as a complete hedonist.

Already dressed and holding her bag, she was about to leave for the clinic when she heard a truck pulling into the yard. A truck with a diesel engine. That narrowed the visitor to a possible few, and not one she was pleased to see. Surprised that her Inuit dogs hadn't howled, she frowned while closing the cabin door. A few fast steps and she was outside.

To her dismay, her hearing hadn't misled her. It was Ian Campbell's truck. Then she noticed her dogs' absence. Dexter had begun his daily morning run with them. What now? There were no sled dogs for Campbell to buy or borrow. There was only one young Alaskan husky female left. When a couple had come to adopt the two huskies, Little Raven had run into Brooke's arms and refused to budge. The people were happy with just the one dog, so Little Raven stayed.

Brooke tried to be professional. "What brings you here so early?"

"I want to buy Seth's Iditarod sled."

"Sorry, it's not for sale. And besides, it is MY sled, paid with MY money."

"Don't be obstinate, Brooke. You don't do much sledding with your mutts. You don't need a high-end sled. Besides, you need the money. I'll pay a fair price."

His calling her Canadian Inuit dogs mutts riled her. "Go back where you come from, Mr. Campbell. The sled is not for sale. Would you like me to spell that out for you? My mutts, as you call them, have no problem pulling it every day. Now, go!"

"Don't be stupid. I need it. You don't. And when the bank repossesses your property, they'll auction it and you'll get nothing."

"If it gets to that, you can be there to buy it. In the meantime, get out of here before I lose my temper."

He threw an envelope at her chest and strode to the shed. Her first reaction was to grab the ice cutter leaning against the wall and go after him. Reason prevailed, and she waited. Not for very long. She heard him throwing the smaller sleds around and watched him emerge from the doorway like an enraged beast. With as much nonchalance as she could muster, she threw the envelope onto his truck's hood.

"Where is it?"

"Out sledding."

A menacing few steps brought him inches from her face. He yelled. She didn't flinch. Her hand fingered the scalpel she had forgotten was still in her pocket from the earlier confrontation. Adrenaline surging into her body intensified her awareness of her surroundings. In the distance, a familiar panting sound filled her keen ears with pleasure. Dexter was coming up the trail. Before she could say anything, the team was rushing straight at her unwelcome visitor.

Her dogs had the reputation of being the toughest dogs going, though not in an aggressive way. Campbell had demonstrated before he didn't trust, or rather feared, her Arctic dogs. There were stories, rumors mostly, about sled dogs attacking people. There were, though it had to be said that in every instance, the dogs had been provoked one way or another. Since Campbell didn't raise dogs himself, he readily believed the old stories.

He leaped into his truck not a second before the team halted in a blizzard of whirling snow. The Inuit dogs, always keen to greet people, howled their disappointment while pawing at the cab's door. It took all her will not to laugh at Campbell's pathetic face at the cab window of the truck. While Dexter tied the snub line to the hitching post by the cabin door, Brooke got the dogs under control.

"What does that guy want?"

"To buy the sled."

"You don't want to sell, do you?"

"I told him no. He took it badly."

The grimace on his face released her laughter. He unhooked the gangline, thus freeing the whole team. "Take them to their pen. I'll have a word with him."

Brooke got hold of the gangline and walked away, surrounded by the boisterous dogs. She noticed Ian had climbed down and was facing Dexter. The dogs gave a cursory lick to the water already in their pails and sat watching the ledge where treats of caribou fat awaited them. She shooed away the chickadees pecking at the fat and gave each dog the prepared treat. The tone of the discussion between the two men had risen. Unfazed, she untied the sled and push it into the shed. The padlock, which customarily hung unused from the clasp, was now snapped shut to secure the door.

She smiled at the thought that a pickup truck can eloquently express the attitude and feelings of its owner. Campbell's was no different. It shot out of her yard with spinning tires that threw a cloud of snow in the faces of those standing near. Normally, Brooke would be offended by such rude behavior. On this occasion, she was highly amused. Ian Campbell had received his due comeuppance for the cowardly bully he was.

"You got rid of him quite nicely. Did you flash him your badge?"

"He doesn't need to know I am a cop. Can you lock your shed?"

"I already did. I hope I can find the key. There should be two of them."

He chuckled while they went inside to look for the keys. Brooke left for work after telling him to take one.

At the clinic, it was back to routine business, until a last-minute musher arrived with his team to be certified for the Iditarod race.

"I'm sorry I couldn't be here yesterday. I had truck troubles."

"Better get it fixed before you set off through the mountains."

The young indigenous man looked distressed. "I am not too late, really?"

Brooke smiled as she pulled the ECG machine into the examining room. "You're always late, TeeJay. Bring your dogs in."

"What about the certificate? It has to show fourteen days, right?" Lara said.

"I signed it yesterday. TeeJay was probably hunting to freeze enough meat for his wife and baby while he'll be away."

"Attenuating circumstances. Don't his dogs look beautiful!"

"I agree."

When all the dogs had been examined, the young musher handed Brooke a rabbit and a cut of caribou wrapped with herbs in a length of cotton cloth, which she took with a nod of thanks.

"Make sure you're not late arriving in Nome, TeeJay."

He grinned on his way out. It was his third Iditarod and had placed in the top ten the previous year, an achievement for a beginner musher. The three women sat around with a cup of coffee.

"TeeJay has never used plastic bags," Brooke said for Lara's benefit. "When the government banned all single use plastic bags, he felt rather smug."

"Good for him. That packaging looks interesting."

"Very efficient. Herbs and woven grass, a recipe several centuries old. It never rots," Erin said.

While Brooke was going over the routine for Lara, the printer clicked and whirred, spewing sheets of paper.

"The ECG from Big Sky Kennels for Ian Campbell's rented team," Erin said. She bundled them neatly.

"How are you getting them to him?" Lara asked.

"I'm not. I'll take them with me to hand directly to the Committee coordinator. Let Campbell sweat a bit when he's asked for them and realized he doesn't have them."

"Has he ever won the race?" Lara asked.

"Nowhere near. He has a history of scratching," Erin replied.

"Why does he bother?"

"He's a sucker for punishment," Brooke said.

They stood as a woman came in with a Bichon under her arm. Before the vet could ask what was the problem, another three came in. Brooke teased them and introduced Lara.

After the women had left, Brooke and Erin burst out laughing. "You can't hide in a small town."

"I found that out. I have so many invitations already."

The door buzzer sounded again, but a man came in. Garth greeted them.

"The Welcome Wagon ladies want to throw a party to welcome Lara. I'll take care of it, but I want to make sure it's okay with Ms. Pelham. They'd like to have a sit-down dessert and dancing after the speeches."

Erin and Brooke laughed again at the horrified look on Lara's face.

"You're just the excuse for a party. Nights are long and cold here. I'm the secretary of the WW which is also the Community Activities Committee and we invent pretexts to have fun," Erin said.

"I'm overwhelmed, but I'm game."

They discussed a few details, and it was time for Brooke to go home.

Home! A home where Dexter would be waiting for her. Her heart swelled with the warmth of love. Desperate love. Did he really love her? Doubts mounted. She so much wanted his professed love to be genuine, but no matter how she tried, she couldn't dissociate his job from his personal life. What would happen when he concluded his investigation? What reason would he have for remaining in Agate Creek? As she drove over the snow-packed road, images of his arrival in Agate sprang up into her mind. Why did he buy the chalet closest to her own? There was another, better house, with more amenities, on the opposite side of the village. Why did he cozy up to her? That she had the answer, playing at being a James Bond. She canceled that thought. He wasn't. Or... was he?

The more she thought about it, the more she convinced herself that he had planned all along to get close to her solely in order to obtain whatever scrap of information she might have about Seth. Talk about being used!

A cold shiver of realization ran down her spine. Could he possibly suspect that she too was involved in whatever crimes her worthless ex-husband had been committing, and that pillow talk would reveal her secrets? After all, it was hard to believe that she and Seth had lived completely separate lives. It was rare for a wife not to have at least some inkling of what her husband was up to. What a fool she'd been! All that time, she had believed in Dexter's true love.

His eagerness to drive her to the seemingly endless bank appointments, driving her and Vicky to Whitehorse hospital to see Ethan, were these merely a ploy to get closer to her? And the offer to stay at Doghaven so that she wouldn't need to purge the plumbing system, to look after her dogs while she was away, was that all part of his grand scheme?

She'd been lulled into giving him carte blanche to search the place for any clues to her late husband's guilt or her own. But why did her heart beat faster when he was with her? She had it all wrong once again.

Disillusion threatened to stifle her reasoning. She fought back tears and swallowed hard. She'd tell him it was over between them. She was too trusting. Once more, she'd jumped into the love realm without looking first.

In just a few days, she was leaving for her stint in the Iditarod race. Maybe it was not too late to tell Dexter she didn't need his help. Alex was still going to come and feed the dogs after school. He would only take one or two dogs at a time for a short outing. It meant they wouldn't get all the exercise they were used to, but they'd adapt. Once she was far away from Dexter, her heart would learn to forget him.

With this resolution in mind, she pulled into her yard. She strode resolutely into the cabin. There was no Dexter. Only a loving note on her plate and the enticing smell of coriander from the curry warming on the stove.

Deflated, she sat to partake of the savory food before going outside to play with her dogs.

CHAPTER NINETEEN

At his kitchen counter, Dexter made a sandwich with one hand while holding his satellite phone in the other. "Can you repeat that, Max?"

—— Our colleagues in Alaska have arrested a mule carrying more than a million dollars' worth of raw diamonds.

"Does it have any bearing on our case?" He chomped on the sandwich. "Excuse me, it's late and I need food to think clearly."

—— The suspect claims he's only the delivery person and was taking the package to a locker in Anchorage. A bank of lockers reserved for Iditarod mushers.

"More and more obscure. I don't suppose he knows Lammers has been bumped off."

—— He wouldn't know anybody. The way it works is he receives a text message, picks up the merchandise and delivers it. His payment is deposited in cash in another locker. He knows nothing more than this.

"And now they're watching the locker. The text message was sent from a throwaway phone. It doesn't advance us."

—— There seemed to be a connection with the sled dog race. You need to investigate those mushers in your area.

An image flashed through Dexter's mind. Brooke, volunteer vet for the Iditarod. Her dead husband, a suspected link to the smuggling. "The race is international. If we're to investigate all the mushers, we need more manpower."

—— Start with the widow. She's going to be on the Iditarod trail. You ought to be suspicious. Her husband's out of the game, but she is with the race. You've got a connection here.

Dexter bit his tongue, then breathed deeply. "I have been entrusted with the keys to her house. She even told me to search it all I want."

—— There we are! She must be pretty sure you won't find anything. I'd say she ought to be suspect number one.

"You forget Lammers cleaned her out. Nothing fake about that. She's on the edge of bankruptcy. If he had been involved, something perhaps happened that he suddenly needed a huge amount of cash.

—— It fits in like a glove. She's about to be bankrupt and she's part of the Iditarod when our colleagues caught a shipment. Why use the reserved lockers if it wasn't for someone in the race?

"She's stationary at a checkpoint, and I believe the veterinarians are flown back to Nome, or is it Anchorage? Don't tell me a musher will collect the bundle from the locker and hand it to her."

—— Hence your connection. Who the hell would suspect an idiot running with a bunch of dogs in sub-zero temperatures through blizzards in the middle of nowhere as you said yourself?

"Good assessment, yes, but the race trail is miles away from here. And Dr. Porter crosses the border as an ordinary traveler. I'm sure the border guards would be checking her bag for drugs. So it's unlikely she could carry raw diamonds or polished ones."

—— You're defending her too much, Dex! Don't forget you're on duty, but I agree, you may have a point.

"I suppose the parcel has been lifted from the locker and replaced with one containing real rocks." Laughter rang in his ears. "Any progress on the black agenda?"

—— Nothing useful yet. Actually, I think you should be taking part in the race. As a musher, you'd be able to see what happens.

"You're kidding! It takes years of training to run a team of dogs in a one-thousand mile race. I can just about handle five dogs, maybe six, on a good day. Those teams have sixteen dogs, pulling through perhaps the last frozen wilderness on earth."

—— The maximum number of dogs has been reduced to fourteen.

"Sure, that would really help me. Don't be obtuse, Max. I can't race dogs." He gave a hollow laugh. "What good would it be, since even if it wasn't too late to apply, I'd be the very last on the trail?"

—— Too bad. I feel if we could have someone in the race, we'd learn a lot.

"Mushers are spread out and there may be as much as two days between the first and the last."

—— You seem very knowledgeable.

"When you live in a community where sled dogs are more numerous than people, you soon learn about racing strategies, sled dogs and veterinary care."

—— For which you have privileged information. Don't let romantic notions get in the way of your work, Dex!

The call ended, but it was too late to go over to Brooke's. She had just accepted him back into her life, barely, but he sensed her hesitation, her lingering doubts about the sincerity of his love. Although in his work he sometimes had to get close to a woman, he always tried to keep a professional distance between them, and because of that, he knew he had hurt some women. Apologies, flowers and chocolates had done little to erase the look of pain in their eyes, even if their pain had perhaps saved countless lives.

What was happening with Brooke was entirely different. He'd been hit with a tsunami of emotion he had never experienced before. He thought he was safe from himself, because she was married and he adhered to a self-imposed code. Acting the good neighbor was a change for him, even when he caught a glimpse of wistfulness in her eyes. It made finding clues more difficult, but not impossible. All that changed when she became a widow. He found himself in a close encounter with a highly desirable woman.

How could he convince her he loved her, regardless of having to do a job that touched her? Without a doubt, he knew he wanted to spend his life at her side. Yet, he despised himself for still deceiving her. His offer to look after her cabin while she was away also hid the motive that he needed to search not just for clues, but the possibility of finding a stash of precious gems. She was quick on the uptake, though. He had to ask himself whether the reason for his offer came from a deep and genuine feeling to make her happy and give her peace of mind while away performing her race duties or the pressure he was under to crack the mystery of this case. Separating the two motivating impulses was beyond his current abilities.

He was aware that leaving her beloved Canadian Inuit dogs had bothered her. This year, unlike other years, she was not able to rely on her old friend Jimmy Redhead, as he too was involved with the big race. When he, Dexter, spontaneously offered to look after her cabin and exercise the dogs, he had no ulterior motive in mind. At least that's what he liked to think. It just happened to be convenient for the both of them. On that score, she was prepared to trust him. Did he really think a search of her property would provide clues? Deep down, he knew the answer was no. Brooke struck him as smart enough to know that she wouldn't have been able to hide anything from a trained and experienced police detective. The fact she expected there was nothing to hide was reason enough to allow him free run of the house and surroundings. Was it proof she knew nothing? For a split second, he wondered whether he was the one being exploited.

Two cups of coffee later, he still hadn't answered his own questions. The only sure thing was that he missed holding her in his arms.

Chapter Twenty

The drive to Whitehorse had been mostly silent until Brooke turned to him. "How come you have the best Jeep they make and a truck now with a transporter? I wouldn't have thought Royal Canadian Mounted Police inspectors got paid that well."

Dexter gave another laugh. "That's true, but I inherited a bit of money and invested it. I bought the truck when I moved to Agate Rock."

"To blend in?"

"I guess so."

"Really? You stand out like a sore thumb, if I may say so."

"Oh, how?"

Humor animated her features. "You dress like a city slicker masquerading as a rural guy. Your clothes are clearly of better quality than those of the Donek sled dog aristocracy. You walk around with an air of quiet authority and discipline. When you help organize the local races or the kids' summer games, you do it in a way that has everybody falling into line without a murmur."

"I don't mean to behave like that."

"No, it just comes naturally, the way you'd expect a general to rally his troops."

Dexter burst out laughing. "Is that a compliment?"

"I suppose it is. The usual way things get done a round here is with a high degree of chaos and petty rivalry. I don't know how, but you had everybody working together with good humor."

"Chalk it up to my early training in crowd management."

"I should have thought of that. I imagine you don't come out of police college and become an inspector right away."

"It takes years of training and preparation and thoroughly knowing police work. It's a tall ladder to climb."

"Do you like your work?"

"Sometimes I do and sometimes I don't."

"Like most jobs. You must get some satisfaction in locking up drug pushers, no?"

He smiled at her use of *drug pushers*. "The drug pushers are the small fry. What gives the most satisfaction is getting the drug kingpins. When you put it like that, yes, I do."

"When you solve this case, you'll be off to another assignment."

"When we deal with international crime syndicates, it can take years to wrap up a case."

"That justifies the investment in real estate and that kind of thing." She turned away to look at the passing scenery for a moment. "You're so good, though, you'll solve your case lickety-split."

Was there a note of regret in her voice? It was true. Once the case was resolved, he'd be assigned to another and that could be anywhere, most likely far away from her and Agate Creek. He could leave the Force. He had already clocked up a sizable number of years of pension. The idea made him feel as if he were betraying a friend. Then Brooke would perhaps not take it as a proof of love. Instinctively, he knew she wouldn't abandon her clinic and this mushing world to follow a man, him, to the end of the world. Relationships can't survive if one partner denies themselves so the other can pursue their passion.

Why was he torturing himself? They hadn't talked about commitment. Since that first night when she accepted his return, she'd made no move to resume their intimacy, and he didn't want to pressure her.

He parked in front of Stephanie's house and picked up Brooke's bags from the back seat.

Stephanie came bounding down the walk. "Just in time for lunch! It's waiting for you."

Brooke returned the hug. "Don't you have to be at the clinic?"

"I've made time for lunch."

Dexter put the bags down. "I'll leave you, ladies. I've business to attend to."

Brooke gave a start, but her friend pounced on Dexter.

"Lunch takes precedence over business." She led her guests into the dining room. "Sit down." Dexter meekly took a seat at the table.

When lunch was over, Stephanie disappeared into the kitchen while Brooke saw Dexter to the door. Her pliant body encircled in his strong arms, he lowered his head. He intensified the kiss, drawing her upward to new heights of emotion.

He broke off. "Have a great time in the frozen wilds of Alaska."

Laughter burst from her. "You should try it sometimes."

"That's an idea."

He left, and she joined Stephanie to finish the dishes.

"Now you look more rosy. Was there some tension between the two of you?"

"He's a cop, and he hadn't told me."

Stephanie gave a low whistle. "Many women wouldn't think twice if their new interest blurted out *I'm a cop*. Maybe a cop's image isn't the stuff of romance novels the way firefighters or mountain climbers and airline pilots are, but it's still pretty impressive."

"Except that all the kisses were a way of finding out if I knew anything about Seth and to allow him to search my place once he discovered I knew nothing."

"Alright, let's admit it may have started out like that. He did fall for you regardless of his job and initial motives."

"Are you sure you shouldn't have gone into psychology rather than veterinary?"

Stephanie laughed. "You're as stubborn as ever."

"Once bitten, twice shy."

"Let's go to the clinic. If I judge by your goodbye kiss——"

"That's what it was. A goodbye. Adieu. Farewell."

"Liar!"

CHAPTER TWENTY-ONE

I n the organized confusion of the pre-race checkup for over a thousand dogs, Brooke met old friends. After her first Iditarod, she'd got used to the inevitable jokes when she held the cup under a dog to collect a urine sample to test for drugs. Like her, Garry had been volunteering for several years.

"Will you dance with me at the banquet in Nome?"

She smiled. "One dance."

"The whole evening, hundred dances."

"Don't be greedy. There are more men than ladies. We have to share ourselves around."

"Can I see you home and take you to dinner?"

Always careful not to hurt anyone's feelings, Brooke shook her head. "That would be a thousand mile detour. It's not worth it."

"Maybe it is for me." He looked at the ground.

She had to stop him for good. An image of Dexter passed in her mind's eyes. "Be reasonable, Garry. I'm not free." He didn't to know that she meant she was committed to animals rather than a man. Because she hadn't committed herself and might never do, but she was committed to the animals, pets or wild.

His head snapped up to be confronted with her contrite air. "I see."

Karel, the rookie vet, approached them with a sheet of paper in his hand. "Do you only need to do the HAWL at every checkpoint?"

Relieved by the interruption, Brooke replied, "I think they ought to add one more L to Hydration, Attitude, Weight, Lungs. They should add Limbs. You have to be attentive to soreness of the limbs. The musher is usually the one to tell you if a dog appears to be limping or has a slight change of gait. The last thing he wants is to run a lame dog. Always check anyway, even if the musher doesn't have a complaint."

They moved on to the next team to inspect. It was Ian Campbell's.

While they bent over a dog, Brooke whispered to Karel, "You always need to be extra careful with mushers who hire a team. There were some I had to remove from the race because, not being their own dogs, they didn't look out for them as they would their own. In fact, they neglected them. Not many mushers, mind you, but you need to watch for that attitude. I know Campbell and I'll give him that. He has always taken care of the dogs he hires."

"That wasn't mentioned in the Idi instructions for vets."

She straightened. "That's where experience comes in. And that's why, as a rookie, you're under my supervision." She smiled at him. "The ink on your veterinary diploma isn't quite dry yet."

He stood straight. "I admit I was a bit miffed at first when they accepted me, but made me dependent on your good will. Now, I'm glad they did. You're very knowledgeable."

She acknowledged the young man with a nod and a smile. She signed the vet book and handed it to Campbell. "Your dogs are good to go, Ian."

He shrugged. "Thanks a million."

A musher swaggered into sight. "Hey, Campbell! Are you going to scratch at Willow again?"

Brooke winced at the rude reply. She took the arm of the newcomer and moved him along with her to the next team.

"Don't go antagonizing people like Ian Campbell. It isn't good sportsmanship."

"Yes, ma'am. But it's true, you know. Five years in a row, he starts and finishes in Willow. That's only the official restart of the race. So, in fact, he never races. He just drives up Highway 3."

Her eyebrows pulled together, Brooke's thoughts whirled in her head. "How do you know?"

"Three years ago, me and a buddy, we had an accident and had to scratch. He did too, just before us. Yet he didn't have an accident. Then we saw him on the highway. Friends tell us he just motors up to Fairbanks."

"Are you sure? What could he do there?"

"Got a girl, I bet. Enters the race just to impress. Has no intention of running it."

Troubled, Brooke set up to examine a team. "Maybe. Excuse me, I've got work to do."

She worked in silence with her helpers. When she finished, she smiled at Scott Walsh. "So this is your last time racing the Idi?"

GENEVIEVE MONTCOMBROUX

"It is. Chris is expecting and I want to spend more time with my growing family. I missed too much of Glenn's early years."

Brooke nodded. Scott's estranged first wife had kept their son away from him for almost five years. Jerome Renard strolled into the little group.

"Scott's going to win this one."

"No, you are! I saw your dogs. Superb, absolutely superb," Scott said.

Jerome winked at Brooke. "Don't believe him. He has years of experience. That counts in this race."

The banter continued. "I'm finishing, here. You had a vet clear your team, Jerome?"

"Yes. I'm parked at the end, next to Jimmy. Did you see Campbell?"

"I just cleared his team. Why?"

"He looked very agitated earlier on and at the pre-race banquet too," Scott said.

She pulled her bag to her. "He was rather sullen. That's nothing new for him."

"He's got loads of mushing experience. He has won mid-distance races and could absolutely win the Idi, but scratches, even though he rents great dogs," Scott said.

"From Big Sky Kennels," Jerome said.

Brooke straightened her back and gave a pat to the dog she'd examined. "They're good dogs and they're well-conditioned, so he has spent time training with them."

"Strange guy," Scott said.

Still holding the sheet of instructions, Karel motioned her over to Roman Cluny's team. "It says here, Roman is an Alaska State Park Ranger. Is he on duty?"

"No, young man, this is my vacation." The broad-shouldered ranger had just strolled in.

"Sorry, I didn't see you. Best of luck. I hope you win."

The next day was the ceremonial start of the race in downtown Anchorage. The cacophony of barking and howling dogs, along with the excited chatter of the crowd, was music to Brooke's ears. Glossy black ravens perched on the roofs of buildings, looking down at the strange happenings below. Silence finally prevailed, and bib Number One was called. No one in the crowd of mushers stirred.

A young, shivering boy tugged at Brooke's sleeve. "Who's the Late Norman Vaughan? What did he do?"

"He's the honorary musher for this year's race. Do you know what an honorary musher is?"

"Is that someone great?"

"In a way, yes. It's a mark of honor for someone who has done good things for other people. Norman Vaughan was an Antarctic explorer. That was very important at the time. And he raced the Iditarod for the last time at age eighty-four."

"Eighty-four? That's old."

She repressed a laugh. "He was fit and healthy. So age doesn't matter."

A woman called to the boy. "Spencer, don't bother the lady."

"She ain't bothered. She's telling me all about the Iditarod."

The woman stepped closer. "You have to excuse my son. We've just arrived from Arizona. He's not used to all this."

Brooke nodded and smiled. "Don't worry about me. I'm a volunteer race veterinarian."

Spencer caught her attention again. "So Number Two is going to win the race since he's the first one to go?"

"Not necessarily. Being the first to start the race isn't an advantage because every racer is timed, that is the length of time he has to wait before his turn to go is adjusted during the compulsory twenty-four hours rest. So Number Seventy-three, the last number, could just as well win as long as he arrives first in Nome."

"Cool. I saw in the paper the race como... commemorates a vaccine for sick children. What does that really mean?"

"The children in Nome——"

"I know where it is, right at the top of the map."

"That's correct. The children needed a serum, a medicine, to save their lives. People couldn't use a plane because in January the weather was really bad, and in 1925, the planes were not as big as now. So, the authorities in Anchorage put the serum on the train to Nenana and from there, dog mushers relayed the serum, each team passing the vital medicine on to the next team all the way to Nome."

"There was no train to Nome?"

"No, no train, no roads, just a vast wilderness with a few scattered settlements here and there, where people used sled dogs to get around. It was very brave of the mushers because it was very cold, with storms as well."

"And the children were saved, right?"

"Right."

"I read that the dog Balto led the team into Nome, but one named Togo ran more miles."

"You learned well. Gunnar Kaasen got to Nome with his team led by Balto. Leonhard Seppala covered the longest distance with Togo leading his team."

"I'm going to the Hall of Fame tomorrow to see it all."

They chatted until Spencer had to go and warm up inside. Brooke went to her hotel to prepare for her flight to Skwentna, the first checkpoint where her team had been posted, along with other veterinarians.

Chapter Twenty-Two

The Inuit dog family curled up, happy after their long run, Dexter went into Brooke's cabin. By now, he had pretty well examined every crack in the floor and walls and pieces of furniture. When he opened the top drawer of her chest of drawers, he found a sarcastic note in her handwriting.

Warning: Underwear below. Don't be shy looking for hidden gems!

It made him feel lower than a garden slug. There had been difficult moments in his career, but none like this operation. He had absolutely no doubt that Brooke knew nothing of her late husband's activities. Yet, in his type of work, one didn't take anything for granted. Now convinced that Seth Lammers had been a very smart criminal, Dexter endeavored to think like him. Lammers had only been an intermediary until he grew dissatisfied with his profits...

His satellite phone beeped.

"Max, what's new?"

—— Those racers who have lockers have been coming and going until they had to be at the marshaling area. There was a crush just before the mushers' banquet. The locker under surveillance was opened by a nondescript individual. The security camera only shows his back, as if he knew he was on camera. He was swallowed by the crowd for a moment. Our American colleagues' spotter finally caught up with him and followed him to a sport equipment store where it was discovered that the he was a she. A woman employee of the store. She isn't a musher, so she passed it on to someone. She's being investigated.

"Is the GPS tracker working?

—— It's working alright and moving, but contact is spotty because of the terrain I guess. We need someone closer. That's where you come in. You're going to fly out there and follow the race. Our U.S. colleagues are arranging for a plane to pick you up in Anchorage and will fly you to a checkpoint. All racers have to stop for a few hours of rest at various checkpoints at intervals, depending on their own race strategy. Then you'll have to follow the parcel until we find out where and to whom it goes.

"Why me? Can't one of the DEA in Alaska do it?"

—— You'll have Olivia Jones with you. It's a joint effort. There's a flight from Whitehorse tomorrow morning at six o'clock. Be on it.

"I'll book now and arrange things here."

Wrinkles creased Dexter's forehead. This affair was becoming complicated. On the other hand, he might have a chance to see Brooke. An imaginary ray of sun had just appeared. He was bound to meet her. He'd make sure of it. He loaded the stove with wood and climbed into his Jeep. First, he stopped at Agate Grocery.

"Tom, I have to go away and I'm going to ask Jimmy's sister to house-sit. Charge my card for anything she needs, will you? Give her little guy a toy or two." He handed the card to his friend.

"No problem. We'll make sure everything is fine, but keep your card. I'll put it on your tab till you come back.

"Thanks. She will accept, won't she?"

"Yashee loves Brooke's dogs. Count on her to take them out for runs."

Dexter chuckled. "I heard she's as good a musher as Jimmy, and her boy is a future musher. So sad she lost her husband."

"It is. He was a brave man."

Dexter drove on to Yashee's house. His mind swirled with questions. Where had the real diamonds come from? Why was the package of fake diamonds going to Nome if it was to have all appearances to come from Canada? It suddenly hit him so hard he had to brake and stop on the shoulder of the road while he absorbed his own discovery. From Nome, the mushers flew home wherever that may be. In fact, custom officers were likely to be friendly with the racers and would be reluctant to do thorough inspections of all their mushing gear. Who could blame them for not wanting to sift through a pile of dirty laundry, smelly dog harnesses, soiled booties and dog coats, next to a pack of howling canines wanting to get out of their crates? It was a brilliant tactic.

Dexter arrived. "Yashee, I need a big help."

"You are going to marry Brooke. I will help."

He smiled. "I hope so, but right now she's in Alaska and I have to fly there tomorrow."

"Good. You propose to her. So what do you need?"

"I had promised not to let Doghaven freeze. Can you come over and stay until she comes back?"

"Of course."

"You buy anything you need at the Agate Grocery."

"No need. I can buy my own groceries."

"No, I insist. It's all arranged. You get what you need and we sort it out afterwards." His tone was firm.

"Yes, sir!"

Dexter laughed. Yashee was smiling. She had been widowed the previous year when her husband had drowned trying to rescue a snowmobiler who'd gone through the ice. Dexter made a mental note to call in at the regional power company's office in Donek and pay for three or four months' worth of electricity for her cabin, because he knew Yashee would be offended at the offer of money for helping a friend.

"I'll leave the Jeep with you."

"I would prefer your truck."

"Done deal."

"Turn the electric radiators down. I get our things together." She moved toward the bedroom.

Five-year-old Gugàn burst into the kitchen. "I finished drawing. We go to Brooke and I get a ride with the dogs."

Dexter and the boy chatted while his mother packed.

Chapter Twenty-Three

L aughter prevailed when the veterinary teams climbed into Marc's Cessna. There were no seats.

"Sorry, ladies and gentlemen, for the lack of seating. This bird is meant to transport teams of dogs, sleds and other equipment, hence the cable with picket lines running from back to front. But you're cordially invited to sit on the straw bales."

The next ten days or so were going to be rough living. They knew it and took it all in their stride.

The plane made a smooth landing on Skwentna's snowy airstrip and Brooke disembarked with her assistants. Mushers were keen on having their dogs' first assessment. At the checkpoint, teams piled up, eager to continue. Close to the start line, but far enough for problems to develop in the dogs, Brooke and her colleagues didn't have a minute to themselves. Every musher wanted to make sure his or her canine athletes could run the remaining eight hundred and ninety-two miles to Nome. An undetected problem could end the race for the musher.

From the Skwentna checkpoint, Brooke and the two members of her team were leap-frogged to Nikolai to await the arrival of the first dog teams. With a smile on her face, she contemplated the huge, brightly colored welcome sign before trudging to the community hall. It was only day four of the race and they didn't expect the first musher until late in the night. Two other teams of vets had also flown in, and among them they quickly organized shifts. At the community hall, a volunteer led them to a recess space close to the main door, and slightly more private, where half-dozen cots had been set up for them. Women were cooking food on the other side of the hall.

After they'd eaten, the vets strolled into the small town. As expected, the locals met them with their dogs. All were healthy, fed on wild meat, but carried a worm burden. Brooke and her team handed out deworming medicine.

***

A bleary-eyed Dexter met the tall, slim woman waiting for him. Introductions didn't take long.

The woman spoke before he even reached her. "Hello, I'm Olivia Jones. Why did they have to send you?"

Taken aback, Dexter stopped in his tracks. What was the problem with this woman? "And good day to you too, ma'am."

"I'm capable of running the show. I don't need help from Canada."

He had met her type before. Aggressive women didn't faze him. In a way, he pitied them, but he tried to keep his tone neutral. "You forget that my country is deeply involved in this particular operation and our agencies always work together."

She huffed, turned round, and ordered. "Get to that plane, just over there."

Dexter stiffened and reined in his instinctive reaction. With a suave, almost humble tone, he articulated, "Do you mind if I go in to use the facilities first? I've been flying for five hours!"

Red colored her cheeks. "Of course."

The image of Brooke superimposed over the aggressive female agent while he walked across the terminal.

The pilot of the private jet that had brought him caught up with him and snorted. "Get a load off that gal! Thinks she's the boss."

"This is her territory. So I guess, technically, she is."

"You've got self-control. I'd have flattened her."

"I have to work with her."

When they were done, they found a fast-food outlet and ordered a meal.

"I see Marc, your Iditarod Air Force pilot, chatting up the girls at the gate over there," the pilot said.

"Do you know everybody who flies?"

The pilot grinned. "I've done the Iditarod with my Cessna, but I also need a steady job, so I try to manage pleasure and work."

"You seem to have the best of both worlds. I wish I could."

They made their way toward Marc. Moments later, they were joined by Olivia and proceeded onto the tarmac again. Once Olivia was seated in the front seat of the Cessna 180, and Dexter perched on a straw bale, she pulled out a black box from her bag.

"A new tracker device. I adjusted the frequency. We should be able to pick up the GPS chip in the bag of fake diamonds without problem."

"How far are the mushers on the trail?"

"We lost contact at about one hundred miles."

Dexter pursed his lips. It didn't add up. He had his own suspicions about Miss Olivia, but chose diplomacy. "Maybe the battery was a dud."

Annoyance bathed the agent's features. "I've got spares now." Her arid tone didn't invite further comment.

Which suited him. His first impression was correct. The woman had to prove she was competent, even if she had forgotten to pack spare batteries. This partnership wasn't off to a good start. Ms. Jones was insecure in her position. As a contrast, the matter-of-fact attitude of Brooke floated across his mind. Feisty she might be and capable of justified anger, Brooke always remained human and ready to acknowledge her mistakes. Olivia's exclamation shattered his musings. He brushed the thoughts away. He had a job to do.

"I got it. It's going strong."

Dexter leaned against the window. "There's only one musher on the trail. Can you turn round Marc and pass over him again?"

"Can do." Marc executed a smooth turn and circled the Cessna back in line with the trail and the lone musher below.

"He's got a dark parka. It could be green, I think. Not much help, lots of them do."

Silence settled for a while. The plane kept on flying and turned round again.

"It stopped moving!" Olivia brought her face closer to the window of the plane. "The signal is lost."

The trail dipped into a gully and disappeared beneath the dense pine cover.

"There's a checkpoint coming up," Dexter said.

Seconds later, she exclaimed, "Look, I can see the musher. He's still alone." She thrust the tracker into Dexter's hands. "Can you get a signal?"

The plane passed a brightly lit camp. "That was Rohne," Marc said. "There's a roadhouse and a couple of big tents. I saw teams stopped. It's a popular place to take the customary twenty-four hours' rest after the mushers have made it through the Dalzell Gorge."

Dexter craned his neck to try to see. Darkness was rapidly falling. "He must have checked in and he's continuing. But no signal!"

Olivia chewed her fist. "Can we follow? He's bound to stop at the next checkpoint. We could be ahead of him."

"There's no signal. Could we turn round?"

"Sorry, can't do. It's too dark already. We've just passed a safety cabin. I've got to turn here and put this bird down. I saw there're a few teams there."

Olivia shook her fist in frustration. "Why did he not stop at the checkpoint?"

"Many do, but regulations state they only have to check in. They're not obliged to sleep over. They can travel all night if they want to." Dexter kept adjusting the tracking frequency without success.

"We'll leave at first light. Don't worry, we'll catch up with him. There's another seven hundred miles to go," Marc said.

Night had fallen, but the expanse of white snow relieved the darkness. The Cessna made a textbook landing on the short and narrow airstrip.

"Thank you, Marc. You're an ace," Olivia said. The compliment didn't flow naturally from her lips. She was obviously trying to erase the unfavorable first impression she made on Dexter.

Marc continued securing the Cessna, but threw her a smile. "The cabin's small and it'll be a bit crowded. You might want to get the tent out."

"Thanks, but I've got my sleeping bag."

Dexter had eaten earlier on the plane and had saved a couple of sandwiches. He saw that Olivia had a sandwich, too. They walked across to the parked teams.

"Weiman! What a surprise," Jerome Renard said. He had finished settling his dogs and was unrolling his sleeping bag on the straw next to them.

It was bound to happen that he'd meet mushers from home somewhere on the trail. His mind made a double-take. Did he say *home*? Was it meant like home is where the heart is? He had to come up with a reason for his presence. "I heard and learned so much about this race that I had to come and see for myself."

Jerome teased him. "Nothing to do with a certain veterinarian, of course."

That was a good clue. "Another thing I learned was how the vets are crucial to the race and, in addition, I now know all about the Iditarod Air Force or the IAF for short."

"Our heroes who look after us from above, hey, Marc!"

"Somebody's got to show you guys the way to Nome." Marc's deadpan face brought a guffaw from the mushers.

With a cup of coffee in his hand, Scott Walsh joined them. "You just missed Campbell. First time he's actually mushing the race."

So that was the lone musher they'd been tracking. Frustrated, Dexter was determined to keep up with his role. "Can't say I'm sorry."

"He made a flying visit and didn't like our ugly mugs. I think I'll sleep in the open too. The cabin's full. Normally, it's just the two of us," Jerome said.

They parted to get a couple of hours of sleep. Jerome wiggled into his sleeping bag next to his dogs.

"I'll sleep with my dogs too," Scott said. "You're welcome to share, Weiman. It's not cold, only zero degree. Fahrenheit, that is."

"I think I will. What's minus twenty degree Celsius between friends," Dexter replied. *Keep up the pretense of experiencing the race. It won't be the first time I slept outdoors. At least here it's cold, but not raining.*

Olivia pulled a face and opted for a spot on the floor of the cabin near the door. Silence settled on the tall spruce forest.

A couple of hours later, an unusual noise troubled the silence of the night and reached Dexter's ears. In seconds, he was out of his sleeping bag, fully alert, tying his bootlaces. It wasn't the swish of the runners and the panting of dogs of a passing team that alerted him. The cabin door banged again against the wall. A sound of retching was heard. Dragging noise followed. And a feeble cry for help.

Dexter ran toward the cabin. Olivia, on all fours, was trying to drag a man out.

"What's up?"

She pulled up onto her knees. "My head! Gas..." She fainted.

"Jerome! Scott! Problem. Come help!"

A couple of dogs let out a few barks. Two dark silhouettes were already shrugging into parkas. Dexter pulled his neck warmer over his nose, took a deep breath and rushed into the cabin where five mushers and Marc had elected to sleep. He bumped into his inert body, bent down and grabbed him as best as he could, hampered as he was by the thick sleeping bag, and dragged him outside. "Come'n, Marc, wake up!" He shook and shook him. His two friends had understood the situation and gone in.

Moments later, everyone was out of the cabin. The three friends were shaking the mushers and Marc.

"Carbon monoxide poisoning," Dexter said.

"How the devil did that happen?" Jerome asked.

Dexter shook his head. "Leaking woodstove, I suppose."

"But Scott and I always stop here rather than Rohne because it's so much quieter. It's in good order. We made sure of it."

Scott raised his head from massaging Olivia's shoulders to help her breathe. "Too many people tonight. That's why we stayed outside."

"When the place is aired enough, I'll go and inspect the stove. There's nothing else in there?" Dexter said.

"Nothing."

Finally, the mushers were regaining consciousness. Olivia and Marc were the least affected, as they had been the last ones to go into the cabin.

Jerome looked at his watch and took note of the time. "We have to report this. I don't think those guys should be going until they are fully recovered and that may take several hours."

Dexter nodded, took note of the time as well, estimated how long it had taken to get the mushers out and wake them up, and wrote it down. He pulled out a flashlight from his bag.

With his mouth and nose still covered, he went back in. A couple of pine logs still crackled in the stove. The beam of light danced on its door and his eyes widened. He noticed that a small stick was caught on the top compressing the gasket and leaving a tiny hole.

Jerome joined him. "Find anything?"

"This stick?"

"It must have been caught when someone loaded the stove, but not enough to poison everybody the way they are."

"It'd take all day with that small a hole." Dexter continued to inspect the stove. The damper was in the closed position. A loud expletive escaped his mouth. "This is a crime. Look at that stick in the back!"

Jerome craned his neck to see the stovepipe bent at the joint and stabilized with a stick similar to the one above the door. "Yeah! It didn't get there by accident." He reached for the stick, but Dexter stopped his hand.

"It's a crime scene. Don't touch anything."

They walked out.

"What on earth is happening?" Jerome asked.

"Someone doesn't want you to win."

"Mushers are competitive, but I can assure you we are all sportsmen. Nobody would resort to a dirty criminal act to try to win."

"Don't be so sure. We need to know who came to the cabin before you, and these guys."

Head tilted, his friends looked at him curiously. "Are you a cop, or have you read too many police thrillers?"

"The first option is the better one. So let's see if any of the mushers can recall who came and went while they were here."

Sprawled in their sleeping bags, the men were confused. The five of them traveled together and had intended to rest for four hours. Their minds weren't clear enough to talk. A mushing team went past and waved. Dawn was approaching.

"You two, get going. Those guys will need maybe three or four hours to recuperate. Don't lose your placing. Besides, you can tell the story at the next checkpoint," Dexter said.

"That'll be Nikolai. Seventy-five miles, we'll be there in the afternoon," Jerome said. "But we can't let you handle those sick guys by yourself."

"They're conscious now, but we can stay a bit longer," Scott said.

"No, you go. I'll find out how to contact Nikolai on my satellite phone. You wrote the time when Olivia tumbled out of the cabin?"

"Yes, did you?"

"Let's compare. Add the mushers' names and my estimate before they can take off again, then give it to the marshal."

"Good. They shouldn't be penalized for that lost time. It's not their fault."

"Now go."

They were already readying their dogs, who were standing and raring to move on. Just as he was climbing on the runners, Scott turned and faced Dexter. "I remember now. The guy before us was Ian Campbell. He didn't stay. He doesn't like company."

"Why am I not surprised!"

Phone in hand, Dexter called Max and explained the situation.

—— I'll get hold of the officials in Nikolai as well as the race committee. Who did you say was the last musher to leave the safety cabin?

"Ian Campbell. An unpleasant character, but he doesn't have a record. I already checked back in Agate Rock."

—— When can you fly out?

"Not until our pilot is completely recovered. At least two or three hours. He wasn't in the cabin as long as the mushers."

—— What are the coordinates of the last time you picked up the signal?

Cold sweat ran down Dexter's back. Somehow, he missed something along the way and that annoyed him deeply. He rattled off the coordinates. "But from that point on, nothing. No signal. And I checked the tracking device. It's working perfectly. The musher we had singled out kept on the trail, but there was no signal from him."

The expletive from the other end seared his eardrum.

"My sentiment, also."

The call ended and Dexter went to make sure the mushers were keeping awake. Olivia tried to stand, but lurched as if drunk.

"I'm so dizzy."

"I can see that. Just breathe deeply. You need to take in as much oxygen as you can."

He turned his attention to Marc, who was sitting on his sleeping bag babbling away.

"Take big breaths, you'll start feeling better."

"I'm alright. I must fly straw bales to... yeah, the next one."

"You're disoriented. You can't fly. We'll wait."

"I can... d-drive..."

"You're sick, Marc. Wait till it passes."

"I'm n-not drunk."

"No, you're not drunk. You've been poisoned."

The pilot mumbled a few more slurred words, but let Dexter straighten his shoulders, and had him breathe deeply on command. A dog team trotted past, the musher oblivious to the drama unfolding at the tiny cabin.

CHAPTER TWENTY-FOUR

A team of sled dogs loved nothing better than to pursue another team. It was in the nature of sled dogs to be competitive. Friends would often take turns leading to encourage the team behind to keep pace. When they sensed a team behind, but didn't hear "trail!" and were not directed to the side of the trail, they'd put on a little more speed to remain in the lead.

Scott was about to signal Jerome to overtake him when he noticed a black spot up ahead on the trail. Fearful of encountering a moose, he gave their agreed signal to slow down, left arm outstretched with the hand pointing down. Slowing a team running at full speed is no easy task, not when the dogs are frisky and eager to run.

When they drew closer, Scott's hunch proved correct. A moose and her calf stood on the trail. Both teams slowed to a halt some distance away. Two mushers were already on the scene and were arguing with each other, and two more waited farther back on the trail. The presence of the moose was not totally unexpected. It would be rare for a musher not to come face to face with one somewhere along the way. The huge animal, like a throwback to prehistoric times, uttered a barking sound to her calf, a warning of danger.

Jerome and Scott secured their teams off the trail. The rule was that when there was a moose on the trail, all mushers would stop and wait until the situation was resolved. They approached the arguing men.

While still a few yards away, Scott sighed. "It's Campbell."

An uncomplimentary word was Jerome's only comment.

"The idiot's got a rifle and Cluny is trying to prevent him from shooting the moose."

They were now close enough to hear the exchange. Campbell was determined to shoot the moose. Jimmy Redhead caught up with them.

"What is going on?"

"Campbell is going to shoot the moose if Roman Cluny can't take the gun away from him."

Jimmy took a couple of steps forward. "I know that rifle. I have seen it before."

Nobody ever disputed Jimmy's assertions. He never spoke needlessly.

"Whose is it?" Jerome asked.

"That is Seth Lammers' gun."

"Did he sell it to Campbell?" Scott asked.

"You don't buy or sell a Mauser 98 Magnum just like that. That, I believe, is the stolen rifle."

The two friends whistled in surprise. It attracted the attention of the other two mushers. About to advance to Roman's help, Jimmy halted as two shots resonated across the trail, down the Takina River, and up the side of the mountain. The moose and her calf lay fallen, unmoving on the trail.

Before the shocked mushers could react, Ian Campbell jerked up his snow anchors.

"Stop! You're under arrest!" Ranger Cluny yelled.

"You can't arrest me. You're off duty." A demoniacal laugh and Campbell released the brake, and the team bounded forward, skirting the bleeding carcasses.

"That's against the law. If you kill a wild animal, you have to dress it." Scott's softly spoken words were met with nods of agreement.

"I scratch. As of now, I'm on duty," Roman shouted. He freed his team while pulling out a satellite phone. "You guys deal with the moose." He had hardly spoken that his team sped after Campbell.

"Be careful!" A chorus of voices shouted.

"I hope that jerk doesn't turn and decide to shoot Roman," Jerome said.

"He won't. There are too many witnesses," Scott said.

"Who wants to volunteer to help?" Jimmy asked.

Jerome and Scott called out they were, so did the two mushers who'd witnessed the scene. More mushers arrived and, as required, stopped.

"We must not waste. So we will not leave the meat here to attract wolves and others animals before the trail authorities can come and retrieve it with snowmobiles. Although it goes against my principles, we will not skin the moose. It takes too long. We shall quarter it and take it into Nikolai," Jimmy declared.

Everyone agreed. Jimmy's quiet ways were more powerful than barked orders. A plane buzzed low, turned round and circled the scene on the frozen wasteland, before continuing on.

"The Iditarod Air Force," Scott said. "He'll tell the officials about the moose."

Finally, the improvised butchers finished and several other mushers helped by taking a piece of the meat on their sled so that they could all keep up a good pace to Nikolai. The column of dog teams set off.

***

In Nikolai, the three teams of veterinarians sat on straw bales. There hadn't been any mushers through for over an hour, and that was unusual. Their chatter was interrupted by Dave, the marshal in Nikolai.

"Everybody grab a straw bale. We have to make a funnel to slow and stop the next team without injuring the dogs. An Alaska Ranger is pursuing an offender."

Puzzled, volunteers and vets carried bales to where the trail emerged from the forest and into the marshaling area, where they were to stop the team.

"Do you think he won't stop?" Brooke asked.

"He might try a breakthrough, though he'd have to stop sooner or later. For the sake of the dogs, we have to convince him to stop here." Dave added a few words to his helpers in their own language. They positioned themselves at the narrow end of the funnel.

They heard the panting and yipping of the dogs before seeing them. Covered in frost and belching condensed breath, like an old steam locomotive, the leaders emerged from the trees and, seeing the straw and the people, slowed down. Yells to *hike* came from behind.

"Goodness! Those dogs have been run hard," Brooke said.

A second later, the musher standing on the runners came into view.

"Campbell!"

"He clearly had no intention of stopping."

Several pairs of hands grabbed hold of the lines. Defeated, Campbell let go of the sled.

"As mayor and law enforcement officer in Nikolai and marshal of the Iditarod Trail race, I place you, Ian Campbell, under arrest," Dave said. His even voice, devoid of emotion, resonated in the cold air.

The children, always on hand to watch the teams, had scampered some distance near the houses after being told there would be danger. They rushed down while the adult helpers put the straw bales back. Resting mushers who had woken up looked on with curiosity. Since there were enough vets to care for the team, Brooke remained next to Dave.

Campbell fumed. "You can't arrest me. I did what was needed."

With the same placid voice, the marshal said, "The only time you can kill an animal is if the animal attacks you."

"It did."

"There are witnesses that it didn't. And here comes Roman."

Campbell's shoulders slumped.

The ranger pulled in and handed his team to the volunteers. His dogs, too, had run hard to keep up with the fugitive.

Brooke addressed a livid Ian Campbell. "You never expected anyone to phone, did you? Or to be seen by an IAF plane?" She could scarcely conceal her own anger at the man's behavior. "You put the dogs at risk running like a mad man!"

"Shut up, woman. I should never have raced. I should have scratched."

"So, why did you bother to enter the race in the first place?"

"None of your business."

As Campbell was led away to the Council Office, Brooke's mind was trying to make a connection with Dexter's work, but came up blank. She had no time to pursue that niggling thought, as there were dogs to care for. After a rest, mushers departed. It grew busy until Dave came up to her.

"There's been an accident at the safety cabin."

The veterinarians within earshot stepped closer, frowning and trying to picture a cabin they only saw from the air.

"At the cabin shortly after Rohne," Dave added. "The woodstove sprang a leak and several mushers suffered carbon monoxide poisoning. I guess they might need care when they arrive."

The grimace on Brooke's face attracted Dave's eye. "What is it?"

"How long since they were exposed?"

"I don't know. The message was relayed, so it's brief. Why?"

"If they started the run too soon, the exertion of hitching up the dogs and driving them could cause seizures." The vets came even closer to listen. "If they breathed it to the point of unconsciousness, the carbon monoxide binds with the blood hemoglobin and can damage the heart and the brain. The longer it remains in the body, the more dangerous it is for those vital organs. How much oxygen do we have on hand?"

"Not much. We rarely need it. CO poisoning is a bit unusual, but our local health clinic must have some oxygen."

"Then, as soon as they arrive, we have to take them there."

His fist against his mouth, Garry was the picture of concentration. "Can you get over the effects of the monoxide in the hemoglobin?"

"The carbon monoxide replaces the oxygen in the cells. Therefore, the organs are starved of oxygen and, if not remedied promptly, death ensues."

"Not something I ever saw in my vet practice."

"That's because you cater to pets. I had the sad experience of a sled dog traveling in a trailer who died shortly after being put in harness. The autopsy showed a high concentration of CO absorbed from the tailpipe of the towing vehicle. There was not enough oxygen left in the body to sustain the exertion of running."

While Brooke and Garry went by snowmobile to the health clinic, the vets who had listened with interest pooled their knowledge and compared the monoxide poisoning to the dioxide gas a deep-sea diver experiences when he gets the bends from surfacing too quickly. They agreed both were equally dangerous.

Eylin, the nurse in charge of the local clinic, welcomed Brooke, who quickly explained the situation.

"I have received one oxygen cylinder for the race. That is all," the young Athabascan nurse said.

"We'll make sure not to use it all. Even a little bit for each musher will help until we get them to a hospital if needed. Would it be possible to get the IAF to fly in another cylinder?"

"I'll get on the radio right away."

At Garry's enquiring look, the nurse added, "Much faster than the telephone and the pilots can also pick up the signal."

They returned to the marshaling area. They didn't have to wait long before children came up running. Two approaching teams had been spotted. Strong dogs made a grand entrance out of the pine forest. Walsh and Renard directed their dogs to the spot assigned by a volunteer. They hurriedly unloaded the hind quarters of moose from the top of their sleds, brushing off the bloodied snow on which the meat had rested. Women were already there and banded together to carry the meat to the community hall where some of it would go into the stew for the mushers.

While Scott and Jerome were watering their dogs and the vets examined them, Jerome called Brooke.

"You heard about the accident, except it wasn't an accident. Someone deliberately blocked the stovepipe. Only one musher had left the cabin."

Although Brooke itched to help Jerome put booties on his dogs, she refrained. The mushers were not supposed to accept help and could be penalized if they did. "Do you know who that was?"

"Ian Campbell."

"Are you sure? I know he's obnoxious, but to try to kill people, that's something at a different level."

"Maybe he didn't realize how dangerous it could be. He probably wanted to disturb our sleep, make us late to give him an advantage," the musher replied.

"You're generous, and I hope you're right. What about the moose incident?"

Jerome stretched and rubbed his back. "You saw the results. Fortunately, both mother and calf were killed instantly with two clean shots. Jimmy said it was a rifle that had been stolen from… Seth Lammers. Sorry."

For a moment, Brooke couldn't think. Her mind was swimming with conjectures. Then Scott called Jerome. Dave checked them out, and they both hit the trail to Nome. She took a few steps toward the Council Office to go and confront Ian Campbell before reason prevailed and she returned to stand next to Dave. Since Roman Cluny guarded Campbell with a couple of men, whether it was indeed her late husband's rifle or not, made no difference. That would be a separate charge.

The other mushers carrying the moose meat pulled in one by one. The villagers were happy to accept the meat. Jimmy sought out Brooke.

"Campbell was carrying Seth's gun. There was no doubt it was his. I would recognize that big Mauser anywhere. You said it had been stolen."

"Yes, it was stolen some two years ago from the cabin."

"So, he did not buy it from you."

"No. I don't understand. Seth and Ian were buddies. Why would he want to steal it? Seth was really mad about the loss of that rifle."

"Maybe Campbell bought it from whoever stole it."

She shook her head. "This is all very confusing." Seth's rifle that had disappeared. The jerk who shot animals with that rifle. Poisoning by carbon monoxide and Dexter after diamonds that Seth supposedly had hidden. "Just crazy, but don't waste time, Jimmy. Your dogs are good to go."

CHAPTER TWENTY-FIVE

A plane landed on the strip at the back of the settlement. Already volunteers on snowmobiles were on their way. They collected the oxygen cylinder and carefully transported it to the clinic.

Later, more teams were spotted by the youngsters. The whole village turned out to greet them, snowmobiles at the ready. It was a convoy that trotted into the open space, demonstrating the sportsmanship and solidarity between competitors. As mushers learned of the accident, they framed the sick mushers to make sure they could reach Nikolai safely. Brooke wasn't surprised at the selflessness of the men and women, even if it meant losing time and placing. She promptly assessed the dog drivers. Two of them, Adam and Niels, were still experiencing bouts of dizziness and shortness of breath.

She accompanied them by snowmobile to the health clinic. The three that hadn't slept as long in the cabin had no obvious side effects, but Brooke insisted on them breathing fifteen minutes of pure oxygen at intervals of fifteen minutes, so they could continue racing. Finally, reassured they were well-recovered, she allowed them to leave, but not before she extracted from them the promise to check their blood pressure, lungs and heart rate with the vets at the next checkpoint. She wrote down their stats for each of them to show to the vets. Although the two mushers most afflicted appeared recovered after breathing oxygen, Brooke wasn't satisfied.

"I have nothing to measure the level of carbon monoxide in your blood. Your blood pressure and your heart rate are lower than they should be. This is an indication there still is some CO in your system. I believe you need to breathe oxygen for two, maybe even four hours to clear whatever is left. You may feel fine now, but could get sick in two days' time or two hours or six months' time, if your brain has been affected."

"My brain..."

The two looked at each other. Adam spoke up. "Do you mean we could go crazy, crazier than we are already?"

She smiled. "Not crazy, just feeling sick, having headaches or dizziness, possibly seizures. If the poisoning was serious, it could take six months before you're back to normal. What time did you go into the cabin to sleep?"

Blank looks were a telltale symptom. Brooke insisted with more questions. They looked dejected.

"I can't remember," Niels said.

"Me neither."

Brooke spoke gently. "Temporary loss of memory is a typical sign."

"Shall I call the plane?" Eylin asked.

"Yes. Please do."

Adam put his head in his hands. "I've spent so much money on the race."

"If we are flown to Anchorage and found okay, can we be flown back here to continue the race? It's still early days," Niels said.

She empathized with the men. "I'm only a veterinarian. I don't know about the organization of the race."

"Even if we could just finish the race, we wouldn't lose everything. Sponsors would understand, but if we have to quit, we could lose our sponsors," Adam said.

"If we could come back tomorrow, it could be counted as our twenty-four hours' compulsory rest."

"What about our dogs? Can they stay here, if we can come back?"

A volunteer reassured them. "We won't send your dogs back to Anchorage and will look after the dogs for you. You phone tomorrow if you are allowed back. You tell Dave to count it as your twenty-four."

The fact they were able to talk rationally was an encouraging sign. Still, she worried. She wrote their stats on the veterinary pad, added a note to the effect that the mushers would lose everything if not treated promptly for the emergency doctors. Brooke hoped that they would be prioritized.

A plane engine was heard. The volunteers on snowmobiles drove the mushers to pick up their essential bags, complete with identification and a change of clothes. They then drove to the airstrip. Seeing their distress, Brooke accompanied them.

"You can boast that you flew out of Nikolai International Airport."

They looked around and at the small building, little more than a shack, in front of which they were standing.

"International?"

"Did you notice the large sign, flanked by moose antlers, just by the trees? It says Nikolai International Airport."

A cough interrupted their laughter. She didn't regret her decision to call for them to be evacuated for treatment. The cough signaled they still had too much carbon monoxide in their blood.

The LifeMed Alaska plane landed smoothly, turned and taxied to a stop.

"Thank you, doctor."

Her charges embarked rapidly. She stood a moment watching the plane disappear in the bluest of skies. Hearing the title was a stab to her heart. Of course, she had the title of doctor, Doctor of Veterinary Medicine, but no one said "thank you, doctor" to a vet like people do to a medical doctor. A flood of what could have been washed over her. Once more, an emergency had her act as a medical doctor delivering the right diagnosis. A tap on her shoulder broke her gloomy reflections.

"Dave here to see you," Garry said.

"Ah, doctor. A plane is coming. It is the pilot who had the poisoning too."

Doctor again! She hardened herself. These good people didn't know. No one did. The hurt had never gone away, but she should stop reacting.

"I'm thankful for the extra oxygen."

Dave smiled. "We communicated with the race committee. Officials will be waiting at the airport to help the two mushers."

He heart filled with warmth for the solidarity and the care that was dispensed to mushers and dogs.

They turned toward the south and soon spotted a dark speck in the sky. It grew bigger and finally its skis touched down on the airstrip.

"That's Marc's Cessna!" Garry's eyes followed the plane as it turn round and deftly parked near the reception committee.

Marc was the first to jump down, followed by Dexter, who turned to help a woman off the plane. The heart in Brooke's chest went out of control. Her jaw dropped and for a second, her mouth remained open.

"Dexter!"

He turned his head, "Don't worry, Yashee is looking after Doghaven." He returned his attention to the woman.

Dexter, here? Brooke couldn't believe what she was witnessing. What was going on? First, she had to examine the pilot, though if he had been able to fly and land impeccably, there couldn't be much wrong with him. She was quite sure that Dexter wouldn't have allowed him to fly if he'd had any doubts. The young woman didn't look as perky, though.

"Marc, how are you feeling?"

"I'm alright now."

"Let's go inside the terminal so I can listen to your heart and lungs."

Marc smiled. "Terminal is a pretty a grandiose name for this shack."

Olivia and Dexter followed. Brooke examined both patients and cleared them.

"You're regaining your color, Ms. Jones," Brooke said. "Are you still experiencing nausea?"

"Not really, but I'll confess that I was scared to death flying here. I didn't know if Marc was still feeling sick. I wasn't feeling all that great and assumed he wasn't either."

Relieved at the satisfactory outcome, Brooke smiled. "The body weight makes a difference in the absorption and elimination of the carbon monoxide. You're a slim woman, Ms. Jones, so you have less resistance."

"I'm glad you told me. By the way, I'm Olivia."

"Brooke."

The young woman nodded in what Brooke considered was a dismissive manner. What on earth was Dexter doing with the Iditarod? How come he just descended on Nikolai where she happened to be? And who was that woman?

Olivia walked over to Dexter who was speaking on his phone. "Dext, are you still picking up a signal?"

Dexter finished his call and slipped the device into his pocket. "Nope, we lost it before we stopped at the cabin, remember? It just vanished."

Olivia frowned. "My brain is still fuzzy." She strode toward the door. "Let's go."

"Ms. Jones, you will go to the health center to breathe pure oxygen to make sure the monoxide gas totally leaves your blood. You too Marc."

Olivia started protesting. Brooke turned her back and asked the volunteers to take Marc and the mystery woman to the health center to inhale some oxygen. Eylin would know what to do.

A big woman took Olivia's arm. "On my machine, now! We do not want you to die here. It is not convenient."

The spectators turned away to hide their laughter at the expression on Olivia's face. Brooke was relieved. The local woman would make sure Olivia obeyed the nurse.

"Climb on my snow machine," Dave said to Dexter.

A glance at him made Brooke's heart beat a little faster. His eyes spoke for him. Tenderness, of that she was sure. But tenderness is not love. Tenderness is what you show to children, friends and dogs and other animals. She still didn't want to believe that he really loved her. If she did, she would be vulnerable again. Her heart couldn't take anymore punishment. He wasn't on the Iditarod trail because of her, but because of his work. That they met was a coincidence. Best take love out of the equation.

The snowmobiles stopped at the Community Hall. Dave ordered everyone to eat. Brooke realized how hungry she was. Marc and Olivia soon joined them. After a satisfying meal, they walked to the Council Office. Garry signaled to her to go. "There're enough of us to look after the dogs. You go in. I'll supervise Karel. I guess you've got a connection to that affair."

"I believe I do. Thanks."

"Where are the sleds and the mushers?" The brittle tone in Olivia's voice attracted all eyes.

Her face expressing her displeasure, Brooke pointed. "This way."

Olivia turned round. "Okay, no racers leave. Stop the race. Racers stay where they are. Who's in charge?"

Stunned, Brooke finally reacted. "The marshal here at this checkpoint is in charge. The Iditarod Race Committee for the overall race is in charge. And this is an international race. You can't stop it."

The woman flipped her ID under Brooke's nose. "Yes, I can."

Deep dislike roiled under the vet's professional calm composure. "No. you can't. You can't, for practical reasons."

Dexter hurried next to the women. "The race can't be stopped. Let's go to the sleds. We'll find it."

"Find what?" Brooke was close on Dexter's heels.

"Hopefully, a bag of diamonds."

A furious Olivia reprimanded Dexter for disclosing information to a civilian, which made Brooke burst out laughing. It was good to relieve the tension and at the same time lower the aggressive woman's authoritarian tone a notch or two.

"Calm down, Olivia. She knows. Brooke's late husband was the other link."

Chastened, the younger officer reached the first of the parked sleds. After the eleventh sleds, her frustration mounted.

"The tracker had to be picking it up. It was on a moving sled and now they're all stopped. So where the hell is it?" She was clearly losing patience.

"The signal disappeared somewhere way back on the trail. Then we stopped for the night." At Dexter's patient tone, Brooke grimaced. She didn't feel at all patient with this overbearing woman in their midst.

"You're still suffering from the effect of the monoxide poisoning, Ms. Jones. It affects the memory pathways. In another few hours, you'll be back to normal." Brooke remembered Campbell's sled and dogs parked behind the administrative building. "This civilian will take you to another parked sled."

Although her tone was neutral, it carried plenty of sentiment. Dexter snaked his arm around her shoulders and squeezed.

"It's Ian Campbell's..." She stopped in her tracks and lifted her head to see that Dexter had also made the connection.

"For Heaven's sake! What's that guy thinking?" He added for Brooke's information. "We have strong reason to suspect he's the one who sabotaged the stove in the cabin."

They searched the sled bag, to no avail. A dejected Olivia slumped in on herself.

"I'm sorry you didn't get your diamonds," Brooke said.

Dexter gave a dry laugh. "The one we're looking for are good quality glass. The real ones are safe."

"I should have known."

Olivia shook herself. "Could it be on a sled that's still to arrive?"

Phone in hand, Dexter kept moving the official map around the screen. "We didn't see another musher since before the cabin when the signal disappeared. There was only one, and that was Campbell."

"Could he have stopped and given it to somebody else?" Brooke asked.

Dexter nodded. She refrained from commenting, sure that he was sharing her thoughts. The trail snaked between trees and rocks. If a musher stopped, he could have been shielded from the fast moving plane. They walked around the dog lot again. No signal and the mushers were growing irritated by the interruption of their rest.

Anger didn't suit Olivia's otherwise pretty face. "Can we go back to the spot where we lost the signal?"

"We will. Too bad there isn't a better map than Google's satellite image. The terrain doesn't come up very well," Dexter said.

"You need a drone," Brooke whispered.

He nodded, half a smile on his lips. "Now, we have to interrogate a certain individual about the stove. You said he is at the Council Office?"

"He is. Let's go."

As a race marshal, Dave didn't have time to stay and watch the interview. Mushers were arriving and departing and he had to check them through. Jack Siteen, his deputy, would have to represent the police until the Alaska State Troopers arrived.

Dexter fell behind Olivia to be next to Brooke.

"Sorry for my lack of a civil greeting when we arrived, but I wanted to reassure you quickly that your house and dogs are being well taken care of."

"It's alright. Funny, I had thought of hiring Yashee as a housekeeper and kennel manager before my problems... She's very good."

For a fleeting moment, Dexter pictured Yashee in Brooke's cabin while he and Brooke lived in his house. It was gone before they took the next step.

"By the way, Dexter, I saw Jimmy. He told me that the rifle Campbell used to shoot the moose was Seth's rifle."

"The one that was stolen?"

She nodded at the same time she poked him to look ahead. Siteen was holding the door open for them. "Jack wrapped the rifle in paper bags with the bottoms cut open and taped up to make a bag long enough to hold it. He doesn't have evidence bags that size."

Dexter chuckled. "It's just as good. We're after diamonds and we end up with a stolen gun. What a cock-up."

From sitting with elbows resting on his knees and a gaze directed to the floor, Ian Campbell sprung upright when they entered. "Weiman!"

"You obviously were not expecting me."

About to speak, Olivia scowled and shut her mouth when Brooke pinched her.

Campbell shrugged. "Let me go now. I've wasted enough time. So I killed a moose on the trail. Big deal, I was in my right. It was threatening my team."

"The moose incident is going to be handled by the State Wildlife authorities. I just want to ask you what you know about a bent stovepipe at the safety cabin."

"I don't know what you're talking about. I didn't stay there."

"You did stop, though."

"So did dozens of other people."

"Witnesses report that the stove was in good and safe condition before you stopped. A leak of carbon monoxide gas occurred after your visit. Do you have anything to say?"

"You're stupid to think I had anything to do with your effing stovepipe."

Incensed, Brooke said loudly, "You're talking to a cop."

Eyes widening, Ian Campbell started.

Dexter stretched his lips into a hollow smile. "Surprised? Make it easy on yourself and tell all."

Campbell resumed his stance, elbows on his knees, but kept his head high. "I have nothing to do with that incident, and you're making me lose precious race time."

Olivia, the epitome of anger, made to go in front of Dexter. Brooke caught her arm in a vise grip and whispered. "Wait!" To her surprise, the woman obeyed.

"There's no escaping fingerprints and DNA. The state troopers will deal with that." Dexter signaled to Eylin, who was also the council secretary. "Could I trouble you for an extra large plastic bag and latex gloves?"

"Right here." She produced a large blue bag and a box of purple latex gloves from a closet. Slowly and methodically, Dexter pulled on the gloves, then picked up Campbell's parka and mushing gloves and dropped them into the bag and secured it.

In a calm and emotionless voice, Dexter turned to Campbell. "That's for the stove business. Now we have another matter."

Ian's body jerked, but he didn't look up.

Dexter continued in the same voice. "We're not finished. Jack, would you bring the rifle out, please?" The young man hurried to the desk where the rifle lay.

Dexter removed the rifle from its wrapping and held it in front of Campbell. "Is this your rifle, Mr. Campbell?"

"Yes."

"You obtained it in Canada?"

"Yes."

"I need to see your firearms license."

"I didn't bring it with me."

Dexter tilted his head. "Really? How do you plan to go through customs on the way back into Canada? What about a bill of sale? You need that too unless you have a QR Code. "

"That has nothing to do with you."

"But it does because this Mauser 98 Magnum is on record as being stolen."

"I bought it... legal and above board."

"From whom?"

"I don't have to answer your questions."

Although Brooke knew Dexter was following some official procedure, she'd heard enough. She stepped forward. "That rifle was my husband's. It was stolen from our cabin. Is that the gun you used to kill him with?"

Clenched jaws and a stiffening of his body were the only signs that Campbell was laboring under duress. He remained silent.

"Did Seth Lammers sell you the rifle?" Dexter asked. His voice had a disinterested tone to it.

A slight hesitation before Campbell replied, "Yeah."

About to deny that statement, Brooke checked herself. Dexter had neatly trapped the man. A plane was heard over the settlement. She couldn't help ask the question that bothered her. "You were racing well enough, already being in line for a good placement in the top ten, actually, so why did you try to murder some innocent mushers?"

The man remained silent.

"I get it. Since this time you were actually racing, you wanted to make sure neither Jerome Renard nor Scott Walsh could challenge you. Isn't it so?"

"I had no intention of killing anybody, just slow them down. A bit of smoke to give them a headache, that's all."

A stunned silence fell over the room. No one said a word. Every musher, every northerner, knew of the danger posed by wood-burning stoves, as most of them lived in remote cabins, many of them without the luxury of electricity. If stoves were not adjusted properly, they could emit lethal carbon monoxide fumes, the silent killer. Brooke shook her head. She never thought Campbell was very bright, but this was sheer stupidity. The silence stretched until it was interrupted by the sound of approaching snowmobiles. Moments later, two Alaska state troopers strode in. They read Campbell his rights and searched him before handcuffing him.

Jack stopped filming with his cell phone and sent the clip to the trooper's phone, as well as to Dexter's.

"Roman, you're coming with us."

"Right on."

"Weiman, Ms. Jones, we hear that you have something more to do with this individual. We'll meet in Anchorage?"

Phone in hand, Dexter didn't take off his eyes off the screen. "We'll be following you. We have one more thing we want to check before we go."

"The rifle you report as being stolen is not in our jurisdiction. We'll leave that to you Canadians, but we're taking evidence from the stove incident."

Garry slipped into the room and nudged Brooke. "Will they send him back to be judged for his Canadian offences?"

"That's how it usually works."

The troopers escorted Campbell to the door.

"He needs a coat," Brooke said.

A volunteer wrapped a blanket around him after he was installed in the snowmobile trailer.

"Dext, are we going back on the trail to see if we can pick up the signal?"

He nodded. "Marc's at the hall. First, let's grab some sandwiches for later. I think It's going to be a long day."

A disgruntled Olivia stomped out. Carefully holding the Mauser, now back in its improvised bag, since it was a vital piece of evidence, Dexter pressed himself close to Brooke. "Campbell lied about the rifle, and I admire your self-control when he said Seth sold him the rifle. Whatever it is, he's in deep trouble." He tilted his head and stole a fleeting kiss from her lips before walking out.

With her mind still puzzled by Ian Campbell's bizarre behavior, Brooke resumed her duties. She would think about Dexter later, when it was her turn to rest.

Chapter Twenty-Six

A few days later, Marc's Cessna took off from the checkpoint with Brooke and her colleagues, as well as another team of vets on board.

"And now to Nome," Marc said.

His words were greeted enthusiastically. "You mean we're finally going to watch the winner pass under the Burled Arch?" Brooke asked.

"You will!"

"I'm thrilled. After all these years of volunteering, it'll be the first time I'll be able to witness a winner's grand entrance. Karel, you lucky dog, your first Idi and you get to see the winner grand entrance."

The high winds shaking the plane couldn't dampen the exuberance of the vets. Marc landed the Cessna smoothly at the busy airport. He waved his passengers on. "See you at the banquet!" He then went to refuel in readiness of his next assignment to fly wherever there was a need.

Karel kept looking around. "Goodness, all these planes coming and going. Who'd have thought this place at the end of the earth would have such a big airport. Where are they all going?"

"Nome is really quite a big city, and it needs supplies like everywhere else. The heavy stuff like building materials and vehicles comes in by sea on a barge in the summer. The rest and all the visitors come by air. So, yes, there are a lot of planes coming and going. Mushers can get a good rate to fly their dogs back to Anchorage, because after the planes unload their cargo, they are mostly empty on the return journey."

"I must say, it's been an experience."

"Let's meet at the Pingo Bakery and Café on Bering Street. I'll take you to see the Burled Arch."

The veterinarians hurried to the terminal, fighting the relentless wind. They were greeted by old friends and offers to take them to their billets. A stocky man cut through the crowd of people.

"Ms. Porter?"

"That's me." She smiled. He must be her billet. His face was familiar, like many others whose paths she crossed each year.

He made a mock bow. "Allow me to drive you to the Gold House."

Karel edged close to Brooke. "What about me?"

"Sorry, young man. It's reserved for Dr. Porter."

Brooke took pity on him. "Go and ask. There'll be a billet for you too." She followed her host.

"I'm Rolf. I run an Airbnb. Your suite is entirely private."

"Thank you very much. After a week on the trail, it'll be luxury."

He chuckled. "It appears that the first musher will pull in the day after tomorrow. Scott Walsh and Jerome Renard are in the lead."

The car stopped in front of a tall white house.

"Great! They're from home."

"You'll be right there to greet them. We have a bet going that Walsh will let Renard win as that would be his first Idi win. What do you think?"

While Rolf carried her bags and opened the door of her suite, she reflected on her friends' personalities. "If you want my opinion, Jerome will let Scott go ahead because this is Scott's last Idi race."

"Well, you know the guys. You're probably right. I'll go and change my bet."

"Don't blame me if you lose."

They laughed, and he left her to settle in. The first thing she did was to take a shower. After sleeping on camp cots and hard floors, the bed with its dark-blue blanket was appealing, but she wanted to use her free time to stroll around town, meet old friends and show Karel the Burled Arch.

After joining up with him, they ambled along Front Street to the dog lot, where the dog teams would be examined, and stood observing the scene. Handlers were already there setting up the dogs' quarters, spreading straw and preparing nourishing snacks.

"It's here the teams recuperate until they are flown home," Brooke said.

"We examine the teams here, right? Not at the finish line."

"Correct. But there's always one or two of us at the finish line to watch the dogs. There's a tendency for the mushers to press harder on that last twenty-five miles since the last checkpoint in Safety, especially if there's another team close behind. That's when trouble could happen."

"Tell me again about the parade."

She burst out laughing. "Parade is a good word for it, I think. Mushers or their handlers walk the dogs in front of a panel of vets so we can determine how strong the dogs are and how well-cared for they've been. It's vitally important for the team to arrive in a good condition, strong enough to carry on running more miles."

"If a team arrives and the dogs are tired, what happens?"

"Even well-cared for dogs can become tired on the last stretch. Those won't be in line for the Leonhard Seppala Humanitarian Award."

"Are you on the panel?"

"Not this year. I was last year, but declined this year because Jimmy Redhead, another musher from home, is running and whenever he runs he gets the Humanitarian Award."

"And you don't want to appear to favor him."

"That's right."

Her attention was attracted by laughter nearby. A young woman, heavily pregnant, detached herself from a group.

"Brooke!"

"Hello, Chris. How's the future musher doing?"

"The way he kicks, I think he's run the Iditarod on foot. He'll soon be ready to pop out, and I'm going to Donek so you can assist me."

Anxiety washed over Brooke. "Be reasonable. You must go to the hospital. I'm not a doctor."

"You're kidding! Me going to the hospital? Baby would be born before we reach Whitehorse and I am not having my baby in the cab of a truck on the side of the road."

"As much as I love you, and because I love you, I insist you get proper medical assistance. I am a vet, not a medical doctor." It was costing her so much every time she had to say she wasn't a doctor. Technically, she was, having been awarded her MD and completed two years of residency. She chased her somber thoughts away.

"There's no difference between birthing a baby and a litter of puppies."

Brooke chose to laugh. "But you are not a dog."

"What if I have an emergency? You'll come, won't you?" There was an anguish note in the future mother's voice.

"We'll call the Star helicopter. They have paramedics and could even have a doctor on board."

"But you will come because the chopper takes too long to come from Whitehorse, and if it can't fly because of the weather, I'll need you."

With her heart beating hollow in her chest, Brook smiled to reassure her friend. "I wouldn't leave you in the lurch. But promise you will do your best to get to the hospital ahead of time."

"I'm not promising something I'm not sure can be done."

"You know Scott is in the lead, don't you?"

"Everybody knows. You're just changing the subject."

They hugged awkwardly around her bulk. Brooke glanced at Karel coming toward her. "Ready? Let's go over to the Arch."

They walked along Front Street to the finish line under the massive arch, where workers were still installing barriers. A front-end loader was spreading two feet of snow onto the street from the dog lot to where the trail joined the street.

"What a massive piece of wood. It looks quite new," Karel said.

"Relatively new. The old one that presided over twenty-five races broke. The race committee found another tree. I think this one has been well-coated to preserve it."

"It must be in the way of the traffic."

"It gets moved after the end of the race."

His cheeks reddened at his naivety. "That makes sense."

CHAPTER TWENTY-SEVEN

I n the noisy restaurant, all eyes were fixed on the television screen tuned into the satellite webcam that followed the mushers on the last part of the trail.

"Still the same two teams ahead, with two more not too far behind them."

Brooke turned to Karel and Garry. "That's Walsh and Renard out front."

"So, when will they arrive?" Karel asked.

"In five to six hours, maybe."

Garry stretched in his chair. "Trust the boss. She's a musher too."

Karel gave a low whistle. "That means they'll arrive at two or three in the morning."

That was also the opinion at the neighboring tables. "Better get some sleep now!"

Some patrons expressed their intention to keep watching. "It could still change, you know."

"It could well. Call me when they are in Safety."

Brooke stood up. "I'm setting my alarm for a quarter to two."

Garry and Karel followed suit. In any case, they'd be on duty the minute the first team passed under the Burled Arch.

After more than a week of waking at odd hours, Brooke was conditioned to being fully awake the minute her alarm beeped. Front Street was filling up with spectators. The air was filled with music and cheering. Bars and restaurants stayed open. Excitement flowed among children and adults, all craning their necks to see the finish line. Brooke had to take her official card out of her pocket to get through the crush. Finally, she stood next to the modest podium where the winner would sit, flanked by his lead dogs, for photos. Two yellow silk-flower garlands waited to be put around the dogs' necks.

Karel and Garry caught up with her. Finally, they could see a bobbing pinpoint of light in the distance, closely followed by another. A blast of sirens competed with the clamor of hundreds of voices cheering and encouraging the approaching mushers. As if the dogs sensed this was the end of the journey, they put on a spurt of speed to pass under the Burled Arch. A shower of ice crystals from the sled's brake flew into the air.

The victory announcement crackled from the loudspeakers, magnified by the cold air. "Scott Walsh, the winner!"

While Scott sat on the podium with his dogs, the crowd grew frantic, waiting for the second-place finisher. The second musher, closing in on the finish line, was being challenged by a third.

"Jerome Renard!" Brooke said to her companions.

The roar of the crowd deafened the three vets. Jerome applied the sled brake just as the nose of the lead dog of the third musher passed the Burled Arch.

"TeeJay's third! Bravo TeeJay!" Brooke shouted.

"Hey, Brooke! Am I late again?"

Laughter erupted. "Go on!" To Karel and Garry, "TeeJay is always late for his veterinary appointments. Okay, back to work," Brooke said.

They made a quick inspection of the three teams and, finding nothing untoward, followed them to the dog lot. Drug testing was at the discretion of the vets at any checkpoint and automatic within six hours of arrival in Nome.

The next few days were busy round the clock, till there was only one musher left on the trail. The rookie young woman was due to arrive at about four o'clock in the morning. To everyone's surprise, an announcement came that there were actually three mushers still on the trail, all bunched closely together. Although Brooke wasn't on duty, she made her way to the finish line. It was heartwarming to see a sizable crowd of supporters who had chosen to brave the frigid night air to greet the stragglers. Although these last teams were far behind the winners, their achievement by merely finishing the most grueling sled dog race on earth was, nonetheless, remarkable.

"Karel, take a look at the Widow's Lantern hanging from the Arch."

"So that's the famous Red Lantern. Well, someone has to be last."

The astonished spectators saw the flicker of two headlamps approaching almost side by side. A question ran through the crowd as to who were these extra teams bringing up the rear? Yet another tiny pinprick of light could be seen even farther back still. The speakers announced these were the mushers who had been airlifted to hospital and had returned to finish the race. Shouts of "Bravo!" and other encouragements exploded from the crowd. Cheers deafened Brooke. She ran up to them.

"You made it! Congratulations!"

"Thanks to you, Dr. Porter."

"I'm happy for you. Is Leni far behind?" She pointed to the other light still on the race trail.

"I guess about half an hour. She had to stop and put a lame dog in the sled."

"I'll see her when she arrives. Go, now. You've earned your rest."

An announcement confirmed that there would be a thirty-minute wait. Someone put on some music, people danced and laughed. From nowhere, a tray laden with doughnuts appeared and was passed around. Time flew by in the midst of the impromptu celebration. More spectators joined the crowd.

Suddenly, cheers went up from onlookers, now swelled to several hundred, as the bobbing light from a musher's headlamp drew closer and closer. Out of the pitch darkness, the young woman's dogs broke into the ring of light around the finish line. As frisky as if they had merely run around the block and oblivious to the fact they were the last competing team, her dogs pulled the laden sled across the line like champions. Brooke's expert eyes quickly assessed the team, now reduced to nine dogs plus the one in the sled.

She ran forward. "Leni, what's the matter with the dog in the basket?"

"She started slowing down. I didn't want to take any risk, so she's been riding passenger for the last fifty miles."

"I'll follow you to the dog lot."

While Leni was with the officials, Brooke explained to Karel. "She took it easy. The important goal for inexperienced mushers is to finish the race. That in itself is the reward."

"Leni McCaffrey. She's all of nineteen years old, according to the listing," Karel said.

"Go and invite her to sit with you at the banquet."

Brooke almost laughed. Karel was already introducing himself and within minutes sharing the runners with Leni on the way to the dog lot. Brooke followed at a more leisurely pace.

After checking the dog and finding it tired but otherwise in good shape, she strolled down the street to the Pingo Bakery and Café. Despite the early hour, it was open. She went in and ordered a hearty breakfast.

CHAPTER TWENTY-EIGHT

Balloons and garlands decorated the hall. Tables had been pulled close together to accommodate everyone. The buzz of diverse conversation rose and fell to allow the emcee to impart the latest news and crack jokes until the start of the awards ceremony. He recounted the moose incident but avoided naming names.

"Well, folks, we all know a moose can be ornery and a danger to both dogs and humans, but on this occasion one community was the lucky recipient of the meat bounty."

Still without names, of course, he lavished praises on the solidarity and sportsmanship of mushers when an accident happened.

Finally, the volunteer servers cleared the dishes and glasses. Some tables were folded and put away to make room for the dancing later in the evening.

Applause and cheers burst on Brooke's ears, but she smiled. This was a happy moment. She leaned back in her chair and watched as one by one mushers came up to the podium to receive their prizes. When it was Jimmy's turn to receive, as anticipated, his Humanitarian Award for the musher who provided the best care for his or her dogs, she clapped louder than anyone. The emcee recognized Scott and Jerome as heroes for getting mushers out of the safety cabin and saving their lives with a special plaque given by the paramedics association. Jimmy was also praised for his leadership role in handling the moose incident.

An energy company representative stepped up to the podium to announce a special award to two mushers who demonstrated the spirit of Alaska when they rejoined the race after receiving medical treatment, even though they knew the best they could hope for was last place. "Folks, they made it together ahead of the Red Lantern."

A thunder of applause echoed to the roof. When the men passed near Brooke, she saw tears in their eyes. The two mushers stepped to the podium. Like everyone else, she joined the standing ovation.

When the noise subsided and everyone sat down again, the pair thanked the Green Company for the award, then Adam took the mike. "We would also like to thank Dr.

Porter. Without her skilled diagnosis and her prompt action in shipping us to the hospital for emergency treatment, we wouldn't be here right now to celebrate. Dr. Porter, please..."

Surprised and not a little confused, Brooke rose to her feet. Heads turned toward her as the applause resumed, this time for her. She bowed as tears welled up in her eyes, and she cheekily blew a kiss toward Adam and Niels.

She was enjoying the evening, yet wondered what it would be like if Dexter were sitting next to her. His job had taken him away again, just as it would always take him away. It was not like a business trip which could last two or three days. His absence could be weeks or months at a stretch. Did she really want to commit herself to that kind of life, a life where absence was an everyday feature? And that did not take into account the constant danger side of the job. What about having children? She was deeply aware that her so-called biological clock was ticking away, true, mere seconds at a time, but ticking away nevertheless. Another few years and she wouldn't feel confident about bringing a child into the world. There was that unfulfilled part of her that called for a child. A need to give and nurture life. Maybe she could adopt a baby. It was becoming somewhat easier for single women to adopt. Chill reality drowned out her daydream. With bankruptcy looming, she wasn't a suitable candidate for adoption.

She had little interest in staying for the dance. Her parka hood pulled up to cut the wind, she set out on foot for the warmth of Gold House. She planned to hitch a ride on an Anchorage-bound plane in the morning. Setting her bag on the stand, she began to pack. She had only just started when she looked up to see a taxi come to a halt in front of the house. It was probably the upstairs tenant. She paid no more attention. To her surprise, there was a knock on her door. So used to the tranquility and safety of Agate Creek, she opened the door without a second glance at the intercom box, and stood rooted to the spot. "Dexter!"

His drawn features lit up with a smile. "Hello, Brooke."

Finally, she reacted. "Come in."

He dropped his bag by the door. "I had hoped to arrive earlier."

"You missed the awards ceremony. The mushers from our small corner of Yukon did well. Have you had dinner?"

"A long time ago."

"Here." She brought out a couple of buns, cheese, a half jar of strawberry jam, a hard-boiled egg and pot of yogurt. "That was for breakfast tomorrow, but we can go..."

She stopped speaking. Had she just invited him to stay? Of course not. Offering a visitor food was a part of northern hospitality.

His eyes shone. He flashed her a cocky smile. "Is this an invitation?"

A troubling heat was spreading throughout her. She longed to feel his arms around her and let go against his broad chest. "I don't suppose you have a place to stay. Every available room has been taken."

For an answer, he reached for her and pulled her against him. She trembled under his touch. Her heart pounded against her ribs. Earlier musings about committing herself sprang back to her mind. His lips touched hers lightly and her mind shut words of reason.

She loved this man. That was something she could not deny.

It was late when Dexter sat down at the makeshift dinner while Brooke made coffee. "I missed you,"

Did he miss our intimacy or me as a person? She recognized that making love was wonderful for both of them. She formulated the question in her mind, but the words that came out were unexpected and surprised her. "I missed you too."

"Am I truly forgiven for deceiving you?"

"I'm still mad at being taken for a ride like that, but I guess I've put it behind me. No wait, that's a contradiction. Maybe I'm just a bit sad that you professed to love me but didn't trust me. Love and trust go together. You can't have one without the other."

Chastened, he lowered his head. "Can we start over as of now?"

She fixed her eyes on him while she pondered the question. An old wives' tale said that you could peer into a person's soul through the window of their eyes. She never usually put much store in sayings like that. To her scientific mind, they belonged to the realm of fortune-cookies. Nor did she see any reason to change her mind. As she stared into his warm brown eyes, all she saw was a pleading look. It could be interpreted as a plea for love. Yet, was that really love she saw? It could just as easily be lust. Perhaps his lust had been satisfied, at least in some measure. And, perhaps, what she saw really was love, love shining back at her from the depth of his soul. Souls did not lie, did they? A small voice in her head whispered that if she was not prepared to take a chance on life, she would never know what could have been.

Her answer slipped out without her being aware of it. "Yes." The single word answer was rewarded by the look of happiness that spread over his face, and the kiss that followed.

"Will you accept that I truly love you?"

"Not so fast. I agreed to start over again, to get to know each other. Properly, this time."

He repressed a sigh. "Fair enough. I'll settle for that. I have to go back to Seattle tomorrow to wrap up my side of the investigation, at least as far as we've got. Will I see you at home?"

She smiled. "Of course, at home."

CHAPTER TWENTY-NINE

They waited in line at the Nome airport. During a lapse in the casual conversation, Dexter pulled her against him. "We talked about trust. I trust you entirely. This is why I'm going to tell you what we know and my part in the diamond affair."

"Fair enough." She listened while he told her about his case and its challenges. The passion that drove him wasn't only the satisfaction of a job well done when catching criminals but that exploited humans, children particularly, would get a reprieve from abuse.

When it was time, she raised on her tiptoe to kiss him. He caught the commercial flight while Brooke wandered to the tarmac reserved for the Iditarod Air Force. She bumped into Scott.

"Hey, Brooke. Looking for a plane?"

"I am."

"I've just secured a cargo flight to Anchorage. There's room for you if you want."

"Thanks."

"This way."

Minutes later, she pitched in to load the half-barking, half-howling dogs into the plane, the sled and the spare that mushers are allowed to ship to a checkpoint. A precaution in case the main sled sustained damage on the trail, particularly after the Dalzell Gorge, with its treacherous switchbacks. It didn't take long to get to Anchorage, and they repeated the operation in reverse. With the help of an employee driving a forklift truck, the dog crates, sleds and bags were lined up in the bush plane area.

"Let's go and get a bite to eat. When Marc is ready, he'll fly us to Donek. He shouldn't be long."

"I'm game. How much——"

"Brooke!"

"I'd have to buy my ticket and I know you're paying Marc."

"Marc and I have been friends for the longest time. We have an agreement. Now no more. Let me go and grab some coffee and a couple of sandwiches."

He was barely back with the food that Marc landed. The Cessna was refueled and the baggage and dogs loaded. They soon were on the way home.

The engine noise didn't encourage conversation, especially as the plane was being buffeted by a strong headwind. That gave Brooke plenty of time to reflect on her last talk with Dexter. Agreeing to meet again at home was not the same as agreeing to commit to each other. If she didn't, would she be passing happiness by? She couldn't really figure out why she held off confessing her love for him. If she kept it bottled inside her, she could easily persuade herself it didn't exist and therefore she couldn't be hurt when things fell apart. Dexter, she knew, was never going to give up his work, not only because it was more than just a profession to him but also because he had a deep commitment to the community at large. Protecting people from crime was far from being just a job, it was a vocation. Work would take him away from her, and any possible children, for as much as a year or more at a time. That was not a figment of her imagination. He had said as much himself. She would have to be content with a flying visit now and then. A deep sigh shook her chest. For her, love had to be unconditional. Like the love her dogs had for her, and she for them.

A slight bump and the Cessna landed, taxiing to a halt. A cheering crowd was on hand to welcome the travelers. Alex and Vicky stood in the front row, waving frantically. Dozens of hands helped unload the plane, to the great delight of the dogs howling their pleasure to be back, on their paws on home territory. Scott's handlers, Marina and Justin, were on hand too with water and treats for the dogs, before loading them onto the transporter for the final leg of the journey.

"How bad is the overflow on Little Gem stream?" Doug asked. As an auxiliary constable for Donek and the unofficial wildlife warden, he was always concerned about the safety of the residents.

"Only a couple of inches," Marina replied.

"Good, but take it easy. Brooke, I'll give you a ride?"

"That'd be great."

Night had long since fallen when she dropped her bags on the porch and hurried over to the pen where her Canadian Inuit dogs were frantically howling and standing on their back legs, front paws against the chain-link fence. Inside, she got mobbed. She sat on what remained of a larch that had to be cut down after a storm. Her canine companions crowded around her, licking and pawing at her. This was pure happiness. She laughed out loud, and they responded with yips and throaty sounds. Finally, she reached for the pieces of moose meat from the shelf on the fence and silently thanked Yashee for thinking about the treats. They instantly sat in silence and took their treat with the most delicate of movements of their strong teeth.

Brooke pushed open the door to her cabin. The soft warmth from the woodstove enveloped her, and a delicious scent tickled her nose. Yashee had prepared supper.

"Did Weiman propose?"

Brooke burst out laughing. "I suppose he did, in a backhanded sort of way."

"You accepted?"

"No. I have to think about it. Think about lots of things."

Consternation spread over Yashee's face. "You are both in love, Early Sun. What is there to think about?"

"Quite a few things, my friend. My financial disaster, for starters. I don't want to say yes to solve my money problems. I'm not a transactional kind of person."

"That is what I always said. You think too much. You need to go to sleep now."

That was a good advice and Brooke didn't argue. She needed thinking time now that she was away from the heady excitement of the Iditarod race. For the moment, thinking would have to wait. As soon as her head touched the pillow, sleep and with it blissful oblivion enveloped her.

Chapter Thirty

On Sunday, Brooke drove Lara to the airport in Whitehorse.

"I enjoyed myself thoroughly. People were very nice. I think I'd like to join a rural practice. If you ever need a vet, let me know."

Brooke laughed to hide how much she was touched. "Did you look to see if there are any openings?"

"I found a locum on a sheep farm in Ontario. I applied."

"It's a good way to start." Her phone rang while Brooke was waving to Lara, before the young woman disappeared into the secure area of the airport.

"My plane will be landing in the next hour. Will you wait for me?"

"Dexter! How did know I was at the airport?"

"No secret. I phoned Doghaven, hoping for a connection. A miracle, it worked. Yashee told me."

"No problem, I'll wait for you. It's beginning to snow here."

"I saw the weather isn't the best. See you soon."

Brooke walked to the arrivals lounge and found a seat. To wait. That would be a pattern if she committed to him. She wasn't enthusiastic about a long distance relationship. You couldn't get to know your partner's little quirks when he was away days, weeks, months at a time. Yet it was those little things of daily life that cemented a loving relationship. Was her love strong enough to endure the inevitable separations? It didn't matter which way she looked at it, heartache was on the horizon. On the other hand, if she didn't take the chance at love, she'd forever wonder whether it could have worked.

The kiss he bestowed on her trembling lips was like a homecoming. Dusk was blurring the edges of buildings. Brooke checked the weather on her phone. "Road travel isn't recommended."

"I'll book a hotel." He was already on his phone.

The snow was rapidly accumulating when the truck pulled up at the Raven Inn.

"They have two rooms," Dexter said.

She looked at him. He was respecting her wish to get to know each other. Was there really anything to know? "Let's save money. One room will do."

He winced, but nodded. She became aware of the impact of her words. Money was at the forefront of her mind. Only while on the Iditarod trail had she been able to push it away and forget about the problem for a while. If they shared a room, they'd make love. That was certain. Did that count as getting to know each other better? In one respect, yes, in another, she wasn't sure.

After freshening up, they went to the hotel restaurant for supper.

"I have to tell you Ian Campbell will be coming back to face charges for attempting to cross the border with an unregistered firearm, plus the dubious way he acquired the rifle. I handed the rifle and Campbell over to the Mounties in Vancouver. We'll get the results of the ballistic examination and find out whether it's the weapon that killed Seth."

"Even if you prove it is. Can you also prove it was in his possession at the time of the murder?"

Dexter lowered his head. "Are you sure you don't want to become an investigator? With your sharp mind, between us we'd solve every case, even the impossible ones."

She averted her eyes. "It's obvious, isn't it? "

"Actually, you're right. Campbell claimed he'd bought it shortly before leaving for the race, but retracted that he bought it from Lammers."

"Only after he was told it had been stolen. He isn't all that stupid. Anyway, what about your diamonds?"

"Nothing new. We can only suspect he was carrying the package of fake diamonds, then got cold feet and ditched it somewhere along the trail. That or he passed it to someone else on the trail. No matter how many times we went over the area, we weren't able to pick up the signal from the tracking chip, and he denies any knowledge of a package."

"Just like you suspected Seth was involved."

He sighed. "I'm not a believer in brick walls, but I must admit this investigation has hit one. Did Lammers ever run the Iditarod?"

"A couple of times, but lost interest. He much preferred the Yukon Quest."

Dexter ran his fingers over the stubble on his chin. "The Quest. Mushers cross the border legally from the States every second year, right?"

"Correct. The race starts in Fairbanks, Alaska, one year and Whitehorse, Yukon, the other. That may change now. The climate is too unpredictable. Ice is not forming on the Yukon river and detours had to be made. Nothing is safe anymore."

"That'd fit Lammers' running the Quest. Easy smuggling possibilities. From what we know, thanks to you, Campbell ran the Iditarod but always scratched the race in Willow, then drove to Fairbanks. Why he did so is a mystery."

"He could drive on and cross the border at Beaver Creek. There's nothing for miles around there."

"Yes, that's where he must have crossed the border. The diamonds have to come to Canada to be cut and exported with all appearance of legality. Custom officers wouldn't look into the dog boxes for contraband if they have no reason to suspect the guy."

"He, and my ex actually, could be very chummy and charming. I can imagine either of them bamboozling the border agents with dog and race stories."

Dexter laughed. "I suppose it gets pretty lonely at a remote border crossing in winter."

With a finger to her mouth, Brooke frowned. "I think Ian Campbell was under great stress when he set out for the Idi."

"How do you determine that?"

"He was always gruff, but his insistence in wanting to buy Seth's sled, to the point that he tried to break open the shed door and had no hesitation in threatening me, was not normal for him."

"What is so special about Lammers' sled?"

"It's a beauty, hand-crafted of the finest ash with a sled bag handmade to fit the sled to perfection. That's what *my* money disappeared into, that and a team of superb dogs, among other things."

"Yet, it's strange that with all that money that he had no qualms commandeering, he should go for a traditional wooden sled. Not when all the other mushers break the bank to buy sleds made from the latest hi-tech materials like fiberglass, carbon fiber and aircraft aluminum, custom made for the Iditarod race."

"I never thought of questioning that."

A deep sigh rose in Dexter's chest. "In the end, we have a musher who wanted to win the race for the money, not the glory, is suspecting of transporting diamonds, the faked ones which disappeared into thin air, and ended up with a wildlife violation ticket. I wanted to press an indictment for attempted murder, but it was not going to stick. You can't press charges against stupidity. It fell back to the Iditarod Committee to put a charge forward, and that is only interfering with the rules of the race. The mushers who were at the cabin declined to press charges. Innocent until proven guilty."

"Is that all?"

"Until I can gather more evidence, unfortunately, yes."

"Agate Creek was once such a quiet backwater. The most serious crime was an attempt to cheat at bingo."

"We'll work hard to return it to peace and tranquility."

A quiet laugh escaped her. He took her hand to go up to their room.

Chapter Thirty-One

Not long after their return to Agate Creek, Dexter announced he was attending the Chamber of Commerce meeting. Brooke expressed her approval, but declined to go. Now back home, all the problems she had forgotten about while on the Iditarod were surging anew. She was running scenarios in her head in the hope one would show the way to solve her problems.

Yashee stood in front of her. "A man came looking for you yesterday. He said he would come back today."

She had hardly spoken when a car was heard approaching the cabin. "It's Ernie's Taxi."

Brooke nodded. Ernie, a retired teacher and star volunteer, drove people where they needed to go. His service was affectionately known as Ernie's Taxi.

A man she didn't recognize, dressed in a sport parka and brown tuque alighted. He paid the driver. The fare was optional and went to the Community Helping Hand Organization. The two women watched while the man walked up to the porch.

Brooke opened the door. *Oh, no! What the devil is this about?* The past had come back to smack her in the face. Her reaction was to slam the door shut and call Yashee to send him away. Anger stiffened her spine. She waited for the man to speak.

"Hello, Brooke."

There were times when instinct took over rational behavior. "I'm sorry, how can I help you?"

He looked mortified. "You mean to say you don't recognize me?"

The problem was that, yes, she did recognize him, but the angry turmoil that his appearance aroused prevented her from acknowledging him.

"Luke, Dr. Luke Petrov."

"Yes, I know perfectly well."

He looked taken aback. "May I come in? I'd like to talk to you."

A disdainful look settled on her features. "I have nothing to say. I suggest you turn and go back the way you came."

"Wait until I've talked to you, but please, let's talk inside." He looked around at the snow-laden pines bordering her yard and made a tight grin. His breath hung in a cloud over his head. "It's not exactly conducive to conversation out here."

She assumed a disinterested face. "Yukon air doesn't agree with you? You shouldn't have come. But I'm not a monster. Step inside, into the warmth, while I call your taxi."

"Not just yet. I really want to talk."

She let him in, her face a stony mask. Yashee pulled out a kitchen chair and motioned him to sit. He glanced toward the living room space. Brooked leaned against the counter and waited.

"I saw that you were a veterinarian on the Iditarod Trail Race and learned you lived in this area."

She let the words evaporate before replying. "Yes."

"I thought I ought to get in touch again."

Her raised eyebrows were the only sign that she'd heard.

"I've done well for myself. I have a practice in Ottawa and employ three doctors." He gave an awkward laugh. "We're outnumbered by nurses and reception staff. I'm going to expand and open a veterinary clinic. I'll employ the best veterinarians, of course. You'd like to work with me, wouldn't you? We have so much in common."

After the accusations and during the trial, she had learned to control her expression when needed. Her blank face and silence appeared to unsettle Dr. Luke Petrov.

"I know you must still be angry about what happened back then, but I was an immature twenty-five-year-old. I know I should have supported you better."

His last words were too much for Brooke. She gave a bitter laugh and spat out her reply. "Better? You jerk! You couldn't run off fast enough. Support? That isn't a word in your vocabulary."

Unfazed by her outburst, he waved his hand as if to dismiss her concern. "I came because I believe we should start over. I was looking for you for years and dreaming. I'm so glad I found you again."

"Found me?" Brooke stared at the man who had caused her so much pain, incredulous that he should have tracked her down.

He gave what she assumed was a benevolent smile. "You are, indeed, the heroine of the Iditarod race. I made a few inquiries and here I am."

She couldn't believe what she was hearing and rolled her eyes.

Although it wasn't lunch time yet, Yashee took that moment to plonk a casserole onto the table. "You will have some rat soup?" She swiftly produced plates and spoons.

Petrov looked at Brooke in astonishment.

"Lunch. I have to go to work in five minutes." Amused by Yashee's deviousness, she sat to serve herself and began eating.

He didn't move. "What does she mean by rat?"

"That's what it is, rat stew. It's very good. You should try it."

His face went pale. "I don't think I should. You shouldn't either. That indigenous people eat it is their culture, not ours."

"You racist pig!" Brooke blurted out. "Get out of my house!"

Startled by her outburst, he reddened. "Okay, okay, I'm sorry."

"Apologize to my friend."

He hesitated. "Alright, I didn't mean to offend."

"And?"

Growing more and more uncomfortable, he looked for words. "I'm sorry. Please accept my apologies."

Petrov's assurance withered at the undisguised contempt on Yashee's face. "*Ts'àkl gishoo!*" From all her not-so-small height stretched to the maximum, she left the room.

Not so cocksure anymore, he looked at Brooke for a translation. Brooke didn't have a mean bone in her body. She took pity on him. "It's an insult as bad as the insulting comment you made. There isn't any real translation, but approximately, we would perhaps say, disgusting fiend. You're no longer a man. You've been demoted to the lowest kingdom of the tree of life, lower than a garden slug, in the realm of dirt and offensive materials."

Red and uncomfortable, he squirmed in his chair. "I had hoped we could talk."

"Talk away. I have another five minutes to spare."

"I'd like to be close to you so we could get reacquainted. Will you move to Ottawa?"

Brooke couldn't believe her ears. "You're out of your mind." She observed a change in his attitude.

"I suppose I could move to the Yukon. I heard there's a dire need for highly qualified doctors. There are several career prospects in Whitehorse. I'll make an inquiry."

Brooke had listened long enough. She took another serving of stew from the cast-iron pot and pointed it to him. "Try it."

"No thanks."

She gave a brief laugh. "Not your standard rat, it's muskrat. But actually, it's the same family. It was accidentally killed on the road and since we don't waste anything around here, we eat it. The fur will make a nice bonnet for a kid."

His face turned ashen. A tremolo colored his voice. "Anyway, I wonder where I could stay."

"The hotel in Donek is very good."

He shook his head. "Outrageously expensive. I was hoping you could put me up. I'll pay, of course."

There must be a way to get rid of the insufferable man. "Yashee, I have a question for you."

Her friend came to stand by her chair, her eyes throwing daggers at the man.

"How much do you charge for your Airbnb, Yashee?" She winked at her friend, who entered the game with a straight face and named a figure over the price of the hotel.

"You're kidding! This is a scam." Color returned to his face.

Irritated, Brooke pulled a face. "Of course it's a scam. Everything is a scam. Your coming here is a scam. You got wind of my fifteen minutes of fame and you thought you could exploit it. Too bad I won't fall for your scam."

Taken aback by her sharp retort, he opened his mouth to speak. Yashee cut him off before he could make a sound. "I tried to call Ernie's Taxi. School must be out and kids on their phone. No internet."

At that moment, the porch door slammed, and a whirlwind entered the cabin. An excited Gugàn brandished a sheet of school exercise paper. "I got everything right." He glanced at the man sitting at the table and ignored him as he was being congratulated by his mother and Brooke. Since he had started half days in kindergarten, he reported on every activity with enthusiasm. He climbed on a chair while Yashee served him stew.

"Would you like a ride to town, Gugàn?" Brooke asked.

The boy was busy stuffing himself with stew. He nodded and soon finished his meal. Yashee turned away to hide the laughter that wanted to get out.

Brooke looked at Luke. "You can hop in the back of the truck, I'll drop you off at the hotel. Bus at eight tomorrow morning. It's not a coach on a regular schedule, just a local entrepreneur, so don't be late. He won't wait."

Dumbfounded, Dr. Luke Petrov picked up his bag and followed the two women outside. In the truck, he had to sit on the cab half bench in the back with Gugàn, who bounced all the way to town chatting and mimicking school happenings, in both languages, unchecked by his mother or Brooke.

Chapter Thirty-Two

"Take the truck back home. I'll get a ride." Brooke handed the keys to Yashee.

"Good. Weiman will drive you. I make supper for him too."

"Go on." She pushed her friend away.

Closing time finally arrived at the clinic. Brooke and Erin cleaned everything, not that it was needed, as there had only been two clients who came in to buy a bag of homemade dog cookies. Alex and Vicky had come to discuss their advanced level biology assignment. Brooke watched them go.

"How are your studies progressing, Erin?"

"I'm doing well. The other students in the remote learning don't have the luxury of a professor at their elbow."

"I'm not a professor."

"What do you want to call someone who teaches and gives practical advice?"

"A friend."

They laughed. "Do you think our clients never come before ten, although we open at nine, because they know I take an online class from eight to ten?"

"Are you surprised?"

"I was really anxious when I replied to your ad for a veterinary assistant. Donek is mostly white. I was fearful they wouldn't accept me, a Tagish."

"And you saw it made no difference. There are quite a few First Nations in the area. You're not alone."

"Here comes Mr. Weiman."

"My ride. See you tomorrow, Erin."

Brooke let Dexter in. "How did you know I was without transportation?"

"A little bird..." He laughed. "Yashee came to the meeting and put in an application to join the chamber of commerce now that she has a business."

"I'm not surprised. She's joined the Airbnb association and duly registered as a business. She's moving fast and already doing well."

"I was most impressed by young Gugàn. He sat quietly the whole afternoon, drawing portraits of the board members sitting at the table. They acknowledged his talent and made him honorary president of the board."

Dexter locked the door, and they drove off. "I'm allowed to tell you a proposition that the chamber of commerce is putting to the municipality. We know it will be approved."

"Of course, most of the counselors are also members."

"The municipality will draft a proposition to lease your kennels as well as the house for a rescue and rehabilitation of pets and wildlife."

"But——"

"I know, you already do that, but in order to keep the bank at bay, it needs to be on a different footing so that you can repay the creditors and keep your home."

"Paying twice for it is like my father's gift is thrown away. He bought the cabin for me."

He parked behind the cabin and shut off the engine. She didn't move. He took her hand and squeezed it. "It's early days. Our lawyers are looking at all possibilities. Lammers was smart in a devious way, but he didn't think like a lawyer."

Our lawyers. He said, our lawyers. A little frisson went down her spine. He was identifying with her. Did it mean..? She shook the thoughts. "Even if he stashed his illegal gains somewhere, it's laundered money, and I wouldn't want anything to do with it. Let's go in. It's getting mighty cold out here."

They jumped out and walked round, only to be stopped by Gugàn sprawled in the snow with his toy bulldozer.

"Stop! Construction zone here."

"What are you building?"

"A big house with kennels for my dogs. I have lots of pebbles, see? It's the bottom of the house."

"That's great. So you're the architect."

The child looked up from his game. "Yeah, an arki... That's me." The bulldozer and a load of pebbles started up the snow ramp with an accompaniment of noises. "I need more pebbles."

"Good luck finding some under the snow." said Dexter.

After supper, Yashee and her son had retired into the annex. By the end of the evening, Dexter managed to convince her that volunteering didn't mean being out of pocket. She had to pay for medications when injured wildlife was brought to her. The Helping Hand organization was very good at raising funds and promised to foot the bill for every injured wild animal brought to her. They were planning a campaign so that a fully equipped wildlife rehabilitation center could be built.

Overwhelmed, Brooked remained silently brooding.

"I should get to my cabin now," Dexter said.

A frown still marring her forehead, she looked up. "Do you want to?"

"No. I just see how preoccupied you are. Maybe you want to think about this new development by yourself."

This was the moment of decision. If she let him go, she'd be torn to pieces and wondering whether she could have coped with the demands of his job. If they went to the bedroom, it'd be a step into the unknown and the unspoken fear that, at times, his work was dangerous.

Blood suffused her cheeks and her lips trembled in anticipation as she held out her hand to lead him to the bedroom.

CHAPTER THIRTY-THREE

It was that time of night when slumber is so deep that noises barely touch the consciousness. Training took over and Dexter was up and pulling on his pants. He thrust his bare feet into cabin boots and shrugged on his parka. All this took mere seconds. The ruckus made by the dogs had also woken Brooke. She could hear muted knocking noises coming from outside.

"It's the shed," she whispered.

His handgun at the ready, Dexter stepped out onto the porch, with Brooke following him. The screen door squeaked shut behind them.

Brooke pointed into the gloom. "There's someone running across the yard."

His footsteps muffled by the snow, the intruder disappeared into the night. Some distance away, an idling snowmobile engine sparked to life. The only thing Dexter and Brooke saw beyond the trees was a headlight slashing the darkness in its escape southward.

They ran to the shed. The intruder had tried to gouge out the wood around the hasp. "This is a stupid way to break in. An amateur way."

"Do you think it was Campbell?"

"Right now, I don't think. We have to find out what is so valuable in your shed."

She tightened her parka around her shoulders and shrugged. "Diamonds, I guess."

He took her elbow, and they walked back to the cabin. "I have examined every nook and cranny in the shed. Nothing out of the ordinary. It's frustrating."

Inside, they found Yashee up and clutching her robe. "You need a surveillance camera."

A nod from Dexter acknowledged her comment. "You're right. I'll get one tomorrow."

Fully dressed, they dozed on and off for the rest of the night. In theory, once disturbed, burglars didn't come back the same night to the same venue. Dexter demolished the theory. "It's precisely because of the saying that a smart burglar will wait a couple of hours and come back."

When the dogs howled again, they were outside in no time, only to see a young fox inspecting the yard. He promptly scampered away when they appeared on the doorstep.

"I've got to fix that squeaky screen door."

"In the winter, the door is not needed. You may as well take it off until spring."

"I'll do that after breakfast."

"By the way, what is happening with Seth's rifle?"

"It's evidence because it's stolen property and has been fired. Since it was in the possession of a person of interest who has no proof of having bought it, the experts are doing a full ballistic test on it."

"I don't want it, except that if it could be sold, it'd repay some of Seth's debts."

"Are you the sole inheritor?"

"He didn't have a will, but I inherited the debts. It's only right I should inherit anything of value to sell."

He cradled her against his chest. "We'll do our best."

Dawn was bleaching the night sky. They were just finishing breakfast when the phone chirped. Yashee came in with a bouncy boy, eager to go to school.

"Sorry, the line is cutting out. Who's calling?" She listened intently. "Okay, I'm coming. Put a big cushion under Chris' pelvis and keep her legs elevated."

White and trembling, Brooke looked at Dexter. "Chris is in trouble. The baby is early and is in trouble. Phone Bill to pick me up with his snowmobile." With measured haste, she packed her vet bag with medicine and instruments.

Yashee handed her a small pouch.

"Hawthorn?"

"Liquid. Very strong. Just twenty drops to stop contractions."

"Thanks."

"Bill's on his way. Would driving be faster?"

"Not by road. Takes one hour. There's overflow on the creek. The snowmobile will get through. I couldn't understand much, but the baby is trying to be born and Scott thinks he saw the umbilical cord. Not good. It's too early." She bundled herself into the oversized snowmobile suit that had been owned by her late husband, that she sometimes used for dog sledding,

"What can I do?"

"Phone the hospital that we'll be bringing a complicated delivery. Also phone the Star helicopter and when I get there, Scott can call in the coordinates. Ah, here's my conveyance."

She gave him a quick kiss through her woolen mask, brought down the visor of her helmet and, to a stupefied Gugàn, rushed out to climb on Bill's big snowmobile, her bag squished between their bodies.

"Hang on tight! The overflow froze."

As a police auxiliary, Bill, the perfect handyman, had outfitted his wide track snowmobile with a siren and two flashing blue lights front and back. He gave a blast of the siren before crossing the road and opened the gas. Just what they feared. The overflow had frozen over. The ice wasn't strong enough to support the weight of the snowmobile and would break, plunging them into the water beneath. It was safer to go through water than over thin ice and suddenly falling through. Bill slowed down.

"Do we attempt it?"

"There's no choice. It'll take too long to get down to the road."

"Okay, let her rip!"

Brooke tightened her grip on Bill's waist and closed her eyes.

At top speed, Bill launched the snowmobile down the incline and across the creek. The ice broke behind it. He and his passenger leaned forward as the machine hesitated, chewed the ice and finally gripped solid ground on the other shore.

They didn't speak until they arrived at Scott's cabin, where they were greeted by his howling dogs. She divested herself of the suit and helmet. In the bedroom, she put her bag on the chair by the bed and pulled on surgical gloves. Already, she could see that Scott had correctly identified the problem. The umbilical cord had slipped through the col of the uterus and was being compressed by the baby's head. By elevating the pelvis, the baby had moved closer to Chris' stomach, and the pressure was slightly less. But if the pressure was not released soon, the baby would suffocate.

"I want to push," Chris said. Pain distorted her face.

"Don't! Whatever you feel, don't push. I'm going to try to slip the cord back. You're only dilated about seven centimeters. It's not enough. Okay?"

After a couple of minutes, Brooke, hiding her fear, called the men. "We have to get Chris to the hospital as soon as possible to save the baby. The Star helicopter should be on its way already. Call in the coordinates of the cabin. I'll hold the umbilical cord and keep the baby's head in place."

"Scott, pass me my stethoscope, please."

Her right hand, maintaining the prolapsed umbilical cord, the other listening to the baby's heartbeat. "It's still strong. The compression isn't fatal at this point, but it won't last. Scott, twenty drops from the vial in my pocket."

"I feel I want to push... get that baby out..."

"Don't. It will kill your baby if you do."

The tall musher reached into the pocket of her fleece. He carefully measured out the medicine.

"Help your wife swallow all of it."

"The chopper is on its way with a couple of nurses," Bill said. "I gave them the cabin coordinates." He switched off his satellite phone. "I'll go and move your truck from the yard, Scott. It'll land right here. There's enough room."

"What about the wood pile?"

"It's low enough. The rotor blades will clear it. Good job it's not the beginning of winter."

The waiting began. Counting down the minutes wasn't helping, but meaningful conversation was possible. Finally, the unmistakable sound of a helicopter was heard, and in moments, the H145 chopper smoothly settled on the snow-covered yard like an enormous bird. A medic and a nurse bounded out. In a few succinct words, Brooke told them about the situation.

"The contractions have stopped." She didn't tell them about the native medicine. Let them believe they stopped naturally.

"I'll get the gurney," the nurse said.

Bill went to help.

"You seem to know what you're doing. Do you have the cord and the head quite secure?" the medic asked.

"I do."

"Then you're coming with us. No point me trying to replace your hand, it might undo all the good work you've done. Baby's heart is still quite strong."

The men slid Chris onto the gurney. Scott arranged the survival blanket around his wife. The nurse added a warm blanket on top and secured the straps. Brooke remained in the awkward bent posture, her arm under the blanket between Chris' legs.

"We better carry the stretcher. Rolling it would shake our patient too much," the medic said.

The cold seized Brooke, cutting her breath, but she ignored it. No one had thought of throwing a blanket over her back. Climbing into the helicopter was complicated in her position, but she wasn't going to let go of the cord and the baby's head. Hands guided her feet and pushed her up without apologies for where the hands landed, but she was inside the chopper. The nurse swung out the stool and Brooke was able to get more comfortable. She shivered.

"I'll ask the pilot to turn the heat up," the medic said. "I'm Nathan, by the way." He checked the rate of the perfusion he had just put into Chris' vein.

"Damn, we could have given you a blanket," the nurse said. She grabbed one and carefully fitted it around Brooke, produced safety pins, and secured the blanket like a coat.

"I'm Andrea. They always mock me and my safety pins, but they do come in handy at times."

Warmth was coming back to Brooke's body. She introduced herself. "Safety pins and duct tape will repair a multitude of tears and breaks."

They shared a laugh. The medic had installed a heart monitor on Chris' chest and belly. "Still good. Take relaxing breaths, Chris. We'll be soon there."

Two hours later, they landed on the hospital helipad. A medical team was waiting just inside the glass doors. They rushed out to take over. Once inside and running, someone took off Brooke's blanket and wrapped her in a gown. A cap and mask were slipped over her head. The gurney was transferred straight away to the OR along with Brooke still holding the baby's head and umbilical cord.

"Relax, Chris. The surgeon is ready for the cesarean section. Your baby is doing well," Brooke said.

Her speech slurring, Chris managed to say, "My baby isn't moving."

"It's alright. Babies don't kick when they're about to be born. The heart is beating just fine,"

"Thank you. You saved my life. Our lives…" She drifted off as the anesthetic took effect.

The portable scan machine assured the obstetrician that there was no other complication. He made the cut. Brooke was finally able to remove her cramped hand and straighten her sore back. She stepped away quickly so as not to be in the way, but watched intently.

The surgeon's eyes were familiar. Then it clicked. Dr. Thompson had been her teacher at Queen's University in Kingston, Ontario. She remembered how fascinated he'd been with the life in the land of the midnight sun. Not surprising that he was now practicing in a northern hospital.

In no time, a lusty cry was heard and cheers went up from the surgical team. "It's a girl!" The baby was whisked away to the neonatal unit.

Finally, Chris was wheeled into the recovery room. The team regrouped in the prep room to discard gowns, gloves and masks, except Brooke still gowned, who was on her way to the NICU. She was stopped by the surgeon.

"Dr. Porter."

She froze. Who told him her name? It must have been the Star paramedics.

"I want to thank you and congratulate you for your quick action in saving Mrs. Walsh's life as well as that of her baby."

"Thank you, Dr. Thompson." It was him, her former teacher.

"Practicing in such a remote area must have its challenges."

"I am not a medical doctor. I am a veterinarian."

His mouth opened and closed, but the astonishment didn't leave his face. "All the more admirable."

"Yes, she's an admirable woman." They turned toward the voice.

"Eileen!"

The two women fell into each other's arms.

"Dr. Thompson, do you remember the case of the baby who received the wrong medicine?"

"Was that eight or nine years ago? In Kingston. The nurse handed the wrong vial to the intern. There was a tumultuous and contentious trial."

A red flush was mounting to Brooke's cheeks under the surgical mask. She gave a subtle kick to Eileen who ignored her and continued.

"What did you think at the time?"

"I recall I was away giving a series of lectures in New York at the time. But I followed the case closely. It was badly handled. The intern should never have been pilloried the way she was and shouldn't have been dismissed. The supervising pediatrician was also at fault. He ought to have stopped the intern to say to always double check what she is handed. I wish I could have freed myself from my obligations. She was my star student. I wrote a couple of letters on her behalf. When I came back, she'd disappeared. I often wondered what happened to her."

"She became a veterinarian."

Dr. Thompson gasped. "Dr. Porter!"

Brooke winced, but said nothing. She did, however, take her mask off.

The surgeon raked his hair and his cap fell off. "Brooke Porter!" He held out his hand. She took it.

"It's comforting to know you wrote letters and that you'd have supported me," Brooke said.

"You would make a fantastic doctor. Would you consider coming back to medicine?"

She shook her head and smiled. "I love the animals I get to care for, be it the budgies at the care home or a grizzly bear with his paw injured in a trap. The time has passed."

"The medical field profession is the poorer for having lost you."

"What Brooke won't tell you is that she keeps her medical skills sharply honed, and this saved a little leukemic boy's life."

"I work closely with the nurse practitioner in Donek."

Looking intently at her, Dr. Thompson said, "Do consider getting an official qualification. There appears to be a need in your remote area. You wouldn't have to abandon your veterinary practice."

"Thank you, Dr. Thompson. I'll think about it."

"It's George."

"Alright, George."

Eileen nodded and took her arm. "I was called at the NICU. Baby Walsh has got over her ordeal. We'll take her out of the incubator in a few hours, when his mama is ready for him to suckle. I had to come and see you. The story is the news of the day around the hospital."

Dr. Thompson leaned against the wall. The rest of the surgical team gathered around Brooke.

"May we have the rest of the story first hand, please?" George said.

"Nothing special, really," Brooke said.

Eileen Lewis tapped her on the shoulder. "The helico medic and nurse told the story from the moment they met the patient in the cabin, but they said something about a wild ride. What was it?"

There was nothing to do but tell the story from the moment she received the phone call from Scott. Brooke did emphasize the courage and dedication of the local auxiliary constable and his skill at getting them over the creek in one piece. She continued with much detail of remoteness and difficulty of access in the hope it'd spark a conversation on wilderness survival rather than her medical skills. It worked until everyone had to return to duty. Eileen guided her to see the newborn, who had just been handed to her mother. The baby was having her first meal.

Brooke sat for a moment, watching in wonder at the new life.

A huge smile on her face, Pat beckoned her friend closer. "First, I apologize for not taking your advice. Second, how can I ever repay you for saving my baby and me?"

"Never mind all that. Everything is fine, and that's the important thing. I'm so happy for you. No doubt Scott must be on his way."

"She's a miracle. That's what the doctors said. When the umbilical cord prolapses, the baby usually dies. So we want her name to reflect the miracle."

Brooke thought for a minute. "Call her Michaela. It means miracle."

"Perfect. Michaela Brooke. Will you be her godmother?"

"Me?"

"Who else?"

Brooke took a long inspiration. "I'd be honored."

Michaela had finished her first repast. Chris handed her to her friend.

A surge of love washed through Brooke as she held the warm bundle whose eyes were trying to focus. So light, so precious, an intense longing submerged her. Tears prickled behind her eyelids. "Love you Michaela."

Dr. Lewis' pager beeped. She called the desk.

"She's right here. I'll bring her down." To Brooke, "Someone's waiting for you at the reception. Let's go. Chris needs to rest."

Downstairs, the tall, well-built man was attracting female looks. Brooke would have smiled had she not spotted Dr. Luke Petrov crossing the lobby toward her. *What's that jerk doing here*? She pointedly turned her head and hurried to Dexter. Not minding the onlookers, she raised her arms around his neck and kissed him. With his hands around her waist, he drew her closer. The kiss lasted just a breathless moment.

"Thank you, my knight in shining armor, for coming to my rescue."

"The pleasure is all mine. Were you, by any chance, trying to avoid the fellow in the sharp suit and cashmere coat over by the reception desk?"

"That too. I was really thanking you for coming to take me home."

"Is he an old flame?"

She shuddered. "Whatever flame there was got quickly extinguished when a tragedy shook my life."

"And now that you're in the media, he's back, hoping to bask in your glory."

Thoughts tumbled through her head. Was Dexter jealous? Her eyes strayed to the chair on which she recognized her overnight bag and her parka. "You are thoughtful bringing my stuff. Due to the circumstances, I'm without a coat and my purse."

"Bill brought back your snowmobile suit and helmet. He said you'd gone with the chopper to Whitehorse. Yashee ordered me to take those to you."

She chuckled. "You were coming, weren't you?"

"I was."

Still held in Dexter's arms, she sensed a presence behind her, and turned her head, her expression no warmer than an Antarctic iceberg.

"Dr. Porter, I heard about——"

"What are you doing here?"

A flicker of arrogance crossed his well-groomed features. "I made an application for the directorship of internal medicine." A brief disgust fleeted across his face. "Now I don't know if it's worth it."

"You need a job? What a comedown for you!" Had he lied when he boasted of his practice employing three doctors? She looked up to see Dexter clenching his jaw. Somewhat amused, she grabbed her parka and pulled on her tuque. Mouth tightening, Petrov stood with his arms hanging at his side. Dexter picked up her overnight bag and led her to the exit.

A reporter from the *Daily Star*, who was engaged in a heated exchange with a security guard, saw Brooke and brandished his camera over the outstretched arm of the guard. "Ms. Porter, can I have an interview? Please?"

"Not now. Tomorrow morning. Promise."

Dexter marched her to his vehicle while the guard escorted the reporter out. In the Jeep, she burst out laughing.

"Your nerves must be shot."

She hiccupped. "Yeah, totally shot. I'm famished and tired. My arm and shoulder feels as if they had been caught in a wringer. How are your nerves holding up?"

"Much better now."

"You showed great restraint. I thought you wanted to flatten that Dr. Luke Petrov's pretty face." She put an emphasis on the name.

"I did. The reporter too."

"The reporter's okay. He's only doing his job. I don't mind talking to him. You bet he'll be at the Inn before breakfast. Just like when you find your quarry, it won't take him long to find out where we're staying."

With a laugh, Dexter pulled up in a parking spot at the Raven Inn and they went inside. "You'll have to tell me more about that Petrov guy."

"Not worth it. Food now, please."

Chapter Thirty-Four

By the end of Saturday afternoon, Brooke was looking forward to a quiet evening. Dexter was staying with her in her cabin, but hadn't moved in any personal possessions other than his day-to-day necessities. Basically, he lived in two houses. She realized that, faithful to his promise, he waited for her invitation. Warmth spread through her. No matter how much she tried to tell herself that her love for him wasn't really love, only an infatuation, the tiny voices in her head kept whispering, "Don't lie, don't lie." She asked herself how she'd react if, after she arrived home and parked the truck, she found that he had left on some work assignment. Her answer spoken aloud was, "I'll wait for his return."

Her voice didn't even surprise her. It wasn't love if she wasn't prepared to compromise. It wasn't love if she wasn't prepared to make sacrifices. It was love if she wanted him to be happy. It was love if she wanted him to be successful.

Her mood darkened when she spotted Ian Campbell's truck on the road, turning into her yard. She stopped alongside him and lowered the window.

Her tone was anything but welcoming. "What do you want now?"

"Can we talk?"

"Say what you have to say. You've got two minutes."

"It'll take a little longer than that."

Now furious, she accelerated to park in her spot behind the house, glad to see that Dexter was home. She strode into the house to find Campbell sitting and Dexter towering over him.

"I came to apologize. I don't know what came over me those last few months. I've been under great pressure."

Dexter's eyebrows rose. "First time I hear this."

"What pressure?" Brooke's voice carried no generosity in it.

A contrite air came over Campbell. "I owe money... lots. And they want it now."

"Who, they?" Weiman asked. His voice was neutral.

"Several ex-friends. I want to start over. I'm a good racer. I can win enough to repay my debts."

"How come you had my rifle? No, not mine, my late husband's rifle?"

"I bought it in Vancouver. I know, from a fence, but I thought he was legitimate. I didn't know it was Seth's."

"Liar! Everybody around here had been shown that rifle. Seth was so proud of it."

"He never showed it to me. Kept me on the hop. We were good friends, but there are things that we didn't share."

Brooke closed her eyes for a second. Then she sighed. "I believe you."

An audible sigh of relief escaped Ian's chest. "Do you think I can start over? Can my stupidity be forgiven?"

Thoughts jumbled and rolled inside Brooke's brain. Something was amiss. She threw a glance at Dexter, whose eyes were imperceptibly narrower, but she knew him enough to tell.

"You'll have to talk to mushers around here. The ones that were affected didn't press charges, though everybody has an opinion."

"I will do. I'll make amends. So now I'm back to wanting to buy Seth's sled and looking for dogs of my own to train."

"The sled is mine and I'm not selling. I have one rescue in the kennel, but she is not suitable to work in a team. Two that were just brought in are even less suitable. They've gone feral and spent too long surviving in the bush. They'll be sent to a specialized rehabilitation center."

A desperate look passed into Campbell's eyes. "Really, the sled is too big and too heavy for your solely recreational team."

In her peripheral vision, she saw Dexter's eyes getting even narrower.

"I said it before, Ian. My six Canadian Inuit dogs are stronger than a full team of Alaskan huskies. I need my sled, period. Okay, we are done, now."

Dexter's next question came like a bolt from the blue. "What do you know about diamonds, Campbell?"

In the process of standing up, the man froze and jerked the space of a nanosecond. If they hadn't been watching him intently, neither Brooke nor Dexter would have noticed. He finished straightening and walked to the door while putting his tuque on, his back to Brooke and Dexter. "Diamonds? Not a clue."

They watched the door close behind him and heard his truck fire up. They didn't move until the noise had faded away.

"Did you notice his reaction when I mentioned diamonds?"

"I did and expected you to grill him."

"At the moment, he believes he's safe. Let's wait until he makes a mistake. It won't be long. The man is desperate. His bosses want the diamonds or the money, I don't know, but it makes no difference. He doesn't have the diamonds, whether fake or real, nor the money."

Followed by his mother, Gugàn bounded into the living room. "Did you bring an excavator?"

"What do you say, Gugàn?" his mother said.

"Please?"

"I did." Brooke held out a package. The little boy's cries of delight warmed up the atmosphere.

"We go outside to excavate."

"It's dark. We'll go tomorrow. I don't work on Sundays."

Yashee stirred the casserole and put it on the table. She took the bread out of the warming oven. "That is a very bad man, Weiman. He has a dangerous aura."

"You're right, Yashee. I think I felt it too." Brooke never discussed her friend's pronouncements. They always turned out to be true.

"Now, Weiman, since you are not using your house. Do you want to rent it? There are many visitors for the dog sledding rides, but nowhere to stay. The hotel is not big enough."

"Yashee's Airbnb's business is doing well, but it's only one accommodation," Dexter said to Brooke.

It was an opportunity for Brooke to take an additional step forward in their relationship. She took a deep breath. "Give her your cabin. It's big enough. The former owner planned to go into the hospitality business, but his wife was having none of it. They went back Outside. It was empty for a couple of years. That's why you got it cheap."

He covered her hand with his. "I'll move out tomorrow. The cabin is yours, Yashee."

"I lease it. You cannot give it to me. I am not your relative."

Dexter inclined his head. "Very well. We'll draw up a lease tomorrow."

"And I shall move in tomorrow," Yashee said.

Chapter Thirty-Five

M oving couldn't start until the dogs were exercised.

"Dexter, climb in the sled for ballast."

"Me too! Me too!" Gugàn threw himself on top of Dexter.

The Canadian Inuit dogs walked back and crowded around the sled to inspect the commotion. They licked the laughing youngster before starting like an arrow from a bow when Brooke released the brake.

Two hours later, the exhilarating ride ended back at the cabin, much to the regret of the little boy. While Brooke and Yashee who had come out to help were taking care of the dogs, Gugàn climbed back into the sled which Dexter was holding until the last dog was unhitched.

"We've finished sledding," Dexter said.

"I know. I want to get more pebbles."

He was happy to humor the child before putting the sled away. Patiently, he watched Gugàn rummage in the bottom of the sled bag. In his search for pebbles, the boy tugged open a Velcro strap. Suddenly interested, Dexter bent over the handlebar to take a closer look.

"There are no more pebbles." For a second, looking disappointed, Gugàn slapped back the flap and ran into the house to get his toys.

"Brooke! Come over here a minute."

She left the pen. "What's the matter?"

"Is it usual to have a sled bag with double thickness of canvas at the bottom held by a Velcro fastener?"

"Where, exactly?"

He demonstrated. "See, it makes a pocket here." He closed the flap. "Totally invisible."

"Odd. I didn't know, but then it was Seth's sled, so I never thoroughly inspected it."

Gugàn ran out of the house and tugged on Dexter's parka. "I've got my 'cavator. Let's go and dig for pebbles."

The two adults looked at each other. "Pebbles? From the sled? A secret pocket?" They hurried behind the child. With their impatience barely contained, they waited for Gugàn to dig the pebbles out of the snow in his play area.

"I'll hold them," Dexter said.

"Okay." He went back to his work with both his bulldozer and his new excavator.

Crouched next to Dexter, Brooke whispered, "Do you think those pebbles were what Campbell was after?"

"I'm no expert. I was shown a piece of kimberlite. That's where diamonds are found, and these look pretty much the same."

"It's worth freezing our butts, then."

His hands were now full. Brooke took off her tuque, and he dumped them in.

"No more. Give my pebbles to build the house."

Thinking fast, Brooke said, "You must be hungry. Let's go in and have chocolate chip cookies."

There was no need to repeat the invitation. On all fours, Dexter painstakingly searched the play area. Yashee joined him, but they found nothing more.

The sweet smell of pancakes wafted in the cabin as Dexter and Yashee came in. Bits of dough in his hair and nose, and flour all over, Gugàn happily mixed the last of the batter. Yashee motioned to the tuque containing the pebbles. Dexter understood and carried them into the bedroom. Containing his mounting excitement took all his energy. When nearing the outcome of a long investigation, the surge of adrenaline made for powerful sensations.

In addition to the chocolate chip cookies and a herb omelet, pancakes with homemade saskatoon berry jam complemented the brunch. The plates were emptied in no time.

As always, Yashee knew without it being spoken that it was best for Gugàn not to see his pebbles again. She cleaned the remnants of the pancake making. "We are going to the skating rink," she said.

"But I don't have any skates."

Quick on the uptake, Dexter spoke. "Your mama will rent some for you," Discreetly, he slipped a bill to Yashee. "Then you can go to the store. I'm sure Tom will find something for you, maybe a dump truck." He knew there was a big red one on the shelf.

With a nod of the head, Yashee showed she understood.

"Then you can go for hot chocolate," Brooke said. She winked at her friend. "I'll do the dishes."

After they had gone, and despite his impatience, Dexter helped with the dishes. Finally, he dumped the contents of the tuque onto the table.

"I know Gugàn loves sledding and spent hours playing in the sled, but how did he discovered the hidden pocket baffles me."

"Kids don't think like adults. Anything is good for a game."

She sighed. "I guess you're right. I know more how dogs think than children. Those really looks like any old pebbles."

"This is kimberlite for sure. We should see some lighter incrustations if there are diamonds in it."

"Don't they shine?"

"Raw diamonds don't shine. They actually look greasy, according to the expert who taught the workshop I was obliged to attend."

For the second time, Dexter's head swiveled toward the window, then shook his head.

A piece, no bigger than an inch, of what to her looked like a rock in her hand, she rubbed an indentation. "There's something there." She kept rubbing the light brown earth, which began to crumble.

"I'll get a bowl of water."

Puzzled, she looked up. "What for?"

"Diamonds are extracted with water. When the rock is hard and dark, it is crushed first, but if the rock is of lighter color, it suggests it's eroding and water will accelerate the erosion and free the diamond if there is one. Diamond mining uses an awful lot of water. Quite destructive of the environment."

"Gugàn played in the snow. Perhaps that acted as water, too."

While at the sink, Dexter leaned toward the window to look outside before placing the bowl of warm water on the table and carefully lowering the piece of kimberlite into it. "I'm not sure I'm supposed to do this."

The dogs' howling signaled an arrival. Dexter froze. A mere second later, the dogs calmed down, but he walked out and looked around.

"Is there anything?"

He massaged his neck, a faraway look in his eyes. "No. I only get a strange feeling from time to time."

"I was going to say you need to ascertain that those are really rough diamonds."

He chuckled. "Imagine if those were only stones, and I sent them to the RCMP diamond cop. I think I'd get fired."

"Does he know all about diamonds?"

Dexter nodded while gently rubbing the kimberlite in the bowl. "He's a gemologist and knows everything there is to know about precious stones and metals."

"Like gold?"

"That's right. Now look, we can see there's something in here." He took it out of the water.

"I can see something different from the crummy rock."

"Tap it to see if it's hard."

Brooke stood and picked up a teaspoon. On second thoughts, she rummaged in the drawer and pulled out a magnifying glass.

Dexter tapped the outside of the stone, then the different-looking part. "I'd say it is a diamond."

With the magnifying glass in hand, she scrutinized the piece of rock. "It has that greasy look you mentioned. Is it really grease?"

"Nature's grease. It makes it waterproof and never erodes like the surrounding rock."

"And to think Gugàn played with diamonds!"

With a frown across his forehead, Dexter lifted his head and listened intently.

Brooke glanced at him and strained her ears. "What is it?"

"Nothing." But the anxiety in the room didn't diminish. "We're getting paranoid because we've got a few millions worth of stuff on the table if all those pebbles, as Gugàn call them, contain diamonds. No wonder Campbell was so eager to buy or steal the sled."

"That means that my worthless husband was up to his neck in that traffic. He's the one who hid the rocks in the sled, in that clever pocket."

With the stones carefully lined up on the table, Dexter took pictures with his phone. "Whether he and Campbell ran the whole race or scratched at a convenient spot, they had it made. Custom officers wouldn't suspect a musher with a bunch of sled dogs to be smuggling precious gems. They'd look for drugs, maybe, but whether the Yukon Quest or the Iditarod, it's sufficiently well known that the mushers are clean athletes. I don't think they'd search too hard, if at all."

"What do you do now?"

"I'm phoning the discovery."

"It's Sunday."

An amused smile on his lip, he looked at her while speed dialing a number.

"Oops! The law never sleeps, of course."

While he talked she went to the bedroom and retrieved a bead embroidered linen bag with a complicated *babiche* closure. She judged it'd be big enough to hold the stones.

A slight noise caught her attention. Without hesitation, she strode to the porch and outside, looking everywhere. The dogs were silent, but moving around. Nothing unusual though after a good run they tended to lie on top of their houses. They were a good alarm and if they were quiet, she need not worry. It might be a wild animal exploring nearby. But she couldn't shake her unease.

Back inside, she put the bag on the table and bent over the stones with the magnifying glass, examining each of them. "Savanah taught Stephanie how to embroider this bag with beads in the traditional way of the Tinglit. It's fitting to put those valuable stones in it."

When Dexter put an arm around her waist, she nearly dropped the magnifying glass. She pointed to one stone at the edge. "This stone is slightly different, isn't it?"

"Excellent observation. I hadn't noticed."

"It doesn't mean much, though. None of them are identical."

"This one looks like a piece of granite, fine granite." He took the magnifying glass. "You're right. Is it the only one?"

"I think so. Should we separate it from the rest?"

"No doubt our expert would see it. But sure, let's put it in a small bag inside the big bag."

She handed him one of the small linen bags she used to sell the homemade dog cookie treats and put it in the embroidered bag's inner pocket.

"Where do those raw diamonds come from?"

He grimaced. "Most likely from West Africa, Especially Sierra Leone. Terrible human rights violations, near-slavery conditions, child labor..." He raked his hair with his fingers. "The smuggling goes on and on. It hurts Canada's diamond industry too."

"How come?"

"These blood diamonds are passed off as Canadian high-value, fully ethical diamonds. When it is discovered they are not, trust in the Canadian industry diminishes, although Canada is a signee of the Kimberley Certification Agreement."

"Which is..?"

"Eighty-one diamond producing nations adhere to an ethical standard of diamond trade."

"How can they be identified as not being Canadian?"

"All the mining companies have their own special logo engraved at the bottom of each diamond they extract. The diamonds are then cut by a lapidary and made into jewelry. The logo at the bottom remains. It's the guarantee."

"Do I suppose right that your crooks make an imitation logo?"

"Or have a shell company, or use unscrupulous jewelers. Now and then a mule is caught at the airport. Small fry. The syndicate I'm after is highly organized."

"Now you're going to have to catch Campbell's bosses and dismantle that syndicate."

His lips lifted in a wry smile. "In a nutshell, yes. Now, I'm afraid I have to catch a plane and take those baubles to HQ."

The kiss she gave him held all her love. "I know. Will they give you a bodyguard?"

"How did you guess?"

"Because if I were your boss, I would."

"I'd love that. Do you think Yashee is about to come back?"

Brooke shook her head. "If I know her, she will make sure to stay out until dinner time. She understood how important this was. I bet they are visiting their cousins and the boys are perfectly content with the new toys."

"Then we have some time for ourselves."

Chapter Thirty-Six

"Is that someone at the door?" Dexter interrupted the trail of kisses he was dropping on Brooke's face.

"Yashee's back?"

They listened. The quiet was unnerving. The dogs gave a brief howl.

"It's time I go, anyway." Dexter stood and got dressed.

The first one to be presentable, Brooke pushed the bedroom door open. "I'll make you a sandwich to take on the road——" A cry pushed out of her throat. "The bag!"

"What?" Dexter said from the bedroom.

"The bag. Did you put the bag away?"

The bedroom door slammed against the wall as Dexter barged into the living room. "The bag?"

"Did you put it somewhere?"

"No."

The finality of the single word hit them. Instinctively, they searched the room. The bag was big enough and heavy. They had to admit the evidence. Someone came in and stole the bag.

"Campbell!" Dexter grabbed his parka and truck keys and rushed out.

Without wasting time, Brooke put on her skis and hurried to Bill's. She had never cross-country skied so fast. Out of breath, she pounded on his door.

Bill came up behind her, carrying an armful of firewood. "Brooke! What happened?"

He dropped the split logs and held her until her shoulders stopped shaking and she got her breath back.

"I want to report the theft of a bead embroidered bag containing valuables, stolen from my kitchen table. Inspector Weiman has gone to see Ian Campbell. He is suspect Number One."

"Come in."

Just then, Bill's satellite phone beeped. He listened. "She's right here. I'll bring her." He turned to Brooke. "Campbell is injured and unresponsive."

"You better call Janice. She's got a snowmobile."

"Donek is an hour away from Ian's place."

A long sigh escaped Brooke's chest. "Take me to my place. I need my vet bag."

Minutes later, she was back at the cabin. She made another quick search, again without success. With a human blood pressure cuff added to her bag, she went back outside and found Jimmy in discussion with Ed. The news had got around faster at the speed of light.

"You walked over the tracks, but there are enough of them."

Brooke bit her lip. She hadn't thought about tracks. "Sorry."

"Two people. One person wore city boots. The other wore arctic boots. Distinctive sole. They walked through the woods, past Weiman's cabin."

"He must have had a snowmobile hidden over there," Ed said.

"Far enough away to avoid noise. I'll go and follow the tracks to where his machine was."

Ed nodded. "I'm right behind you on the snowmobile. I'll try to avoid messing up the tracks just in case."

"I'll take Dr. Porter to Campbell's place."

Jimmy and Ed agreed. On the back of Bill's snowmobile, Brooke marveled at Jimmy Redhead always turning up when he was most needed. Of course, his cabin on top of the hill served as an excellent observation post over a large area. He probably spotted an intruder and came to investigate. Since she had come back to live in Agate Creek and delivered Savanah's first baby, he had made a point of looking after her.

Campbell's cabin on the other side of the creek wasn't too far, but it was isolated. Dexter had wrapped a towel, now blood-soaked, around the man's head and was on the phone. With great care, she opened the towel and grimaced.

"He needs to go to the hospital. This is beyond my competence or Janice's. The bone is exposed. There could be a fracture. His blood pressure is dropping."

While talking, she sprayed a disinfectant over the wound. After some consideration, she shaved the hair around the wound and put two temporary sutures on the head to prevent the skin from pulling off the skull any farther, then applied a tight bandage. When she finished, she looked up to see the nurse practitioner watching.

"Good job, Brooke. I'm glad you got here first. I asked Ernie to come with his minivan." Ernie's Taxi acted as an ambulance when needed. "We'll take this idiot to the Whitehorse hospital."

Brooke closed her bag and looked at Janice. "Did he bother you?"

"All the time. He has the stupid notion that a woman being single isn't normal. As if I was going to fall into his arms."

They chuckled. Ernie pulled in next to them.

"No... hospital," Campbell mumbled.

"You don't want to die just yet," Brooke said. "So off you go."

With Dexter's help, they managed to get the patient into the back seat. Brooke didn't have a cervical collar and instead slip a neck cushion to hold his head and prevent it from moving. Ernie tied the cushion to the headrest.

"I carry a few of those for my less than young patients," Ernie said.

Janice sat next to the patient to monitor him on the long drive.

"Bill, you better get yourself to Whitehorse. This is a police case," Dexter said.

"Yep. I'm on my way home to get my truck. You come later, since you're a witness." He secured the nurse practitioner's snowmobile and left.

Brooke turned to Dexter before climbing in his Jeep. "Any idea what happened to him?"

He raked his hand through his hair. "He managed to say thug. I pressed him a bit, and he said something about paying. I insisted... okay, I shook him and before he passed out, he said the thug had risked his life for a stupid woman's bag. What do you make out of that?"

"They wanted the sled, but realized they couldn't break the triple heavy padlocks." Her hand went to her forehead in a resounding slap. "I got it all wrong. The dogs made relatively no noise, yet any time someone comes close to the yard, they howl like an operatic chorus."

"But they did."

She shook her head. "Not very much, because I think Campbell went to pet them and probably had treats of meat for them. They know him so they wouldn't have made much noise. I bet he held the treats out at the bottom of the drive. My dogs would have detected their scent and obediently sat as I've trained them to do. That's why we only heard a few woofs and not the alarm they usually are."

A deep sigh came from Dexter's chest. "I think Campbell's accomplice is a professional thief, if you can call that a profession, who'd be confident enough to act in full daylight. They must have been watching the cabin. But where from without getting the dogs to howl?"

"From the ridge, with binoculars. Campbell saw us at the sled, then groveling in the snow. later, they saw Yashee and the kid go, but didn't know whether we'd gone too."

"At that distance, could they see we carried something inside?"

"It's possible."

"So the accomplice sneaked down and looked in while Campbell kept the dogs quiet. He saw us at the table with the pebbles and reported to Campbell."

"That's why you had that odd feeling?"

"I chucked it to paranoia. I suppose they went away, but the accomplice came back later to check on our movements and saw the bag on the table."

"And we were out of sight."

His fist against his mouth, Dexter stared at the ground. "He saw the bag on the table. There was an article a week ago on those special ceremonial bags, which mentioned a high price for them. They're much smaller than yours, though, being ceremonial."

"A photo in the local gazette doesn't give a good idea of the size."

"True. So our thief got the bag believing he could sell it. It seems odd that they, at least Campbell, wouldn't know those were raw diamonds, or maybe he did and wasn't telling his partner. Actually, I'm quite sure Campbell knew what was in the bag, but wasn't going to tell his accomplice."

Brooke was dismayed. "The thug must have wanted to know why he was risking his life stealing a stupid woman's bag full of stones. The thug suspected something fishy and wanted more than the agreed payment."

"My reasoning too. It escalated into an argument and the thug struck Campbell with some weapon before taking off with the bag."

Brooke scrunched her face. "Now he has a worthless bag full of stones. He dumped the stones and went to sell the bag to a pawn shop. Give me your phone."

In a flash of understanding, he handed her the satellite phone, while he inspected the cabin and then the outside.

"Hi Stephanie. Someone stole the bag you embroidered for me ... Yes, that one. I need you to search all the pawn stores and if not there, all the thrift stores. Oh, and the bag was full of pebbles. I want all of them back too ... They belong to a five-year-old and he'd be very upset if he didn't get his precious rocks back. You know everything is covered in snow so we can't replace them ... No, I'm serious ... Okay, you're too smart for your own good. They could be of interest in a police case, that's why it's important to get them all back ... Thanks. I trust you."

Brooke joined Dexter outside and handed back the phone. He made a call while Brooke went over the snow covered ground around the cabin where an unhappy man could have ditched rocks. Nothing. "What do we do now?"

"I have told Max. He's putting on extra surveillance at the airport, on the roads and the usual places. What we don't know is whether the thug knew what the stones were. If he didn't, he could have dumped them anywhere. I've checked the cabin and the outside up to where he must have parked his vehicle. Nothing. If he did know, he'll try a fence, but maybe in Vancouver."

"We're going home. Jimmy found tracks and has gone with Ed to see where he parked his machine. Trust Jimmy to find where he went."

The whine of a snowmobile stopped them right where they stood. They waited. Dexter fingered his pistol in its shoulder holster.

The snowmobile came to a stop. Dexter relaxed. Ed and Jimmy jumped off.

"The tracks circled back here," Ed said.

"It proves our theory." Dexter frowned. "Where would he dump stones if he didn't do it right here?"

At Jimmy's inquiring look, Brooke briefed him on the situation and the diamonds issue. Ed listened carefully. The two First Nations men looked at each other and nodded.

"Now he has a special native bag with ordinary stones, but he knows that we have rituals. He does not know anything about our way of life," Jimmy said. "So he does not throw the stones away. He thinks it will get more money that way."

Ed agreed with him. "He went to Whitehorse first and if he cannot sell there, he will go to Vancouver. You will be going, right?"

Dexter nodded and thanked them. They drove home. He parked and stood for a while looking around the house and the kennels where the Inuit dogs were pleading for more treats. Dispirited, he went in and sat with his head in his hands while Brooke busied herself in the kitchen. "This is the end of my career. To have recuperated the diamonds only to lose them again because... I can't show my face at HQ."

"But," she lifted his hand and sat on his knee, "there is no law against making love. Do you regret it?"

He kissed her before replying, "No, not at all."

"Besides, I know we're going to find them."

He let out a long sigh. "In the meantime, we go to Whitehorse hospital to interrogate Campbell."

"I've prepared some snacks for the road seeing we didn't have lunch."

The door opened. "Can I help?" Yashee asked.

She steered a sleepy Gugàn to the bathroom to brush his teeth before putting him to bed, too tired to protest it was too early. Quietly, she sat in front of Brooke and Dexter. They told her the story.

"Go to Golden New and Used Emporium. He buys native craft. A professional thief would know that. Go, now."

"Do you think we can make it in five hours?" Brooke asked.

She picked up her purse while he took the basket of food.

"We'll take the Jeep. It's filled up."

They soon were running smoothly on the snowy road. Brooke reached for Dexter's phone and put it on speaker to call Stephanie.

"Can you go to the Golden Emporium? Yashee believes the thief could go there."

"Sunday, it'll be closed, but I'll try just in case."

"Thanks. We'll tell you all. We'll stay at the Raven Inn. They always give us the VIP suite. I think we'll make it to the restaurant before closing time. I hope so anyway."

At the wheel, Dexter was lost in thought, and Brooke kept quiet so as not to distract him. When they arrived at the restaurant, Stephanie was already seated at a table. "I ordered for you to make sure you'd get something in case you were late."

"You're a treasure!"

After listening to the story, Stephanie tapped her lip with her index finger, thinking. "The Emporium is closed on Sundays, so your thief still has the bag. He'll go there first thing in the morning. Nobody sets off on the road to the Outside this late in the evening and there are no night planes."

"You're so right. We're too close to the affair to think logically," Brooke said.

"Yashee was right," Dexter said. "Since the thief didn't get the payment he wanted, he'll try to get the most money out of the bag, and that'll be at the Emporium."

Mindful of imponderables, Dexter phoned Max to request surveillance of the Emporium at least one hour before opening time.

Exhaustion and worry marred Brooke's features.

Stephanie took her leave. "I'll do another round of the pawn shops tomorrow, all ten of them."

"And I'll be at the hospital," Dexter said.

They moved to the elevator.

"My assignment is the Golden Emporium, I guess. I'm placing a lot of hope there."

"But the thief may not have gone in yet, if it was closed today."

She shrugged. "Then I'll be there to see him arrive."

"No. You're not to hang around that place. It's dangerous."

She tapped his arm. "I won't put myself in harm's way."

"Maybe you should be the one to interrogate Campbell, and I stake out the store." He swiped the card and opened the room door.

She put her hands on her hips. "On the other hand, a woman in that kind of store stuffed with knickknacks would not attract attention, even from the most wary criminal."

"How come you're always right?"

Brooke burst out laughing. "Genetics?"

"Are you tired?"

"Not that much."

"Me, neither." He swept her off her feet and into the bedroom.

Chapter Thirty-Seven

With his head propped up on pillows, Dexter's eyes followed Brooke. "Despite what we agreed last evening, I think you should go and interview Campbell. He won't see you as a cop."

"Okay, I think you're right, but you'll have to come to the hospital so that I can be let in on police business before visiting hours, since I'm not a relative."

He jumped out of bed. "Done deal. Breakfast first. But unless you get a full confession, I'll interview Campbell. Afterwards, I assume I'll find you at the Emporium when I'm finished with Ian?"

"You guessed right."

At the hospital, the receptionist told Dexter there was a police constable outside Mr. Campbell's door and no visitors were allowed. Dexter showed her his ID and Brooke was waved through. The constable stood when Brooke approached. He nodded to her and opened the door.

She lifted the chart at the foot of the bed and grimaced while discreetly switching her phone on camera. Not that she'd take a picture, but it would record what he had to say and stream the interview to Dexter's phone. "Morning, Ian."

He opened his eyes. "Brooke?"

"How are you doing?"

"Not so good. I think I'm going to die."

Taking his hand in hers, she sat by the bed. "No, you're not. You've got a nasty bump on the head, but I don't think it is life threatening."

"They told me you sewed me up."

"I only gave you first aid. Do you remember what happened to you?"

He hesitated. "No."

"I'm sure if you think about it, you'll remember. Beside the big gash on your head, you have a hairline fracture of the skull. It doesn't affect your memory."

"I fell."

"Is that what you told the doctor? You're not convincing me."

Ian made no reply.

In an even voice, Brooke continued with her questioning. She hoped Dexter would be proud of her interrogation method.

"You fell after a thug bashed your head. What did he want from you?"

"Money."

Although she wanted to shake him, she kept a compassionate tone. "We have to make a police report."

He looked terrified. "No. It was my fault. I don't want to press charges."

"I understand, but by law, the hospital is obliged to report this was no accident. It was an assault."

Ian shrank back on the pillow.

"What did he want? Money, of course. What else?"

In front of his tight mouth, she played a trick she'd seen in a movie. "Lupin told us he'd taken the bag from my cabin to give to you, but he decided to ask for more money and you refused."

Campbell's body jerked and his breathing became short.

"What's his real name?"

"He goes by Toledo."

She smiled. "Ah, a man of many names. Do you know any of his other aliases?" She couldn't believe he had fallen for the old movie trick. Maybe he wasn't the brightest person in Agate, but he wasn't completely stupid, either.

Ian was brooding. "He couldn't get it. Couldn't get the sled. Then he watched you in your house."

Wheels were turning in Brooke's head. That was no help. Did the man understood what they were doing with what looked like pebbles? What would Dexter want to know? "You stole my bag. A gift from a dear friend. What did he do with it?"

About to shake his head, Ian pulled a face and exhaled a sigh. "Ask him."

Anxious that her plot was backfiring, Brooke wracked her brain. "He's not telling. I don't want to wait until he gets a lawyer and wait for the court and all that involves. I want to get my bag, that's all. It's a precious keepsake."

Ian's eyes kept shifting around the room. He remained silent. Seconds before Brooke continued to press him for answers, he spoke. "There's a store in town where they buy native craft. Toledo would know about it, unless he took it to Vancouver. That's his turf."

Her heart beat accelerated. "You mean the Golden Emporium? Then I'll go and check it. I think he'd want to get rid of it as soon as possible, don't you think so?"

"When I saw you... He doesn't know about... I told him it's native stuff."

It took Brooke all her strength to remain calm. "What does he not know about?"

The silence lasted such a long time, Brooke was frantically searching her mind how to break it without getting Ian to suspect she knew anything regarding the stones. "Do you mean he doesn't know about my late husband?"

"No."

"How come he entered my house and took the bag? How did he know it has some value?"

His eyes shifted to the side. "I wanted him to get the sled."

The interview was beginning to go somewhere. Brooke forced indifference. "Well, you know I am not selling it. Besides, what's so special about it? There must be at least half a dozen dog sleds for sale in the area."

He remained tight-lipped.

"Since he couldn't get the sled, he looked in and saw a native bead embroidered bag."

"Yes... Brooke?"

"I'm listening."

"I'm sorry."

Brooke tensed up, but remained quiet. He might be ready to confess the whole scheme.

"In the Iditarod, I wanted to get out of it all. My brain got scrambled... Big debts... I'm relieved nobody died."

If he wanted to rehash all that episode, she'd listen. It might lead to the diamonds in the end. "Did you carry an illegal substance or illegal goods?"

Once more, he remained silent. She waited.

"Your husband cheated me. We'd carried valuables across the border for years. Lammers hid one package in the sled, but got himself killed."

After a moment of silence, she realized he wasn't going to volunteer any other information.

"So you entered the Iditarod, and you carried another package of precious gems that the woman at the sports store gave you. So what did you do with it since you didn't have it at the Nikolai checkpoint?"

His eyes opened wide. "I have a headache."

"Not surprising with your injury. Just tell me what you did with it. Better tell me before your boss sends someone to ask that question."

A sudden terror contorted his features. "I was stopped by a guy on a snowmobile. He took the package... at gunpoint. I'm sorry... sorry I got involved in Lammers' stupid scheme. They'll kill me now because I don't have Lammers' package... The stones in the bag... They were supposed to be diamonds. We've been cheated. They're just pebbles."

Her mind a jumble of thought, Brooke remained speechless. Ian Campbell didn't know what he transported. He expected diamonds to be the shiny stuff from a jewelry store. Under the surge of adrenaline through her veins, her heart beat faster at the enormity of what she just heard. If that guy Toledo didn't know about raw diamonds, he might have dumped the stones. Jimmy didn't think so, but she wasn't so sure.

"You rest now. I have to go."

"They'll kill me."

She couldn't help feel sorry for him. "Stay calm. There's a police officer at your door. Nobody will kill you."

Her compassion was exhausted. She hurried out. Dexter would now have received Ian Campbell's interview and would be waiting for her at the Emporium. While she made her way to the store, she tried to put order into her thoughts after Campbell's revelations. Her scarf over her nose and her parka hood tightened around her face, she entered the store. It had just opened. She saw a buckskin outfit, decorated with beads and feathers, on a mannequin, indicating the native craft section.

For what felt like a long time, she pretended to browse while keeping an eye on the door.

"May I help you?"

She pulled her scarf down. "I'm looking for something practical like a bag, but I'd like some bead embroidery on it."

"You're in luck. I just acquired one beautiful bag yesterday." He held out his hand. "I'm Geoff."

Wheels turned speedily in her head. Yesterday, Sunday. The store was closed. "Nice to meet you, Geoff. You have a lot of lovely things here." She eased her hood off her head to look like the casual, interested shopper who had time to browse.

"I'm pleased you think so. The beaded bag is still in my office, if you'd care to follow me."

Although she knew there were police keeping the store under surveillance, an uneasy feeling niggled at her. Not going into a secluded place flashed through her mind. "Please go and bring it out. I want to look at a few more items."

His smile was genuine. The smile of someone who sees a couple of sales in the offing. He hastened to the back. After a cursory glance at a display of beaded mittens and moccasins, Brooke leaned against the counter facing the door, where she felt safe, trusting she was being watched. Geoff came to the other side of the counter and deposited the beaded bag on the counter, a large smile on his face.

"It's a beauty. We don't often see beaded bags of that size with such artistic value. It isn't cheap, but you understand it's rare."

"Indeed it's beautiful. Do you mind if I take a picture to send to my husband?" She stopped a gasp just in time. She had said husband! Was that indicative of something her mind was trying to send her? Something that she was not yet ready to acknowledge?

He raised his eyebrows. "No, of course. Go ahead."

Brooke switched on the video and took views of the bag from various angles and made sure to include parts of the store and the store owner himself. She put the phone down, but didn't switch off to stream the pictures and whatever was being said to Dexter's phone.

"I used to have a beaded bag, just like this one. A friend embroidered it for me. Who sold this one to you?"

An imperceptible tightening of Geoff's lips didn't escape Brooke's attention. "I cannot name the seller's name, due to privacy concerns, you understand."

Where is Dexter? He should be here. What am I going to do here on my own? Keep the owner busy. "I should show you the pictures of my bag." She picked up her phone and scrolled through the album. "Here it is. That's me holding the bag."

His face darkening, he leaned over to look at the picture.

"And this is me and my friend Stephanie who embroidered the bag for me." *Dexter, where are you?*

"Very nice. Now, are you buying this one?"

"I have to consider it. As you can see from my photos, my bag is identical to this one." She paused to give emphasis to her next words. "Unfortunately, my bag was stolen yesterday."

The owner became agitated. His face hardened. "Look lady, I'm a busy man and have things to attend to. Either buy the bag or leave the store."

Much to her relief, Dexter chose that moment to enter, closely accompanied by another man in civilian clothes, with 'cop' written all over him. Brooke watched them approach. Panic flooded Geoff's face. Obviously, he saw what was coming. He raised his hands, then dropped them back to his side.

"What's going on?"

Brooke began to relax. Now, the law could take over.

"You do understand that this bag was stolen," Dexter said.

Geoff was visibly in the grip of fear. "That's what you're telling me. I didn't know it was stolen. I bought it fair and square."

"On a Sunday? When the store is closed?" Dexter's voice was calm, almost bland.

"With an online business, there are no Sundays. When I get a call, I take it. And if it means driving up to the store, then I go."

"You understand you'll be charged for reception and possession of stolen goods."

"But I didn't know it was stolen!"

Dexter was inflexible. "You'll tell that to the Mounties."

Impatience mounting, Brooke stepped forward. "And I'm taking my beaded bag back." Her hand shot out, ready to lift the heavy bag. The momentum carried it as high as her head. A desperate yell burst out of her throat, "No!" Her hand slammed onto the counter. "It's empty."

Dexter frowned at Geoff. "What did you do with the stones inside the bag?" His tone remained indifferently casual.

Brook noticed a sheen of perspiration on the man's forehead.

Geoff cleared his throat. "The seller claimed this was a ritual bag. I told him native don't put dirty old stones in those ceremonial bags. He said they did. I know they don't. After he left, I threw them out. Why?"

The other cop, propped up against a shelf, watched the development with interest.

"The rocks belong to a five-year-old who is very unhappy," Brooke said. "Where I live up the mountain, everything is covered with snow. Absolutely no way to dig up any more for another three months."

Geoff Golden's look of annoyance irritated Dexter. He put his fists on the counter, leaning on his rigid arms toward the store owner. If there was a more threatening stance, Brooke didn't know of it.

Words tumbled in a hurry out of the scared man's mouth. "At the back, next to the dumpster." Geoff didn't need to say more. Brooke was flying to the back of the store, aiming for the green exit sign.

At the threshold, she paused and look. The snow hadn't been cleared and she could see indentations where the stones had landed. She pulled a nylon shopping bag from her purse, bent and retrieved the first stone. She worked systematically from the farthest spot toward the door and dumpster, carefully clearing the snow. Minutes later, Dexter joined her.

"Twenty. I already have the twenty big ones," she said. "What's the situation inside?"

"Mitch, my colleague you saw in the store, is keeping an eye on the gentleman. We did a background search. Geoff is clean. Let's find all the damn stones."

It took them half an hour, groveling in the snow to find the smaller ones. Dexter made a call. Brooke exhaled a long sigh. "I'm glad they are all accounted for."

"We're missing one."

She lifted her hand. "No cause for alarm. It's the one that looks different and that we put in the pocket of the bag."

"What if it's been thrown somewhere else?"

"No one sees the pocket until they're told it's a pocket."

A police car pulled up in the alley.

"My ride," Dexter said.

"I'll go and get the other stone from the bag's pocket."

She ran into the store. The cop was standing half sitting on the corner of the store counter, arms crossed over his chest. Geoff stood apart at a respectable distance.

With haste, yet precision, Brooke opened the pocket under the interested look of the two men. She retraced her steps to the backdoor and handed Dexter the stone in its Doghaven Cookie bag. "I'm glad this is over."

"I'll second that. I must go. They're waiting for me."

"Do you get an escort all the way to Ottawa?"

"Yes, but a little more discreet one. Here are the keys to the Jeep."

He tied the handles of the shopping bag and put it inside his parka.

"You look pregnant!"

"I'll make sure I don't have a premature delivery before I get to police headquarters."

The joke help released the tension they both felt. He placed a fleeting kiss on her lips. A Mountie was holding the cruiser door open.

Brooke went back inside to retrieve her beaded bag. To her happy relief, Stephanie was holding it and was in an animated conversation with Geoff. They shook hands. Her friend took Brooke's arm and led her out. The cop followed them. He told her that he had been appointed as her security guard and his name was Mitchell and they could call him Mitch. They told him they were going to the restaurant. He went with them.

"What was all that discussion about with Geoff?"

"I told him I had made the bag, and he wanted me to make more. He thinks they would sell well. I won't make the same. We agreed on small items."

"Now you have a paying hobby."

"With three kids, there never is enough money!"

Lunch over, the friends parted. Mitch followed Brooke to the Jeep, then climbed in his own vehicle. Having an unmarked police car behind her was unnerving, especially when a vehicle tried to overtake and Mitch closed the gap to prevent the car from pulling in between them, obliging the vehicle to overtake both.

Chapter Thirty-Eight

The first thing Brooke did on arriving at Doghaven was to go into the pen housing Julot, Nana and their four youngsters. She was mobbed, pawed and licked, while rolling in the snow with them. The accumulated stress of the past few days evaporated under the effusive show of affection. She buried her nose in Spitzweg's thick neck fur. The big male sprawled over her lap, pushing his siblings out of the way. When she uttered the magic word "treat?" they instantly rolled over and sat up, waiting almost patiently. She got to her feet and distributed the bones she had bought in the city. Then she went into the rehab pen to be greeted with effusion by the dogs. The wild ones were making progress and no longer ran and hid when she came in. As for Little Raven, barely a year old who was found starved and scared, wandering on a trail, it had been love at first sight. Three dogs injured when a snowmobile had harassed their musher were recovering nicely. Their musher would be coming in the next few days to put them on the sled to help them rebuild their strength under her supervision. They were shy and hunkered down in their houses when people came, but they came out for her. In the meantime, they all loved their bones.

Mitch, lounging against the cabin's wall, had watched her. Slightly disheveled, she approached him.

"My best friends."

"It was a pleasure seeing them. Will you introduce me?"

"When they're finished with their bones. Where are you going to stay?"

He smiled. "I have orders to stay in an Airbnb."

"My friend Yashee has two. Which one? No, let me guess. You're staying in Dexter's cabin."

"You guessed right. Let's go in and talk about what you can and cannot do."

Her frown would have frozen anyone, but not this tall, muscled man with his phlegmatic demeanor. His gray eyes ran over her like a laser, scrutinizing her. No one was going to tell her what to do. He must have guessed, for he laughed. "Safety first, Brooke. The people we're dealing with are not kindergarten pranksters."

She sighed. "Alright, you win."

A lovely baking smell greeted the pair as they went in.

"Yashee, you have baked a chocolate cake. I am just about eating the aroma."

After she had introduced her friend, they got down to the serious business of eating supper. Finally, Brooke couldn't delay the talk any longer. Mitch had an amused curl to his mouth.

"I'll be out of your way until you sleep. Then, I will be in the bedroom annex doing paperwork, not to sleep. When you go to work in Donek, I will follow you, and while you're at the clinic, I'll get back to my assigned quarters to sleep. Doug will take over and keep an eye on the clinic."

"Surely, the constable has other things to do than watch over me, no? What danger am I in? The diamonds are on their way to where they need to be. Case closed. Why all the fuss?"

He picked up the cup of coffee Yashee just put in front of him. "It isn't over until we get the boss of the syndicate. When we do, it will save the lives of many children, at least for a while."

"You mean until another criminal rebuilds the network or whatever it's called?"

He sighed. "Yeah, that's just about the way it goes. And for a while, the authorities in Sierra Leone will put pressure on the mine owner. But..."

A silence fell.

"You've identified where the stones come from?"

"Not yet for certain. It takes the lab a while to analyze the rocks. Any guess is a good guess. Sierra Leone is likely." He rubbed the back of his neck. "We're just chipping away at the problem. For all the resources at our disposal, we're relatively puny against the tide of criminality."

Brooke squeezed her temples with the fingers of both hands, willing the fatigue to go away. "I don't understand what it has to do with me now."

"We've tricked the syndicate into believing that Campbell still has the latest shipment, as well as the missing shipment, which Lammers spirited away. We think they'll come after Campbell when that Toledo guy tells them Campbell is hiding the gems."

She straightened on the chair. "And in the process, I'm the bait."

"No, Campbell is. Texts from his phone showed that he was lying to that man, Toledo, telling him the sled was of no importance. It was only of value to a musher. In the reply, his acolyte then accused him of double crossing him and the boss."

"Charming!"

"Unfortunately, you're tied to Lammers. I wouldn't put it past those felons to come after you in the belief you were in with his schemes."

"Because they'll soon realized he doesn't have the gems, but the widow must have Lammers' package. Right?"

He nodded. "This is why we're taking precautions and you won't go anywhere without telling me, though I'm pretty sure you won't be in any danger."

That didn't comfort Brooke. She argued that the evildoers weren't going to make the distinction. Especially after they discovered that Ian didn't have the diamonds and that the package he was supposed to deliver went missing on the Iditarod race trail... where she was, too. This whole affair was more than she had signed on for. If only Dexter could come back right away. She was out of her depth in this police, smuggling, syndicate and whatever else was involved. Someone would have to explain how it all worked, but right now she was so tired, all she wanted was sleep.

CHAPTER THIRTY-NINE

For the next few days, Brooke could almost convince herself that her life was back to normal. Although she knew that Mitch was close by, she never actually saw him. She skied to the clinic. Once, she even hitched up her Canadian Inuit dogs. How he kept up with her she couldn't imagine, but sensed she was being watched, nonetheless. There was always someone turning up where she was. When she went for a ride to exercise her Inuit dogs team, Jimmy always met her on the trail right behind her cabin. How did he know she was about to go? She'd always thought the moccasin telegraph was a joke. Now, she wasn't so sure.

One morning when Yashee had come in to prepare breakfast, she had to ask. "That constable Mitch, is he still around?"

"He is. He is good. He can ski too."

Brooke nodded. "Well, I have to live a normal life. Don't I? I don't always drive to work."

"Of course, and if you looked behind, you might spot him."

"Just a moment. Yesterday I sledded to work. What did he do?"

"I showed him how to sled with three of the new rescues. They're old sled dogs and know perfectly what to do. By the way, the new owners are coming next week for them."

Brooke laughed. "You went with him to show him the ropes."

"He is a quick learn."

Still amused, Brooke shook her head. "You devious woman, you."

It was Yashee's turn to laugh. Then she became serious again. "Weiman is coming back."

"I hope so!"

"Now eat, Early Sun. You are not eating. I have to come every morning after the school bus picks up Gugàn to make you eat."

The aromatic omelet was so fluffy and light, nobody could have resisted it. Despite that, Brooke had to force the first forkful. The second was easier as her taste buds sprang to life. This, she reckoned, was what life with Dexter was going to be like. Him away. She waiting. Waiting, not knowing where he was, when he'd be back, whether he was in danger or lounging in some office somewhere. Or, and this sent a chill down her spine, dead. She choked on the last mouthful of omelet. The coffee was hot and burned her tongue.

"Tsk! Don't fret. He is coming back. I told you."

"I know, but it's hard——"

The radio burst to life. "Hello Doghaven, Travelers calling. Are you receiving me? Over."

Travelers was the call sign for the hotel in Donek. In her haste to snatch up the microphone, Brooke's coffee spilled and her chair fell backward. She tripped as she grabbed the microphone. It sounded urgent. Sprawled in an inelegant position on the floor, she managed to gasp a reply. "Doghaven speaking. Receiving you loud and clear. Over."

"A visitor and his company are on their way to you. Is your phone working? Over."

She blanched. After what Mitch had explained to her, Garth wouldn't call on the radio and have the whole area listening unless it was an emergency of sorts and he wanted everyone to be on alert.

"Doghaven, a suave individual by the name of Oleg Austin checked in yesterday and asked for the house of Mr. Lammers. Two less suave individuals also checked in separately. I sent this Austin guy by road, the long way round road. ETA one hour."

A slight trembling began in her limbs. A satellite phone was pushed into her hand. Mitch was at her elbow.

"I have a phone, Travelers. Over."

Seconds later, she was connected to Garth, and sat more comfortably on the floor.

"I'm glad we can talk," he said.

"Thanks, Garth. My personal bodyguard is right here."

"I don't know what's going on, but the rumor has it that you discovered some trafficking and got someone arrested."

"Not altogether like this. My ex was involved, and I did however give a bit of help to the police."

"Yeah, Doug mentioned something about having to keep an eye on you. Those people on their way to you are carrying. Please, keep safe."

"I'll try. Thanks for the heads up." She disconnected.

"Keep the phone. I've got another one. I'll be in the annex. Everything is falling into place." He looked down at her, still sitting on the floor in front of the desk. "That is, if you will excuse the pun."

Brooke got to her feet and dusted herself off. "I'm not sure I like this new development."

"There'll be help arriving shortly, though you won't see them. Keep your cool. Yashee, you'll be in the dog pen."

Bewildered, Brooke tried to regain her composure.

"From the dog pen, one can see the road before you hear an engine. When I do, I'll tell the dogs to howl. So you know cars are four minutes away," Yashee said.

"Marvelous." Brooke's heart beat faster under a surge of adrenaline. It appeared that everything had been arranged for her protection without her knowing. Maybe just as well, she would have been a nervous wreck. Now she was sure that the police knew all along that these individual would be coming. She willed herself to a calm state. And Dexter? Would he be there? "What do I do when they arrive?"

"There will be several pairs of eyes on you. Act as if the guy was an ordinary visitor and we'll see how it develops. I have recording equipment set up and a camera over the porch door if you can keep him there rather than let him come into the cabin. What we hope is that he will say something incriminating. If you could talk and make him say the word diamond, that would be a bonus."

Instinctively, her eyes searched the room for hidden cameras.

Mitch smiled. "You can't see them. The wonders of modern technology."

"If you say so." Not completely reassured, Brooke glanced at her plate. If this was turning badly, she wasn't going to let the last of her meal go completely cold. She sat and ate. It didn't slow her heartbeat, especially when the dogs let out a long howl. Swiftly, she tore the protective sleeve from a surgical scalpel and slid it into her pocket. Its tiny blade could inflict alarming damage if she was forced to use it. And use it she would if necessary.

Mitch looked at his watch and vanished into the annex. The howling rose in pitch to become the signal that strangers were about to enter their yard. Being territorial, they were ready to defend their space from anyone invading. Besides, Yashee was spurring them on and they loved nothing better than howl to the wind.

At the knock on the porch door, Brooke sucked in a deep breath and, snatching up her parka, opened the cabin door, her finger touching the shaft of the cold scalpel in her pocket. She faced the man standing on the porch.

"Yes, how may I help you?"

CHAPTER FORTY

O leg Austin looked the part of the perfect corporate executive. The legs of a pinstriped suit protruded from under a long camel-hair coat. He wore no hat but sported fine leather gloves. His clothes, perhaps fashionably practical for a southern city, were absurdly inadequate for the Yukon winter. His driver stayed in the car.

Brooke determined that if she could keep him talking long enough outside in the frigid morning air, with its biting north-east wind, he would become hypothermic. That should give time for her watchers to get a good look at him and intervene. Her confidence dropped a few notches when she spotted a car stopping half way along the driveway. That must be the pair Garth called the 'less suave individuals.' Bracing herself against the cold, she stood on the porch and looked down at the man standing on the lower step. A hypothermic person, even only slightly affected, would lose their concentration quite fast. An advantage for the alert police.

"Are you Mrs. Lammers?"

"No."

"To whom do I have to honor of speaking?"

"I'm Dr. Porter."

"Does Mr. Lammers live here?"

"I wouldn't know. The cabin was empty when I bought it. That name wasn't on the title deed." Of course, she knew, and she hated lying, but at least the rest was true.

"Where can I find Mr. Lammers?"

"You'd best ask at the municipal office in Donek."

He clenched his jaw. "May I come in? It's getting cold out here."

"No. I'm sorry, but there're no Lammers here. You should ask in town."

A line of frost crystals began to form around his nostrils. "I have been told by a reliable person that Lammers used to live here."

The tremor in his hands and legs didn't escape Brooke's professional eye. "If he did, he no longer does and hasn't for a very long time."

"You see, he had in his possession something of mine."

She noticed the use of the past tense. He must know Seth was dead. What was he playing at? "You should ask him, not me."

"That doesn't appear possible."

"Why? Is he dead?" His spasmodic movements were proof she'd touched a raw nerve. "If he is dead, that means you can't get back whatever he has that you say belongs to you."

"He used to live in this cabin. The item must still be here."

"I can assure you there is absolutely nothing but my belongings here."

"My associate wasn't being straightforward."

"Sorry for that. But I repeat, there's nothing to interest you here." Was she on the right track? If she kept delaying him, would he blurt out something that could prove his involvement?

His nostrils pinched, Austin lurched forward, clumsily knocked her aside, and stepped into the cabin's large front room while she clutched at the door to regain her balance. To the right was the kitchen and to the left was the clinic area with a couple of white rolling storage cabinets. She didn't expect his move. Unsteady, he flopped onto the nearest chair, eyeing the living room with its woodstove and welcome heat. She could see his legs trembling, suggesting he wasn't even wearing thermal underwear, which more than anything marked him as an outsider. Hypothermia, a condition that set in quickly to those not properly dressed for the cold, was fast acting. She wondered where he came from and how he had managed to drive the Yukon highways clad in a city suit and black oxfords. Brooke supposed that Mitch and whoever was helping him knew what they had to do now.

Glad that no one had reloaded the stove, she went to it and opened the damper while opening the regulator wide. That meant it would soon go out, drastically cooling the cabin. As for getting him to incriminate himself, more than he already had by forcing himself into her house, she followed her instinct and remained standing. Soon, a cold draft snuck under her legs. She almost smiled. Mitch, in the annex with the door ever so slightly ajar, must have understood the hypothermic idea and would have helped by opening the outer side door. That is, unless someone else had come in. Dexter, perhaps? Yes, it had to be him. He would know about the hypothermic idea and would know why she shut off the stove. She'd given him several lessons on heating a cabin with wood, as well as the danger woodstoves pose when not used properly. That was why he'd been so helpful during the carbon monoxide poisoning incident on the Iditarod race trail.

By now, the man's teeth were chattering, but he continued speaking, trying to control it. "Lammers and I were good friends and business partners. But he cheated on me. That happens in business sometimes. He departed taking something of mine, and I would just like to get it back."

"I can only wish you good luck. You're probably right, he must have lived in the area, maybe here. I heard he died in a dog sledding accident."

He looked mildly contrite. The tremble in his voice told her hypothermia was progressing fairly fast.

"Then maybe I could search his rooms, if you don't mind."

So, he knew that when Seth lived here, he had rooms to himself! "There's no point. The police already have."

He was taken aback for a second. His being chilled didn't help his concentration. "Why would they do that?"

"We had been married, did you know?"

A look of incomprehension came over his face. He might be heading a powerful syndicate, but he knew little about its employees, if one could call them that.

"Why did the police come here?"

"They thought I had killed him. So they searched the place."

"What! I paid one of his debts so he could get credit to buy a sled. Perhaps I could take the sled in repayment?"

That sled again! So he didn't buy Campbell's explanation. "I have several sleds, but none of them belonged to him."

He shivered. "Lammers bragged it was a custom made sled, a big one. I'll buy it from you."

"It is not for sale." She carefully articulated her words and almost laughed at the notion of this puny man, who probably could not tackle a one-mile hike, wanting to buy a heavy-duty sled that required a full team of powerful sled dogs to pull.

Annoyance spread over his face, but his words were soft. "Look, I'm a business man. I came all the way here to find the package that Lammers stole from me. I know he hid it in the sled."

"I use that sled every day, and I can assure you it is totally empty." That was no lie.

"As I said, I'm a businessman. It must be tough making a living around here. If you'd agree to hand over the package, I'd give you a generous cut. "

Now he's talking about a cut! Anyone else would have mentioned a reward. "Package of what?" she had to get him to utter the word 'diamonds.'

He assumed his earlier air of superiority, although by now he was shivering uncontrollably. His nostrils were getting narrower and his words were becoming slurred. The sound of his teeth chattering gave her some satisfaction. She herself wasn't feeling very warm, but she had her parka on and her padded pants and was at no risk of hypothermia.

"It's a package of samples, er, soil samples, rocks. Prospecting, you know."

So he knew the package was raw diamonds. If he wasn't going to utter the magic word, she had to provoke him. "You mean a package of diamonds?"

He jumped from his chair. "What? You know! Then where are they?" He paused for a second. "How do you know about them?"

She was now out of her comfort zone and decided to risk all. "How do I know? Lammers and Campbell were not exactly discreet about what they said. The whole town knows."

All pretense of politeness fell away. His voice turned ugly. "I want the package back now! The diamonds are mine. Hand them over. Enough stupid talk."

"I don't have them and have not the slighted idea where they could be." She pointed to the annex. "That was his living quarters."

"Move out of my way!" He swung his left arm to push her aside.

Scared that he was going to hit her, her fist brandishing the scalpel lunged forward. The small blade pierced his gloved hand. He let out a scream as the sharp point cut through the leather glove and sank into the flesh beneath. She saw a trickle of blood run down under his shirt cuff.

He drew back his wounded hand against his chest. He glowered at her. "You bitch!"

Brooke shrank back. She waited to see what he would do next and raised the scalpel to protect herself.

At that precise moment, the annex door burst open and slammed back against the wall. Out of the corner of her eye, she saw two burly men rush forward. Her eyes widened.

Dexter let out a yell. "Police! Don't move."

She took a step back. But before she understood quite what was happening, Austin had made a grab for her. He missed. In a blur of motion, she found herself facing the muzzle of a pistol. Her heart pounded against her ribs. Stay calm! Don't panic! she told herself. The scene of frenzied action changed as everyone froze. No one made a move.

"Drop that gun, Austin!"

With the men, a blast of cold air had invaded the cabin. Austin made no reply. What could she do? Nothing in her training or past life had prepared her for such a scenario. Her mind went blank. Fear was preventing her rational brain from working. Like the hapless heroine of a detective movie, she absurdly speculated about where the bullet would hit. The head, no, she was as tall as her assailant. The torso, then. Gunshot wound to the chest. That was how the police report would read.

She became aware of Dexter's steady voice.

"... You're only a two-bit player, Austin. Do you really want to take the fall for your boss? I doubt it. That guy Peetera doesn't care about life, certainly not yours. You fail, so you fall. Add a firearms offence to the rap sheet and you'll get a lot of extra years. You can help yourself by dropping that pistol right now. We can talk..."

A buzz in her ears alerted Brooke to a change in her body. *I'm not going to faint.* She breathed in deeply. The ringing in her ears faded. A strange, serene calm came over her. Thoughts ran through her mind. Is that what hostages feel? Do they suddenly give themselves over to fate and hope nothing will happen? After all, the gunman is just a human being. He has a mother. He wouldn't shoot women, right? No, wrong. They have no qualms about shooting women and children or anyone else. A hysterical laugh bubbled in her throat, but she realized what it was doing to her. *I mustn't interfere with the speaker. He's the negotiator. Hostage negotiator. I am the hostage. Yes, negotiators are successful. Everything will be alright.*

She took another deep breath. That settled her nerves, but she couldn't switch off her mind. What did soldiers experience when they went into battle? She supposed the same as what she was feeling right now? Soldiers faced death again and again, yet they kept going back to the frontline. Was there a technique to tamp down the fear a person experiences in the face of the danger that was coming at them? Why would someone join the army knowing it might mean facing potential death? Why did they join the police? Silly question. Because there were a lot of bad men out there, like this man holding a pistol to her ribs. Soldiers went to war to protect the innocent. Police put their lives on the line to prevent aggressors from terrorizing women and children. To prevent drugs from killing more youths.

She glanced down and focused her eyes on the black object in the man's hand. Alarm spread over her. There was a perceptible tremor in the hand holding the pistol. His body was so cold, he had no reserve left. He was at the point where the shivering was about to become uncontrollable. The firearm could go off at any moment. She closed her eyes. Until this moment, she'd never thought about her own mortality. Not even when her beloved father drowned after his sailboat was caught in a freak storm, so soon after her mother had lost her battle against cancer.

A shout from outside the cabin swept her thoughts away. Her body stiffened into a new state of alertness. Shots rang out. She caught the frightened look in Oleg Austin's eyes as he half-turned toward the door.

At that point, noise and movement seemed to merge. Her brain didn't register the shot fired from the pistol, only Dexter jumping on her. She landed hard, Dexter on top of her. Her eyes followed Mitch flying across the room. Oleg Austin was face down on the floor before she could take her next breath. She scrambled to her knees.

"Dexter!"

He didn't move. Blood seeped through his fleece jacket. He coughed and coughed again. He coughed blood. Numb with shock, yet immediately in professional mode, she palpated his chest toward the shoulder where the blood seemed to come from. Something was broken. She unzipped his jacket and reached for her scalpel to cut the material when a pair of sewing scissors was thrust under her nose. Without losing a second, she cut away the jacket and woolen shirt. She grimaced at the sight of a bone protruding through his thermal undershirt. Yashee was kneeling on the other side, holding open her veterinary bag. Dexter was unresponsive, his breathing hard, and a gurgling sound coming from his throat.

"Dexter! Come on, wake up! I love you! Come back to me!" She finished cutting away the clothing to expose the wound.

"He took the bullet for me. I have to see where it came out." A pair of hands slipped under his ribcage.

No exit wound. "Beretta Pico," a voice said.

That funny name must be the firearm name. Pico, small, her mind recalled. She concentrated. "The bullet hit the lung. The lung is collapsing. Help me turn him on his side."

"But that's his wounded side."

"Yes, for the lung to fall open and at the same time force the air out of the cavity between the lung and the thorax. I must stop the air coming in by the hole between the lung and the rib cage." Yashee was handing her a spray vial. A glance to ensure it was the antiseptic, and she sprayed the wound. She grabbed a waterproof dressing and taped three and a half sides of it to seal the bullet hole and prevent any more air entering the chest cavity.

"You didn't finish taping the dressing," Yashee murmured.

Her voice barely penetrated Brooke's hearing through the commotion in the room and outside with dogs howling and barking, men's voices yelling and pounding noises.

"He breathes with his other lung. When it fills, it puts pressure on the chest cavity and the unwanted air escapes through the side of the dressing that is not taped."

While talking, she inserted an IV in his arm. "A bag of human plasma."

Her friend rushed to the fridge and got the plasma out. "So, you did get some."

"After Ethan's emergency, yes."

"Dog plasma is good, too."

Brooke nodded.

"I called the Star," Mitch said. "The chopper is on its way."

Brooke suddenly realized everything had gone quiet. Dexter's eyelids flickered. She leaned over.

"Dexter! Stay with me."

"D'you mean it? Ouch..!" He coughed more blood. His eyelids closed, but he fought to keep them open.

"Don't try to move. Everything's under control. We're getting you to the hospital." She leaned over a little more for her lips to touch his. "I love you."

Brooke became aware of Jimmy's presence.

"I take care of the dogs," he said.

She lifted her head. She hadn't heard the helicopter, the rush of people. The paramedics were crouching next to her. "You did a good job yet again, Dr. Porter."

She let out a half-laugh of relief. "Thanks, Nathan. Call me Brooke."

The second paramedic smiled. "And I'm still Andrea, you know, the emergency nurse with the safety pins."

The familiar voices soothed Brooke. Everything was going to be alright. "Shot in the chest and a collapsed lung, as far as I can tell. A broken rib, too. Maybe it pierced the lung. The bullet hit him as he was coming down on top of me to protect me."

Nathan was already at work. "The bullet appears to have followed a vertical trajectory. How many shots?"

"Just one, as far as I remember. Mind you, everything was chaos for a while."

He took a large-bore needle and inserted it between two ribs. Air escaped. "Good so far."

Andrea had a pressure cuff on Dexter's arm. "Pressure unstable."

Fear spread over Brooke's face. "He's bleeding internally."

Nathan took the vial Andrea held out and connected it to the IV.

Brooke leaned in. "Antifibrinolytic?" She had to ask and check as a haunted image surged behind her eyelids.

"Right. Aprotinin. That should help slow down the hemorrhage. Now we need strong hands to ease Dexter onto the gurney."

Five pairs of hands moved Dexter onto the emergency gurney. Brooke watched as Nathan put a cervical collar on Dexter to prevent undue movement. Andrea wrapped him in a survival blanket covered by a wool blanket before tightening the straps. Brooke leaped to her feet and looked around for her purse. Yashee was already there holding it out to her. "You go. I take care here. I prepare the wedding."

A laugh alleviated the tension that had gripped her. Brooke gave her friend a hug and ran to the chopper, sitting like a friendly mammoth bird in the middle of her yard. She hardly saw the cars and trucks and the people crowding around. She stopped in her track when she saw Jimmy carrying the inert body of Little Raven, the gentle dog to whom she promised a permanent home at Doghaven.

Jimmy motioned with his chin. "Stray bullet. Go. I take care."

Her heart in her mouth, she had to choose between her dog and Dexter. He was in good hands. But so was Little Raven unless... No, if anyone could save her, Jimmy with his ancestral skills would be able to. But a bullet needed a surgical intervention. In a flash, she knew this was just the situation that would arise if she qualified as a medical doctor. The choice to be made. Two hands pushed at her shoulders. Yashee's voice in her ears, "Go! Now! She'll be okay."

With a spurt of speed that defied her state of exhaustion, she made it to the helicopter.

Nathan was securing an oxygen mask on the patient. Brooke squeezed herself between the pilot's seat and the gurney. Her hand lightly caressed Dexter's forehead. She brushed back his hair and willed the helicopter to fly faster. Close to his ear, she whispered again and again, "Stay with me, Dexter. I love you. It's okay. Everything's going to be okay. You can go away to your job. I'll wait. Hang on. You're going to make it."

She was vaguely aware of Nathan on the radio describing the wound to a doctor at the hospital. "GSW... yes... hemorrhaging... pneumothorax... yes."

Alarm blew through her. GSW? What was that? Her mind went blank. Then her brain kicked in, of course, the abbreviation for gunshot wound. Fear and anxiety prevented her from relaxing. Silently, she talked to herself the way she would to someone in need of reassurance. Think of life. Imagine grandiose mountains. Listen to the sound of tumbling glacial streams. Think of love. It worked. Calm returned to her mind and her breathing steadied.

The helicopter made a smooth touchdown on the hospital's helipad. A team was waiting behind the glass doors and rushed forward with a gurney. In no time, Dexter was transferred and whisked straight to the operating room. For Brooke, the drama was over. The long wait had begun.

She phoned Stephanie.

Chapter Forty-One

In the hushed atmosphere of the OR waiting room, Brooke sat, nervously exhausted. "He threw himself in front of me. It should have been me that got hit."

"I'm glad you didn't. Dr. Fisher is a splendid surgeon. He'll save Dexter. Trust him."

"It's taking such a long time."

Stephanie put her arm around her friend's shoulders. "Not all gunshot wounds are fatal."

"But it nicked the artery. He bled to death."

"No, he didn't."

The surgeon wearing scrubs came out of the operating room. "Just to let you know, Mr. Weiman is out of danger. I extracted the bullet. He received a transfusion and everything will be fine. Now, a long recovery is in store for him."

"You know he saved my life by stopping the bullet for me?"

"I've been told that." He gave a wide smile. "I also hear there's a wedding in the works?"

"If he proposes, yes." For the first time, she, too, was smiling.

Dr. Thompson joined them. "I assisted Dr. Fisher. I'm happy for you, Dr. Porter. Now, how about taking up where you left off and finishing your qualifications? Your skilled action saved Mr. Weiman's life."

She sucked on her lips. "I'm a vet and quite happy being one."

David Fisher beamed at her. "The Donek area will be left without medical care when Janice Miller marries Dr. Lawrence. He's finishing his internship in the spring."

Somewhat inelegantly, Brooke opened her mouth and closed it again. "I heard the rumors, but didn't know she'd be leaving the community."

"Anyhow, think about it. I'll call you when you can go and see Dexter."

"Thank you, Dr. Fisher."

After he left, Stephanie hugged Brooke. "Now you have a duty to fulfill. You have to qualify."

"But it would take at least a couple of years. And I don't want to abandon my veterinary practice."

"Let's be brutally honest, my friend. There really isn't enough demand in the area for your vet services. And there's maybe not enough work for a full-time family physician. Is there no way to combine the two? Combining the jobs would benefit everyone."

"I'm afraid not. It could lead to tragic consequences and put an enormous strain on the individual involved. Imagine if I were called out to tend to an injured sled dog and at the same time I receive a call that a person is in need of emergency care. How do I choose between them?"

"Officially qualified or not, you're doing that already. You're the first person in the district to respond to a human in distress. I'm thinking of Chris and her baby."

"Yes, but no animal needed my urgent care. Right now, my main concern is Dexter. I'm also worried about my poor dog. In the few moments of chaos at the cabin, one of my new rescues was shot. She's such a small thing. I chose to come with Dexter. Yet, in truth, he didn't need me. He is in the hands of the best medical people you could wish for. But my dog..."

"But Jimmy is taking care of her."

After a silence punctuated by sobs, Brooke blew her nose and shook herself. "I'm staying a vet. We'll manage to recruit another nurse practitioner. There are always young qualified people looking for a job who are willing to come to rural communities like ours. Good nurses too. Resourceful types who can handle any situation you can throw at them. They'll travel, too. Not everyone comes into town, even if they do need medical care. Sometimes, those living in remote cabins along the creeks can't leave their animals to seek attention in town. The practitioner's job is to go to them."

"I see your point. Yet, if you're a fully qualified physician, the practitioner would be able to call on you when the situation is beyond her capacities."

Brooke shrugged. "Janice did just that. And I gave her the only advice I could."

"Which was?"

"To call the doctor's help line."

"With the unreliable internet you have and the crappy cell coverage?"

Brooked sighed. "It's fine in town. It's a moot point, anyway. I'm about to lose my house to the bank. Then I have to find the money to pay the lawyers. How could I afford the med school fees and pay rent to upgrade anything?"

"No rent, at least. You'd stay with me. The kids would be so inspired! To them, you walk on air."

"On air, not water?"

"As my six-year-old pointedly remarked, water is frozen much of the time. Anyone can walk on water. It takes someone special to walk on air."

They shared a laugh.

"Seriously, get married to Dexter and he'll help you keep the house."

"Absolutely not!"

"But I know he'd want to help."

Brooke shook her head. "I'm not getting married simply in order that my debts can be paid. Actually, the town is setting up a kind of trust fund under which my entire property becomes a wildlife rehabilitation center, a non-profit organization. That's wonderful, but it doesn't change the fact that the scuzzball of a man who used to be my husband took a hefty mortgage on the place and that it has to be repaid. It's just a way on paper to help me get by. It's unlikely that the bank will see it that way."

The conversation was interrupted by a young nurse. "Mr. Weiman has been moved to the intensive care unit. He's awake. You may visit for a few minutes."

Brooke almost knocked over the nurse in her haste. Dr. Fisher was with Dexter. "You'll be in ICU until I'm satisfied that your levels are all where I want them to be. Don't argue. Even when you get discharged, you won't be able to do anything strenuous for the next three months. That's how long it'll take for your lung to recover its shape and full function."

Brooke touched the doctor's arm. "I'll make sure your orders are obeyed."

Fisher squeezed her shoulder and walked to the door. "I'm confident you will. Only two minutes. I don't need to tell you why."

"Brooke..."

She pressed Dexter's hand. "I'm right here."

"Tell me again."

His breath was short through the oxygen mask. She was relieved he hadn't been intubated and could breathe on his own. "Thank you for saving my life. I'll never say it enough."

"That's not quite what I want to hear."

"Oh... you mean you want me to say I love you?"

"Louder. I didn't hear it."

"I love you. And I'll never get tired of saying it."

"Nor me hearing it. I love you, too." His eyelids fluttered.

"I'll be back." Mindful of the monitoring wires and tubes, she placed a kiss on his forehead and tiptoed out to find Stephanie waiting alongside Mitch.

She looked at her friends. "You two go and have lunch. I'm going to donate blood."

They walked the blood donor lab. Mitch made to roll up his sleeve. "I will too." Stephanie raised her hand. "Woah, there! I'm not going to stand here on my own. They can probably use my platelets too, unless they find my blood is full of guinea pig, cat and parrot cells."

The lab staff exploded with laughter. Half an hour later, they were released.

"John texted me that the kids decided we were all to meet at Antoinette's for dinner. You too, Mr. Bodyguard."

"Mitch."

"Okay, Mitch. You come too."

The fatigue, the fear, the adrenaline all suddenly seemed to drain from Brooke's body. She shook. "Let's hurry, I'm starving!"

CHAPTER FORTY-TWO

"Nice of you to drive me, Mitch. Now that the boss of the syndicate has been eliminated, or was he the underboss, whatever difference that makes, there are no more threats on my life. Do I assume you'll be getting another assignment, which will take you to the other end of the country?"

"He was only one of the underbosses. True, it's over as far as you're concerned. With Lammers and Campbell dead, no one is going to try the mushing trick——"

Brooke jumped up in her seat. "What do you mean, Campbell dead?"

"Of course, you've been extra busy this past little while. You didn't hear. When the hospital declared he could go home, he was transferred to the prison infirmary for his protection. It didn't save him."

After a short silence, Brooke gave a groan. "He didn't deserve to die. He was in above his head, caught up in someone else's nefarious doings."

"Possibly."

"For you cops, a hood is a criminal and whether he lives or dies, it's all the same."

Mitch checked the rearview mirror before replying. "No, it isn't quite like that. We care greatly about people or else we wouldn't be in this line of work. We actually do help some of these offenders."

"Like paying them to become informants."

A quiet laugh was his only response.

"Isn't that true?"

"Again, not entirely. Some former offenders go through rehabilitation programs and do well. They go back into society and are never heard of again. Which is what we want. For others, it doesn't work because of their personality, temperament and general attitude to life. Those are the people we'd like to put in a dungeon and throw away the key. Then there are those in between, the types who don't fit in society and who agree to work with us. Informants help keep ordinary citizens safer, as they render an invaluable service to us. Police alone can't thwart criminal activity. With informants' help, we can."

"Now that you explained it, I realize I didn't see the whole picture."

They arrived at Brooke's cabin. She ran to the dog pens and hugged every one of the happy dogs. Little Raven was missing. Her heart tightened. Hope soared anew as she glanced at the board and saw her dog's name. Jimmy would have removed it if the poor animal hadn't survived. She smiled at Mitch. "Coming in for some lunch?"

"With pleasure."

Brooke opened the front door. A residual fear washed over her. Her being held at gunpoint flashed through her head, along with the image of Dexter slumping forward, spilling blood. All traces of that had vanished. The house was warm and inviting. An aroma of coffee mingled with the rich cooking smell of a stew in a cast-iron pot on the stove. As if by magic, the table was set for three. The tension eased and joy took its place. "Yashee, *gunalshéeh.*" But her friend's eyes were on Mitch. Brooke looked at him to see his vanishing smile.

"It smells lovely. I'm famished," he said.

Gugàn ran and threw himself at Mitch, who picked him up and threw him in the air. "You're back."

"Of course. I told you I would. I always keep my word."

The undercurrents between Yashee and Mitch became palpable. A large smile spread across Brooke's face, but she chose to remain quiet. Let them enjoy whatever secret they were hiding.

With a crooked finger, Yashee beckoned Brooke across to the cabin's veterinary corner. There on a thick blanket, Little Raven lay half asleep with her nose between her paws. On seeing Brooke, she whimpered and stood up on shaky legs. Brooke dropped to her knees, holding her arms out. "Sweet darling, you made it!"

The dog's legs gave out when she placed her head in Brooke's lap. Brooke gave the dog a long hug. "If you have no objection, Little Raven, I'm adopting you. You'll stay here with me forever and you'll have house privilege."

After a few wet kisses, the young female made herself comfortable again and watched Brooke go to the table.

"Now that the job is finished, will you get a few days off?" Brooke asked Mitch.

They sat down for supper. "Not really, but until I get the word, I'm still keeping an eye on you."

"Surely, I don't need a twenty-four hours watch now."

"No, I will only be close at hand should something happen." He stood and retrieved a phone from his parka pocket. "Satellite. This is your emergency button."

"And you can find me anywhere?"

He nodded.

She slapped her forehead. "GPS, of course."

"Though when you drive to the Whitehorse Hospital, I'll be driving with you."

"Fair enough."

Chapter Forty-Three

The next morning, Brooke drove to the veterinary clinic in Donek. Her amazement knew no bounds when she saw Lara come out of the examining room.

"I was at a loose end when I got a call that you would be busy for a while."

A weight was taken off Brooke's shoulders. "Thank you. But you know I can't pay you more than what you take in from the practice."

Erin led Brooke to the office. "We thought of something. Tell her, Lara."

"I'm pretty good at grooming. We had six dogs at home. Long-haired mutts that needed constant grooming. If you think it's a good idea, we could offer grooming services. Some clients are driving all the way to Whitehorse to get their little dogs primped and shampooed. They want their pooches beautified."

Brooke had to laugh. "Beautified, that's one way of putting it. But you're right. For some dogs, not to mention their owners, it's essential they get a haircut and a pedicure. I guess we could set up a grooming salon in the spare room."

"I told Lara we've been keeping the door closed because the radiators are only turned on one degree above freezing."

Brooke leaned back, looking at Lara. "You could set up a practice elsewhere where you'd get full wages for your work."

A blush crept into Lara's cheeks. "Only, I... I like it here."

A quiet laugh from Erin drew Brooke's attention. "Maybe I should explain that Lara has a good reason for wanting to stay. A certain young gentleman has received his permanent certification as an RCMP auxiliary constable. He has also been elected chief of the firefighter brigade. On top of all that, he has a thriving business manufacturing top of the line dog sleds."

"Doug!" She recalled he had attended the Mounties school in Regina and a special session for northern members of the Force. "I guess congratulations are in order."

"Thanks. Donek is growing. I believe it'll work."

Brooke gave the young woman a hug. The door opened, and a client entered the clinic. It was back to work for everyone.

***

Brooke thanked Mitch at the hospital entrance. She knew why Dr. Thompson wanted her to come with him on his rounds. He was going to press her to finish the last step to become fully qualified. Although tempted, the decision not to accept was pushing strongly at her mind.

"You had almost finished your residency, correct?"

"I had a mere four more weeks left."

They stopped and talked to a patient and got a smile from him.

"Do I remember correctly that you had won the NSERC postgraduate scholarship to go into surgery?"

He must have looked into her old file with the College of Physicians and Surgeons, where she had already made an application. She pursed her lips. "That's correct. Before you ask, I was to sit the Medical Council of Canada Qualifying Examination, Part One, but didn't."

"You have the ability to take both parts in succession. It will take you less than a year to prepare. I recall how brilliant you were at diagnosis."

She sighed and looked somewhere in a distant place beyond the walls of the hospital. "I had years of experience when taking care of my mother. But no, I'm not going back and sit the exams. My life has moved on. I'm a vet and I care for animals. Of course, I'll help people if faced with an emergency, but will not take on responsibility for their general health. If I did, there would be no time left for the dogs and other animals that I so much love."

"I think I can understand. As long as you're not acting out of fear of the unknown. Or the fear of making another mistake."

"I am pretty sure I am not. I've come to believe that veterinary work is as much a noble calling as medical practice, even if we don't swear the Hippocratic oath."

While he chatted with an elderly patient, Brooke let her mind mull over his words. When they left the ward, she turned to him. "I appreciate what you are doing to help me. I don't fear making a mistake. At least no more than any doctor confronted with a difficult diagnosis. When I was looking into the muzzle of that man's pistol, I realized what life is really about. Regrets, past injustices, are just a moment in time. For me, they were a heavy baggage that I carried around. Unnecessary baggage that threatened to suffocate me. I realized at that moment that if I survived, I would live my life to the fullest. The past is really only a teaching tool that points to the future."

"Well said."

They arrived at the door of Dexter's room. George Thompson put his hand on her shoulder and turned to face her. "You're a brave woman and a splendid doctor. I respect your decision. What I will do is make sure you get an advanced paramedic kit. You and I will talk to the Medical Council to have you licensed in advanced critical care, with no demands for additional training."

Emotion choked in her throat. "Thank you, George." She swallowed hard. Something like what he proposed would end the need to improvise or use veterinary products to help people in urgent need, the way she had for little Ethan. As an advanced critical care paramedic, she could intervene if and when called upon in an emergency or just urgent care. As for routine medical matters, those she could leave in the capable hands of the nurse practitioner. Outside of those situations, she would remain, as always, the regional vet. Also, now that Lara was going to live in the community, she would never have to choose between an animal or a human emergency. A smile hovered over her lips.

The accumulated weight of the years she'd spent hungering after what could have been fell from her shoulders. Of course, as a fully licensed medical doctor, all the debts her late husband had accumulated would be quickly repaid, but that was a different issue, not one she was allowing to color her decision. She pushed open Dexter's door.

Dexter was sitting propped up with pillows. He was smiling at Dr. Thompson.

"Well, doc. When can I go home?"

Dr. Thompson laughed. "Do you have any other words in your vocabulary? That's all we hear from you from morn till night."

Brooke leaned over and gave Dexter a light kiss.

"See what you're keeping me from, doctor?"

"Seriously, Dexter. You were super lucky. The bullet chewed up the tissues, but it could have been a lot worse. The latest x-rays show much improvement, but you're not out of the woods yet. There's healing taking place, but that rib has not fully knitted yet."

"You don't trust me to sit in bed at home."

George threw a quick glance at Brooke, whose cheeks were becoming pink. He adopted a jocular tone. "I have good reasons."

With that, the doctor left them alone.

"I want to ask you to marry me, but I can't get down on my knee."

"Silly, you don't need to."

"I'm kneeling virtually. Can you picture it?"

"Yes, I can."

"Will you marry me?"

"Yes, of course."

He beamed. "I'm feeling a hundred percent better already."

"You must understand I'm not marrying you because you saved my life. That would be pure sentimentality."

"Just a moment. Just who saved whose life? I was told it was you that saved my life."

"I only gave you first aid."

"Nah, that's not what the doctors and nurses said. Are you going to finish your medical studies to get licensed?"

Her smile was confident. "No. I am a veterinarian and I will administer first aid to anyone who needs it, and I hope it'll never be you again."

He strangled his laugh. "I can't laugh. My side hurts."

Noon came all too soon, and Brooke had to leave. Mitch was waiting for her, with his phone to his ear. "Okay, I'll tell her."

"You tell me what?"

"Dex got a call seconds after you left. You met Toledo? Right?"

"Not exactly. I met the results of his visits to Campbell."

He inclined his head, half-amused. "Ha! The busted skull. Toledo has been arrested and has admitted to killing Seth Lammers."

"A low-life killing another low-life. All that on my front doorstep, so to speak. I hope he gets what's coming to him. I would opt for life without parole. I'm drained of emotion."

"The murder weapon was a Mauser 98."

Shock stopped her in her tracks. She exhaled a long breath. "My late husband owned such a rifle. It was stolen from him."

"I know. The thief used the very same rifle to kill Lammers."

Unable to speak further, Brooke stared wide-eyed at Mitch.

"Dexter believes Campbell showed Toledo where to meet Lammers on the trail. Toledo was smart enough to sell the rifle to Campbell. Like that, he'd be in the clear if the police traced it and Campbell would take the fall."

"Did they ever find the casing?"

"No, but the conservation officers have taken it as a personal challenge to find it. They found and marked tracks, two tracks almost on top of each other, like someone following another on snowshoes."

Brooked tilted her head back to look up at Mitch's face. "When Conrad and Byron get annoyed by poachers, they're as tenacious as a pair of bulldogs. They don't let go. Right now, they are pissed off that a murder happened in their territory. They'll find that casing with enough DNA left on it to prove Toledo was the one holding the rifle."

On those words, they drove back to Agate Rock.

Chapter Forty-Four

S pring arrived in the Yukon's creeks and valleys. It arrived too early, much earlier than usual. That was the consensus among the inhabitants of Agate Creek. Mud was the subject of every conversation. Brooke relished this time of year, mud notwithstanding. It was the time of renewal, of births, new shoots and the return of thousands of migrating birds.

With Toledo behind bars, the threat to Brooke's life was no longer an issue, and Mitch had to take his leave. Though he planned to be back to make a life with Yashee.

"I'm so happy for you both, Yashee. When will he be back?"

"As soon as he gets his transfer from undercover work to regular officer duties. It has been decided that Donek was growing and was in need of a permanent RCMP detachment."

"Wonderful."

"And when is Weiman coming home?"

A smile danced on Brooke's lips. "Tomorrow." Her phone buzzed at that moment. "It's Byron from Fletcher Creek."

With a nod, Yashee went to attend to her Airbnb clients.

—— To give you a head-up, a pregnant moose has been hit by a car. Conrad thinks she has a broken back tibia. She's in shock. We sedated her and got her on the trailer and are driving to your place.

"Was she agitated?"

—— No, rather lethargic, docile. That's what worries me.

"What about the fetus?"

—— It appears to be alive.

"Go straight to the enclosure near the creek. I'll meet you there."

—— Half an hour.

Brooke gathered some bio-degradable bandages. Not that she thought she could repair a broken leg. Perhaps it was a clean, straight break, in which case it would heal as long as the animal didn't put weight on it. She also packed a bottle of Phenytoin-pentobarbital, as she feared she might have to put the animal out of its misery. Collisions rarely resulted in good outcomes for the wildlife. If only drivers would slow down in the areas marked as deer or other animal crossings, there wouldn't be so much carnage. People got hurt too. She eyed her Marlin. The wildlife officers would have their rifles. Sometimes a clean shot was a kinder death. The last thing she did was to pull on a clean overall, whose smell she hoped would be neutral for the animal she was going to attend to since she only used a plant-based detergent made by a woman in Donek.

Ten minutes later, she surveyed the one-acre enclosure built by volunteers. It included part of the creek. Plenty of willows, grasses and trees made for an ideal moose habitat. She slid open the two panels that acted as gates.

The Yukon Wildlife Service truck with its trailer arrived. It turned and backed into the enclosure. Conrad and Byron jumped out, followed by four robust men. The moose, secured in a sling, lifted her head and Brooke took note of her bright eyes before loosening a strap to look at the leg. To her relief, the break was a closed one. Now came the dangerous moment. She leaned over and ran a light finger along the lower leg. A gritty sensation under her fingers confirmed Conrad's assumption. That was where the leg was broken. The fibula must also be cracked, but she couldn't feel it.

The men stayed well away from the moose so it wouldn't get anxious, as the sedative was soon going to wear off. The bio-degradable bandage made of boiled, crushed plants soaked in beeswax had been Jimmy's idea. It was both pliable and strong. It wrapped up around the leg neatly. Brooke melted the end of the bandage with a lighter and pressed it down to mesh with itself. It wouldn't move now. In three or four weeks, the bandage would disintegrate, by which time the bone should have repaired sufficiently for the moose to walk on it. The animal still wasn't reacting. Brooke released the other straps and palpated the fetus, still high into the mother's abdominal cavity. She slid her stethoscope over it and smiled when hearing a strong heartbeat.

At her signal, Conrad approached on tiptoes. "Verdict?"

"You were right. Cracked tibia, still aligned. Which is good. The baby's heartbeat is strong. It has a good chance of survival."

"Let's take her out of the trailer. You drive." He motioned to the helpers.

The men seized the handles of the sling, lifted the six-hundred pound animal, while Brooke eased the truck and trailer some distance away. With infinite care, the men lowered the moose to the ground and left it sprawled on the sling. They closed the gate panels and stood behind the trailer to watch whether the moose was going to stand up. Time ticked away.

Conrad tugged on Brooke's sleeve, keeping his voice to a whisper. "By the way, you'll be interested to learn we found the empty casing."

"No way! I knew you would keep trying."

"We pretty well had narrowed the area down to a few square yards. Don't tell the Mounties, but Byron hitched up a couple of dogs and we reenacted the scene a dozen times over in slow motion, much slower than the speed Lammers would have been traveling with sixteen dogs."

"You make a pair of great detectives!"

"Maybe, but just a moment, we are not cops." He strongly emphasized the negation.

"No, you aren't. Forgive me."

"Ah, love you, Brooke. What helped too was that the snow was beginning to disappear with the warmer spring air."

"And did they find any DNA on it?"

"Lots. All of it Toledo's."

The moose was now alert, with its head up. The expectant mother warily eyed the humans who had rescued her. At long last, she made a couple of feeble attempts to stand. On the third, she succeeded and stood to her impressive height, with her injured leg lifted off the ground. She hobbled on her three good legs to the creek, where she took a long drink.

Conrad and Byron slipped into the enclosure and dragged the sling out.

"I won't be there tomorrow to check on the moose. You can park at my place and walk to the enclosure. The least engine noise she hears, the better," Brooke said.

"Is Dexter coming home tomorrow?" Byron asked.

Brooke could not conceal her excitement. "Yes, he is."

They all gave a thumbs-up and clambered into the Conservation truck.

Chapter Forty-Five

B rooke was up early on the day she would bring Dexter home. Thrilled at the prospect, yet still with some lingering doubt over what she was committing herself to, she fired up the Jeep, only to notice the gas gauge was reading close to empty. On the road, she turned toward Agate and waved at the school bus as it went past, with Gugàn putting both hands to the window. After filling up at Elmer's garage, she got back on the road. As she drove close to her driveway, she spotted a car turning in. She wondered whether Yashee was at the cabin, but she better investigate in case someone had a pet in distress.

A young woman, tears streaming on her face, was standing in the yard when Brooked pulled in.

"May I help you?"

The young woman sniffed and brushed her tears off. "I'm sorry I get emotional. I hit a moose yesterday. The wildlife people took it away. They told me you were a vet. I... want to know if they shot the moose. Because that's what they do when wildlife is injured." Another flow of tears wetted her cheeks.

"Let me assure you the mama moose is alive and well. She has a fractured limb, but I've treated it and, with luck, it should heal up properly."

The woman's eyes opened wide. "It's not going to die?"

A smile spread over Brooke's face. It wasn't often that a driver took the trouble to find out about wildlife involved in a road collision. "No, she's not going to die. She has a very good chance of a full recovery. We've put her in a large enclosure where she can heal without being bothered by other animals." Spontaneously Brooke asked. "Do you want to see her? No guarantee, as she could be hidden in the trees at the other end of the enclosure. We can at least go and take a look."

"Please. I'm Sylvie."

"Brooke." She glanced at Sylvie's feet. "It's a ten-minute walk on a rough trail."

"My running sneakers will do. I'm fine."

They set out, chatting along the way, until Brooke lifted her finger to her lips. The enclosure came into view. Broke directed Sylvie to the viewing spot, a low rise behind a clump of wild roses full of buds. The moose was coming from the creek, limping on three legs, but walking with assurance. Brooke saw with satisfaction that the bio-degradable splint was still in place. The moose browsed for a moment before ambling farther away. The two women retraced their steps.

"That was wonderful! I've never seen such a big animal so close... that is until it towered in front of my car. I couldn't avoid hitting it."

"This female is pregnant. I'll let her have her calf here as long as she's calm. She doesn't appear to be stressed, even though I'm quite sure she has discovered she's fenced in for the time being."

"How long before her leg heals?"

"About eight weeks. In time for her to deliver her calf. I have hopes for her. She's young, probably just over two years, so that must be her first baby. Not all big animals' broken bones heal and unfortunately, some die."

Sylvie was thoughtful. "I'm going to be twice as careful now when I drive. Thank you so much for letting me see the moose. And thank your for showing such compassion for a wild thing."

The woman left and Brooke went to the Jeep just as Yashee came out of the cabin.

"I will make supper for your return."

"You don't have to. You must be busy."

"Early Sun! You are not going to open a can of baked beans for Weiman's first day back home! Now go, you're late."

With a wave, Brooke put the Jeep in gear and drove down to the road. There was a song in her heart, and she surprised herself by singing aloud. When she arrived at the hospital, she stopped in front of the entrance, in the parking space reserved for those picking up discharged patients.

A nurse spotted Brooke heading down the hallway leading to Dexter's room. She poked her head into his room and gave a shout of triumph. "Get ready, she's here!"

Eileen and Dr. Thompson were chatting with their patient, who was seated in a wheelchair.

Dr. Lewis gave her a mock frown. "What took you so long to get here?"

In a flash, Brooke realized that if Dexter's job would take him away at odd times, hers was no different, with its missed suppers and midnight calls. She smiled. "Sorry. You can chalk the delay up to the need to care for a moose with a broken leg."

After the story was told, Brooke emphasized how important it had been for the young woman's state of mind to see the injured moose making a recovery. George pulled Brooke aside. "Can you spend three days to come and prepare for the exam? You'll pass with ease."

"Absolutely. Lara, my locum when I went to the Iditarod, is back... she has a heart condition."

"Heart condition?"

"Yes, a romantic heart condition, not one that you can treat."

He gave a laugh. "Here is the Equipment Standards booklet, the Clinical Practice Guidelines and the Program Skills Reference Manual. Not that you need the last two but they have to be in your kit. I checked myself that it's complete. I'll go and get it while you take Dexter out."

"I don't know how to thank you."

"No need for thanks. I'm grateful for your efforts. When patients arrive here, the outcome is often touch and go unless they have received critical care in the field. If Dexter hadn't received that level of care before the paramedics got to him..."

Their eyes locked. They read the same thought in each other's regard. He may not have survived the wait for the helicopter.

A nurse wheeled out a Dexter already champing at the bit.

"I can walk!"

"It's a hospital rule, Mr. Weiman. We don't want you falling on your way to the door. It wouldn't reflect well on the hospital."

His complaint was replaced by a smile when Brooke put her hand on his shoulder.

"Did they feed you at the hospital?"

"I couldn't eat."

"So, you won't mind if we grab a sandwich chez Antoinette?"

"We could even sit inside to eat. I need to reconnect with the outside world. And I have another tidbit of news for you."

"Tell me."

"That stone you pointed out was different?"

"The granite?"

"Right, it is a beryl, an extremely rare red precious gem, so far found only in the mountains of Utah-New Mexico."

"Does that mean there's more to the trafficking than raw diamonds from Africa?"

He snorted. "Like crooks cheating on crooks. But it isn't our concern."

On their arrival at the cabin, Gugàn ran up to Dexter but halted a foot away. "Are you still hurt?"

"Not as much, now."

"Good. Tomorrow I'll show you all my pebbles and my construction site."

Knowing looks and smiles were exchanged between the adults. The child's happiness knew no bound since he had been given the large, brightly colored glass beads to replace the others. Brooke picked up the mail on her desk. She grimaced at the letters from her lawyer and from the bank and tore open the one from the bank with a muttered, "what now?" A smile crossed her lips, but before she could speak, the door opened on Mitch in the blue uniform of the RCMP. Gugàn threw himself at the newcomer. Dexter looked from him to Yashee to Brooke.

"Are you..?"

Mitch nodded. "I accepted the posting to Donek. I'm the new detachment head."

"You crafty old dog! Congratulations. Tell me all about it."

Yashee raised a hand. "Tomorrow, *Kàa tlein*. Your food is getting cold."

Eyebrows raised, Brooke nodded her appreciation at Yashee. The puzzled look on Dexter's face delighted the women. When Mitch and Yashee left, Dexter put his fork down.

"What did she mean? I'm always Weiman to her."

"You've proven yourself worthy of a Tinglit traditional name, a title if you like."

Impatience showed. "Tell me who I am."

"It means Big Man. Not just physically big. One who does big things for others."

A humble air came over him. "I'm so honored. I'll have to thank her."

"There's no word for thanks in their language."

"Right, you told me. Can you teach the equivalent?"

"No, accept the name and wear it proudly. Now, listen to this. It's the latest letter from the bank."

He frowned, taking it from her. "What? They're apologizing!"

"The bank official who approved the mortgage to Lammers overlooked the fact that the title for the cabin is in one name only and therefore only I could sign. She also forgot to write in the insurance on the mortgage. As a result, the mortgage was never insured. She's been sent back to bank school for more training. Seth must have charmed her. That's why she made a double mistake." Brooke waved the second sheet of paper. "This is the confirmation that my cabin is mortgage free and there are no liens on the title. The other debts remain, but I can cope with those."

Sharing her happiness, he pulled her into his arms.. carefully.

Later in the evening, Dexter invited Brooke to sit next to him on the sofa. They contemplated the flames dancing in the stove. "I have tendered my resignation. I mentioned to you earlier that I had a business project in the works. This is what I'll be doing..."

Shocked, Brooke couldn't speak. Finally, it hit her that he was abandoning his job for her, a job he was passionate about. Tears sprang to her eyes. "But you love your job. You can't quit."

His arm drew her closer. "Life is like a house. It has doors which are closed or open. If you ignore an open door, it closes behind you. There's no going back. With the climate changing, there's a need to find better solutions to housing, particularly here in the North where the permafrost has started melting. An open door. That's what the company I've been working with is doing, UAD. Urban Alternative Development. It will involve quite a bit of travel, down south and to various indigenous communities, but never for extended periods."

"You've got it all organized already. What will you do?"

"Help municipalities implement ecological ways to cool cities in summer while retaining heat in winter, as well as where and how to build. I'm not an engineer, so my role will only be to explain."

"So simple when you put it like that."

"And tomorrow, I want to see a certain moose I've heard so much about."

Her laughter was smothered by a kiss, and more.

About the author

Born and raised in France, she was involved in writingfrom an early age, Geneviève has written a score of books: children's fictionin French and English, romances and historical novels published in France,Canada and the US, non-fiction books and numerous articles for Dogs in Canada.Her poetry has appeared in the Anthologie de la poésie Franco-Manitobaine, andin several short stories anthologies. She also worked as a translator.

In 2003 she received the Queen's Jubilee Medal

In 1983 she was nominated for YWCA Women of the Year

Also by

TRANSLATIONS

L'héritage de la guerre, translation from A Touch ofMagic, June Gadsby.

Quand la nuit tombe, translation from When DarknessFalls, Rachel Wesson

Lorsque l'aube se lève,translation from Light Rises, Rachel Wesson

OTHERS

Where the River Narrows, with Kathy Fisher-Brown

www.ingramcontent.com/pod-product-compliance
Lightning Source LLC
Chambersburg PA
CBHW051641260626
47170CB00004B/1268